MW01147046

RIVER OF THIEVES

CLAYTON SNYDER

Copyright © 2019 Clayton Snyder
All rights reserved.

❀ Created with Vellum

To me. If not for my ego, this never would have happened.

PART I

I said the joker is a wanted man,
He makes his way all across the land,
See him sifting through the sand,
So I'll tell you all the story,
About the joker and the thief of the night

Wolfmother, Joker and the Thief

And everybody knows
That the world is full of stupid people
Well, I got the pistols, so I'll keep the Pesos
Yeah, and that seems fair

The Refreshments, Banditos

FUCK, HE'S DEAD AGAIN

AS CORPSES GO, Cord proved a constant thorn in my side. Don't get me wrong. I liked the old thief, but dying merely inconvenienced him. Dealing with the mess after, however, dug into my ass like a persistent nettle. Given the choice of a nettle in your ass for years, or a small beetle that bores into your guts and then chews its way up your torso like a man slathered in horse shit runs to a bath, most people are going to choose the quicker, less annoying option. Fortunately, I am not most people. I might even be a saint. Or an idiot. I guess I'll find out when the gods hand out prizes at the end.

I sank down against the wall, avoiding the still-glistening blood. I lit a cigar and watched curls of blue-white smoke drift off into the summer night. My brain drifted with them, wondering what a normal life might look like. House, field, two kids, husband. Dog? Probably a dog. I snorted. None of that fit me. Even if my family made the choice to keep me, the path of life veered like a bird caught in a high wind.

I shook myself and looked down at Cord. After a minute, I poked a finger into his empty eye socket. It came away with a wet squelch and I wiped it on my trousers. Gross, sure. But caring about gross passed me by roughly eighteen months ago, and little in the way of squeamishness remained. I still don't know how he talked me into it the first time. I thought back to that first conversation.

"Look, it's easy, one quick jab in the eye, and we're in the money," he said.

"Why not the lung? Or the heart?"

"Because it hurts." He rubbed his chest. "It *really* hurts," he muttered.

"A knife in the eye doesn't?"

He shrugged. "I mean, only for a minute, then it's into the brain, and plop, splat, I'm dead."

"What if I only jiggle up your noodle?"

"Then you'll be changing my trousers for a month."

"Right, so the long knife."

He raised an eyebrow, and I mimed jabbing a blade into his face.

"So it goes deeper. Might need to scrape the back of the skull to be sure," I said.

"That's the spirit. The disturbing, way too eager spirit," he said, and went about packing our gear.

Wind rustling paper under the bridge snapped my attention back to the present. I looked up at the poster of King Mane plastered to the brick and shot it a sneer. The royal propagandist's work impressed me as an example of sweetening horseshit to make fudge. The royal twit appeared on the poster sporting a bulging chest and suspiciously well-endowed codpiece. The art depicted the king handing out gold coins to waifs in rags. They held shining faces uplifted and beaming in thankfulness.

I suspected the reason Cord chose this spot to die sprouted from a tree of simple spite. He hated Mane with a passion that bordered on obsession. His favorite epithet for the king remained The Royal Shit, despite his ever-rotating vocabulary of disdain. I didn't blame him. Even a short tour of the kingdom gave you an idea of just how much bullshit those posters peddled. Still, some of the king's policies proved useful. Opposite the lie of his largesse stood the truth of his paranoia. As a result, Mane employed a great many mercenaries to patrol even small cities and roads. Rumors abounded that he saw enemies around every corner.

Which brought me to my next task - calling the guards. Our take sat on a boat about 300 yards away, along with my bloody clothes. I didn't have a scratch on me. Cord did the dirty work - well, maybe the painful work. If you think stabbing a guy in the eye doesn't make for some interesting dreams, I'd like to speak to you about the definition of *disturbing*. But I didn't envy Cord's part--committing the robbery and ensuring someone spotted him so I could point out his corpse. After, constables being what they are in the backwaters of the Veldt, they'd mark it as a bad deal and close the case. We'd even leave a bit of gold around Cord's body to let them think he'd been the victim of a double-cross in the end. Lay low for a bit and repeat every couple hundred miles.

I tossed the cigar into the canal. I mussed my hair, then knuckled my fingers into my eyes until the whites went red. I ran for the local guard shack just up the road, sniffling. Once I let them calm me down—weeping women make even big guys with pointy swords uncomfortable—they followed me to the body. Over time, I've perfected my role as distraught citizen to the point I expected them to melt down Gunter Horvath's awards and recast the shiny gold in honor of my performance.

Once they left the guard station, I slipped away and hid in the shadows until they passed from sight, carting Cord's body off like flotsam washed up in their clean little hamlet. No littering. Mind the dung. Thanks for visiting. I hopped in the boat and rowed out of the berth, the water sending a chill froth over the bow in the night air. A clear dark night with a bright moon hung before me, lighting the river.

———

THE MORTUARY STOOD at the edge of town. I beached the boat just up the river, and crept out, tugging it into the reeds. They'd eventually find it, but by then, then we'd be long gone. Once done, I straightened, wiped my face clean, and checked my clothing. Rough, but passable. I strode into the building. A teen sat behind the counter, idly twirling a pencil. I gave him a bright smile, and he glowered back and rolled his eyes.

"What?" he asked.

He clearly possessed dickish tendencies. Not the most charming trait. Or maybe just stupidity. In which case, I pitied him a little. We'd all been there. I thought of Cord's advice: never attribute evil to dumb. So I smiled through teeth I wanted to use to bite him in the face.

"I'm here to pick up a body."

"Look, I can't do anything without my boss's say-so," the kid said.

"Sure, sure."

"I'm not even supposed to be here today. You think I want to spend the night with a dead guy?"

I shook my head and let the smile drop. "Look at it this way - I sign the paperwork, take the dead guy off your hands, and we're both on our merry way. Your boss can't bitch about that, right? I mean, he'll have my signature, and you'll be short one corpse."

The kid's eyes shifted to the steel door behind him, uncertainty twisting his lips. He shuffled his feet and let out a huff of air.

"Fine. Your signature and a fiver."

The smile slid back to my face. "Sure, sure."

I signed his parchment with a name that meant something like Bearded Taint in Gentian and plopped a crown worth at least five lesser gold on the table. The privilege of screwing with people in charge paid for itself. When you're handling dead guys and dealing with bureaucracy, you have fun when you can. He pulled the sheet back without looking at it. I felt a pang of disappointment at his inattention as he turned and unlocked the door, but squashed it. Some battles you won after you left the battlefield. One of Cord's sayings. Like most of his little nuggets of wisdom, it carried the double edge of horseshit and truth.

A chill rippled across the room. Low mist clung to the floor, carrying the mingled scents of dried blood and slow rot. We toted Cord's body out of the building and onto a small cart waiting in the yard. We dropped the dead man with a shared grunt. He *probably* wouldn't wake up with a headache. When we finished, the kid leaned against the wall and reached into a pocket, pulling out a tobacco twist and setting light to it with a small striker.

"Your guy's all fucked up. Chiurgeon said it looked like someone was playing with his eye after they stabbed him."

"Gross."

"Yeah. Sick. What's wrong with people?"

I shrugged. "Lotta weirdos out there."

"Yeah."

I wheeled Cord around the building, and chucked the bag of gold down beside him. Then I headed down the street, keeping to the shadows, the soft squeak of the cart's wheels keeping me company.

THE FIRST TIME you cart a body down the road in the middle

of the night, and the dead guy farts, you scream a little. And pee. About the eighteenth time, you sigh and keep downwind. The walk back to the rented cottage wound through town, and I spent a lot of it humming under my breath. Something nonsensical--Dead Hon and the Elephant Boys, or Sketchy Gan.

I crested the slope of a hill, the roof of the rented cottage showing. I managed to drag Cord's body through the front door, and after a bit of flopping about and grunting, propped him up on the divan, then sat down to wait. He used to come back quick. After this many deaths in a row though, his resurrections crept forward in increasing increments.

The first time Cord woke up in a mortuary, the damn chiurgeon tried to drive a stake through his heart. Nothing like rearranging a guy's organs a second time to delay his flight back to the real world. On the upside, it allowed me time to retrieve the body and avoid nastiness like that. On the down, I wondered if the slow return marked a decline in his overall health.

I'd made it halfway through an article in the local one-sheet about the proliferation of morons in government. (Granted, the editor probably wouldn't have let them print those exact words, mostly because they would have ended their career at the end of a rope.) They'd somehow managed to transfer the monthly farm subsidies to a fund meant for young debutantes. Now the crop yield flagged, but the would-be princesses wore diamonds the size of their skulls. Leave it to the rich to fuck the country over with an impressive tidal wave of shit and still come out smelling like roses.

Cord sat bolt upright, screamed once, and vomited up a lump of purple flesh, interrupting my train of thought. The thing squirmed against the rug, smearing crimson on the cream-colored wool, and stubby limbs sprouted from its sides. I smashed it with the hammer beside me. Cord coughed, blood spattering the floor, and vomited again. This time only vomit, no creepy living organ.

His chest heaved, and he made a sound like a sick dog. I waited for a minute. This passed for normalcy these days - the resurrections grew worse, each one taking something out of him. The first death I'd witnessed had only been his third death. He'd come back so easily then. Now we'd reached fifteen or so. A life of running and robbing sucked the sense out of the days. Nailing the exact number down felt like more than I wanted to trouble myself with. Especially when what I really wanted was a warm bed and a night of sleep. Cord sucked in one more breath and sat back, his face pale. He reached shaking fingers for the mug of water on the table beside him and took a long swallow, then finished with a small cough and a wan smile.

"How long?"

"Three days."

"Gods."

"Yeah." I set the paper down. "Look, we gotta take a break. If you die for real, the gravy train's over."

He nodded and waved a hand, tipping the mug up again, draining the dregs. He set it down and leaned forward.

"I've got a plan."

"I hope so. That looks like your spleen on the carpet. But your spleen had legs. I don't think I've ever seen a spleen with legs."

He looked down and grimaced, then back at me. "One more job. Then we can break."

I nodded. My gut knew better. One more job is never just one more job for people like Cord. Or worse, it really *is* the last job, ever. Retirement looked like death or prison. I didn't know which held the greater likelihood. If death continued to avoid Cord, he'd find himself vying with stone walls in a contest to see which rotted first. On the other hand, if the slowing rate of his resurrection indicated anything, true death loomed nearer than either of us expected. Neither of those things mattered much. The question that hung over both of us, like a sword suspended by a hair, was *how many more deaths did he have left?*

"THE GENTLEMAN BASTARDS," Cord said.

"What?" We'd been quietly preparing for the next job, and Cord's statement took me by surprise.

"Our name," he said.

"I'm a woman. Also, I think that's taken."

Cord looked up from lacing his boot. "Oh."

"What's the plan here?"

"I go in, take the gold from the safe, and we live out the next few months someplace sunny. You know, nice beaches, pretty women."

I shook my head. "Not what I meant."

The question reared its head before, but Cord dodged it the way you dodge a bit of snot someone's spat on the walk.

"Why do we need all this gold?" I asked. 100 pieces provided a modest, but comfortable retirement. 1000 might buy a small castle and servants. 10,000, a duchy. We probably had enough for a few duchies by now.

He frowned and straightened, boots laced tight to his ankles. "I don't understand."

"This is more money than you can spend in one lifetime."

He cocked his head to the side. "Ah."

"Ah, what?"

"Well, who here has a bit more than one lifetime?"

"That it? Planning well into your low thousands?"

"Well..."

"What?"

"Rich people piss me off."

"Why?"

"All that money. What do they do with it?"

I thought about. "Well, there's upkeep for their properties, pay for the staff, food, ponies, weapons, armor, maybe a wizard—"

"Think about that. They have a wizard on retainer. How many of the guys in the Dripping Bucket could say that?"

"To be fair, if those guys had a wizard, they'd just use it to make an endless beer fountain."

"Would they? Fet would have paid the guy to keep his crops growing. Al, his children healthy. Yellyn – she would have made sure everyone in her parish had books. But these guys – 'ooh, my sword's on fire' – does that sound all that bloody useful?"

"What about the staff? They've got to have jobs."

"Jobs they wouldn't need if their high and mighty lord of the taint hadn't annexed their land and used it for his personal sewer."

"Are you proposing a redistribution of wealth?"

"In a way," he hedged.

"There really should be a word for that."

"There is. It's called justice."

"No... look – what do you get out of this?" He'd led the conversation in a circle, and I didn't like it. I didn't like that this felt urgent, though I didn't know why.

He looked up at me, then at the moon, hanging in the sky like a weight, and promptly changed the subject.

"Time to go."

THE ROBBERY WENT the way they always do. That is to say, a combination of chaos and blood and short moments of terror.

Cord grabbed the money, let them see his face, let them give chase, and slipped his pursuers before the second turn. We left behind an obvious trail. We happened upon one of the rare hamlets without a constable station, and needed to make our path clear enough to follow. Without Cord's body and evidence of a robbery, the possibility of endless pursuit became more likely.

We stepped into a glade not far from the main track, sweat dripping from the strain of carrying the gold. We broke branches and stomped prints into the dirt as we went, leaving a path easy enough for a blind bear to track. Cord set the bag down and leaned against a tree, wiping a palm across his forehead.

"Okay, that shoul-"

An arrow sprouted from his eye mid-sentence and he collapsed. Men in dark leather appeared as if from nowhere and filled the clearing. They bristled with weapons, potential violence, and some sort of perfume. A man with a pinched face and a hungry look in his eye stepped toward me. He held a naked blade in his hand, the heavy edge glinting in the moon-light. His eyes gleamed with menace. His codpiece hung limp.

"We are the Knights of Axe!" he proclaimed.

I waved a hand, trying to dispel the stink.

"That is a powerful scent, sir knight," I said.

"Yea, the alchemist what sold me it assured me it would attract only the finest of maidens."

I coughed. "It's certainly attracting something."

A fly landed on his trousers and buzzed frantically before falling to the ground. We watched as it spun a circle on its back, wings fluttering like an erratic heartbeat. Finally, it died. He looked up, eyes meeting mine.

"Tell no one of this," he said.

"I wouldn't know where to start," I replied.

I heard the clank of coins and saw the bag disappear into the trees, one of his men toting it. I looked from it to him, and he narrowed his eyes.

"Not a word," he said.

"My lips are sealed," I replied.

He looked me over once, then turned and disappeared into the woods, leaving me alone with Cord and the sound of running feet. I put on my best crying face and sobbed as the constable burst into the clearing.

"Ma'am. Ma'am!"

I looked up. "Yes?"

"What happened here?"

I widened my eyes and tried to look shocked. "Thieves!"

"Where?"

"There!" I pointed to the tree line.

He glanced around, noting Cord's body, the fletching of the arrow still pointing to the sky. He looked back to me and narrowed his eyes.

"And how did you survive?"

I batted my eyelashes and gave him a smile. "They thought me too fine to despoil, sire. But they have my broach. If only someone could retrieve it. It belonged to my gran, and I'd be sore glad to have it back."

He looked from my chest to my eyes and back again. I coughed, and he lifted his eyes once more, face bright red. He cleared his throat.

"Ah, yes," he raised his voice, "Men, search the trees! We must have these scoundrels! Not to worry, ma'am. We'll have your jewels back to your bosom in no time."

My eyes strained to not roll into the back of my head and cause permanent blindness. "My hero."

He grinned and left to supervise the search, shouting orders as he went, chest puffed like a rooster. They quickly forgot me in the bustle. I slunk away.

WHILE THE GUARDS were busy beating the bush, I circled back. I'd stolen the uniform of a worker of Gren. Thick overalls, black mask, and heavy boots and gloves. I hauled Cord's body into the cart and wheeled him out, nodding to the same captain who'd stopped me earlier. He averted his gaze. Workers of Gren were considered bad luck in the smaller backwaters--stupid country superstition. It was like being afraid of the trash men. No one wanted a flood of maggots in the streets. These guys should be getting parades. The guard turned back to his business, and I hauled my partner's dead ass back to the cottage.

Cord woke sans one arrow in his skull, as is the preferred way to wake for most of the known world. He coughed, choked, and spat up another little critter, this one near in size to the last. Again, I hammered it with a mallet, and let Cord recover. He sipped his water and looked out the window over the long field of summer wheat and wildflowers.

"Penny for your thoughts," I said.

"That's a weird saying. Are you implying my thoughts are worth only a single cent?"

"Just an expression."

"Yeah, well, next time offer a crown," he grumbled.

"What were you thinking?" I asked, trying to keep the exasperation from my voice.

"I was thinking it's time we go for bigger fish. This last job—well, I've had more successful shits. *Fuck* those guys."

"Sadly, I don't think anyone ever will," I replied.

"What?"

"Nothing. You were saying?"

He gave me a look with one eye squinted, then shook his head and went on. "I think it's time for a change of pace, maybe time to set us up for retirement. There's an old Gentian saying: 'Why borrow from men when you can steal from gods?'."

"What is *wrong* with the Gentians?"

"A lot. You're ignoring my point, though."

"Are you suggesting we rob the gods?"

"Are you suggesting we shouldn't? What've they given us? Aside from an insatiable blood lust, a horrible curse, and thread-bare socks?" he held up one foot, toes poking from the stocking.

"Hey, it's not insatiable. I'm just saying, if *you* want to spend the rest of your life with a dick for a face, go ahead."

Cord waved it away. "One bridge at a time. The point is, all this small shit is exactly that. Rabbit turds."

"And?"

He fell quiet for a moment, gray eyes searching for something out beyond the flowers. I followed his line of sight, to the ribbon of the river cutting across the Veldt and beyond, to Midian, the capitol.

"Okay," I sighed, "crown for your thoughts."

"Better," he muttered.

"Well?"

"You ever wonder if there's more?"

"Like less horseshit and blood? A little less of the flux and a little more flesh?"

"Yeah, something like that. I just... look, there's no reason for this to go on as long as it has. I'm getting older, and these deaths, they're taking something out of me. And you. You've got a long life ahead, if we pull this off, you can live it in a place that isn't covered in shit."

"Like a king?"

Cord grimaced for a split second. "Yeah, something like that."

"Okay, so what's the plan?"

"First, we're gonna need a crew."

Inwardly, I groaned. He gave me one of his lunatic grins, and my stomach dropped. I knew that look. Outwardly, I groaned.

2

CAT SHIT AND VIOLENCE

WE'D MOVED up the river again to a hamlet called Cait Ap Sith. The locals referred to it by a more colorful name, Cat Shite City. Mostly because of all the cats. They swarmed the local fishery, lounged in alleys, and occasionally pounced from eaves and trees like tiny stupid panthers. I watched a fat tabby chase a small mouse across an alley, giving up halfway through and sitting on its haunches like a winded mule. Further into town, the growls and painful cries of cats in heat echoed through the small alleys. I turned to Cord.

"We're not robbing this place, are we? I'm already going to be picking cat hair out of my food for weeks."

Cord shook his head. "No one here to rob. No, we're here for a friend."

"Friend? You?"

Cord shrugged. "We had mutual interests once upon a time."

"What's their name?"

"Rek."

"Uh huh. And what happened?"

"We had a falling out. I thought we should rob a Harrower, he didn't."

"So what makes you think he's going to want to see you now?"

"We're going to blackmail him."

"*You're* going to blackmail him, you mean."

"Yes. We."

I gave up. "And he'll be so grateful he'll follow us like a puppy?"

"Hopefully. If not, I'll tell him we paid a Harrower to curse him."

"You think he'd fall for that?"

Cord shrugged and led us down a path into the greater part of town, a dirt rut that wound its way between fields of nodding sunflowers. Green clumps of catnip sprouted between the stalks, and the flowers swayed with the passage of perpetually stoned cats. To our left, the river ran south and east. Through the drowsy midlands, it pushed its way toward the sea and Midian, *the* city. Here, most everyone bore pale or slightly tan skin tones, some taking on the blue and green hue of the great algae farms to the north. There, between the tall mountains and the wide snowfields, they grew the snotty stuff in glacial lakebeds. They fed it to their cattle, their children, and themselves. I'd tasted it once, leaving me wishing I'd just licked a snot toad.

The fields gave way to more muddy ruts and ramshackle homes pressed tight like syphilitic lovers, leaning on one another for support. Farther in, the roads made a circle. Rough stalls served as Cait's market. Fishmongers and farmers hawked their wares, stalls of fresh and dried fish, roasted sunflower seeds, and thick clumps of algae sending up a peculiar stink. We took a quick left, back toward the water, and entered a long series of alleys marked by small homes with tin roofs.

"Tell me about this guy," I said.

Cord shrugged. "Rek? Whaddya wanna know?"

"What's he like?"

"Mostly big."

"Big?"

Cord held his hands apart, and then adjusted so he took in the width of one of the houses.

"You pissed him off? *And* you're going to blackmail him? I thought you were supposed to be some sort of criminal genius."

He shrugged again. "Harrower contract law is interesting. You'll see. Besides, he's a softy."

He led us to a house only marginally larger than the others, which in Cait is like saying four sardines fit in this can rather than three. Cats infested the small garden out front, lazed on the steps, and peered from a rough window. They looked like a furry tribunal, and I ducked my head, tried to look innocent. Cord snorted, then raised his hand and knocked, sending a few scattering and at least one hissing. I tried not to think about tiny claws ripping me a new sphincter.

No answer came, and he knocked again.

"Go away." The voice inside sounded like someone taught a boulder speech.

"Rek," Cord said.

"Nuh-uh."

"Rek, open the door."

"No Rek here. Just cats." A pause. And then, "Meow."

Cord shifted as silence from the other side of the door met us. "Quick Rek! Mr. Meowington's in danger!"

"MR. MEOWINGTON?!"

The shout made my ears ache. I stepped off the stoop in time to see a fleshy mountain the color of sandstone nearly tear the door off its hinges. He bounded into the yard, peering into every crevasse and corner, shouting the cat's name. I fell back further while Cord stifled a laugh. Rek turned to him, brow beetling, and the smile died on Cord's lips.

"Where is the kitty, Cord?"

Cord raised his hands. "Look, I had to get you out of the house, Mr. Meowington is fi-"

One of Rek's turkey-sized hands grabbed Cord by the throat and squeezed. Cord's eyes bulged and a croak escaped his throat. His neck gave a thick *snap* and he went limp, limbs flopping to his side. Rek dropped the body into the mud, Cord hitting the ground with an unceremonious *thump*. The big man turned to me.

"You like tea?" he asked.

I eyed Cord's body. "Yeah. What about him?"

Rek waved a hand. "Leave him. The cats give him new cologne, he learns a lesson. When he gets up, he can have tea, too," he shook a finger at the body. "If he behaves."

I followed Rek into the house. It teemed with cats and overstuffed floral print furniture. Small wood tables dotted the place, heaped with boxes of tea and cookies and cat treats. He wedged himself into a chair and gestured for me to sit. He loomed over the room from his chair, bent slightly so to reach the tray on the table beside him.

"Tea?" he asked.

"Yes, please."

He fiddled with a small pot, filling first one delicate cup, then the other. He handed me one. "Sugar?"

"Yes, please."

"FUCK," Cord interrupted as he stomped through the door.

An angry purple bruise still lingered on his throat, and the sclera of one eye nearly glowed bright red with burst blood vessels. I looked up from my tea. Rek dropped two lumps of sugar in and gave a grunt. He didn't glance over. Cord's recovery time surprised me.

"I thought you were dead," I said.

Cord shook his head, winced, and rubbed his neck. "Bastard just paralyzed me."

"Take off your boots," Rek said.

Cord sputtered. "The whole place is covered in cat hair. A little mud isn't going to-"

"Take. Off. Your. Boots." Rek glared at Cord and dropped the last bit of sugar into the tea.

I stirred my drink as quietly as possible while Cord tugged his boots off, tossing them by the door. He muttered under his breath.

"Why are you here?" Rek asked him.

I took a sip of tea.

"I need your help, Rek," Cord said and sank heavily into an overstuffed chair decorated with bright pink floral print and cat hair.

"Why should I care what you need?" Rek asked. He turned to me with an apologetic smile and patted my hand. "No offense, dear."

"None taken. He's a bit of a shit."

Cord shot me a withering glare. I returned a smile.

"Because I'm gonna make us rich."

"Nuh-uh. Last time you told me that, you ended up cursed. The time before that, I ended up in debt."

"I bought your debt."

A frown creased Rek's forehead. "Bought my debt?"

Cord nodded. "You owe me now."

Rek grumbled low in his chest, the sound like a bass drum. "What if I just take it out of your hide?"

Cord spread his hands. "The debt defaults back to the man you owed before. Remember the Harrower? Who would you rather owe, Rek?"

Rek cursed and tossed his teacup at the wall. It shattered,

peppering the room with tea and ceramic. Cats scattered at the explosion, scurrying under chairs and into the kitchen. Cord smirked, and I raised an eyebrow at him. He ignored me.

"Is that a yes?" he asked.

Rek heaved a sigh. "Yes. But when the debt is paid, I'll kill you for real."

Cord looked a little queasy for a moment, and then cleared his throat. "Deal."

We filed out of the house, leaving the big man behind to gather his belongings. He'd meet us at the boat after. On the way there, I stopped Cord.

"You going to blackmail everyone we recruit?"

He shook his head. "Rek just needs motivation. He's really a decent guy."

"Aside from the murdering you in the street thing."

Cord shrugged and continued down the path. "Technically, he didn't kill me. And I deserved it. Probably more. I really screwed him with that Harrower job."

"Yeah? Did you really buy his debt?"

"I did."

"From the same man who cursed you?"

"Yeah."

"That can't have been comfortable."

"He's really proud of that curse."

"I would be, too." I considered. "It can't be good being in debt to one of those things."

"Nope."

"So really, you did him a favor."

"That's how I see it."

"Will Rek?"

"The world is full of unknowable questions, Nenn."

"So?"

He shrugged. "Probably not."

WE MADE IT QUAYSIDE, finding Rek in the bow of the boat, the back poking out of the water. He wore a scowl and held an oar. We waded over and climbed in, settling the craft, and Rek pushed us off, moving the boat forward with powerful strokes. We rode in silence as Cait dwindled, and then disappeared past the first bend.

"Kitties better be okay," Rek said.

Cord just swallowed and watched the trees pass.

3

THAT ONE TIME A HORSE ALMOST FUCKED ME

"THE OUTSIDERS," Cord said, apropos of nothing.

I shook my head, watching the riverbank roll by. We'd made good time with Rek pushing the oars, and Cait was already far behind. The river was busy with merchant ships and day trippers, and we kept closer to the bank to avoid the worst of the traffic, our little boat ill-equipped for an encounter.

"Why not?"

"Sounds like we should be wearing leather, struggling with our identities," I said.

"Fine."

"Where we going, anyway?"

"To see Lux."

Rek groaned from the front of the boat. "Not Lux."

"What's wrong with Lux?" I asked.

"Nothing," Cord said.

"Creepy," Rek said.

"Okay, yeah, she's a little creepy," Cord acknowledged. "We still need her."

I looked around the small craft. "We're also going to need a bigger boat."

Cord smiled. "Trust me. I have a plan."

Rek groaned again, and I joined him.

LOOKING BACK, Rek was the easiest of all the things we'd set to ourselves.

I asked myself then what Rek really wanted. He seemed content with his cats, with his tiny cottage. I wondered if any choice other than blackmail existed, and realized that even in his cozy home, a dual feeling of restlessness and inertia hung about the man. It clung to him like cheap perfume, and watching him in that cottage, among his knickknacks and doilies, he paced like a caged cat. Sitting in that boat, watching the man work the paddle as the riverbank flew by, the set of his shoulders spoke of a joy he hadn't experienced in years.

"How'd you two meet?" I asked as Rek pushed the boat along, powerful arms moving like clockwork.

Cord groaned.

Rek rumbled a laugh. "The idiot tried to rob me. I was working this club in Midian, one of those places that pop up overnight and is gone the next day."

"That's a thing?" I asked.

"For a while. It's a cheap way to make a killing. Buy cheap booze, hire some musicians, charge an arm and a leg for exclusive access--"

"Some people have more money than brains," Cord muttered.

Rek continued. "Which leads to the next bit. Here comes Cord, walking in like he owns the place, ordering bottles of Gentian wine and a girl on each arm."

"How did you know he didn't?"

"The owner was the one who hired me. So, I pick this short little shit up, carry him out like luggage, and toss him on the street. Three hours later, while I'm chaining the doors, he comes back with four guys."

"Oh no."

Rek nodded. "Cord's the only one who got back up. When he did, took him a minute to talk, but he offered me a job."

"And you took it?"

Rek shrugged, the motion rocking the boat.

"The club was closing down at the end of the week, and I've always been good at making people not be people anymore. Besides, he might be an idiot—"

"Hey," Cord protested.

"—but it paid the bills."

"And we've been friends ever since," Cord said.

"And we've been acquaintances ever since," Rek corrected.

The conversation got me thinking about my own reasons for following Cord on this errand, and I slipped into memory during a lull in the conversation.

———

THEY'D NAMED the bar The Dripping Bucket. It smelled of cheap cigars, cheaper whiskey, and boiled feet. On the upside, drinks stronger than an ettin knocked the more offensive of those scents right out of your head. Halfway through my second glass of a whiskey the color of bloody piss, a stranger sat down and bumped my neighbor's elbow. My neighbor, on drink four and looking like the breeding result of a particularly stupid bulldog and a snake, stabbed him in the throat.

Hed, the bartender, glared at the stabber, then at the stabbee. The latter slipped to the floor, arterial spray making a mess of the woodwork. I stood and took my drink three stools down to keep my drink untainted.

"What the fuck, Zef?" Hed asked, eyes flicking back to the killer.

Zef shrugged. "He touched my purse."

Hed grunted, and the rest of the bar managed to make a six-foot hole to give the new guy room to bleed out. Call it country hospitality.

Hed spoke up, addressing me. "Nenn, you gotta get this guy out of here."

It took a minute for the statement to sink past the booze-soaked layer of my brain. Despite the whiskey already in my guts, I realized I remained the most sober. Empty glasses stood on the bar like husks of soldiers drained by a wight. I hated touching corpses. I'd done it for a summer, picking up unfortunates for the morgue. The forgotten and the destitute left there by drug and blade. They squelched and jiggled, and sometimes, if they'd been in the sun long enough, bloated and stank. The especially dead ones liked to slip their skin when you tried to pick them up. I enjoyed touching dead guys like most people enjoy eating scabs. I made a face I hoped telegraphed my distaste.

"I'll pay your tab."

Some arguments however, are airtight.

"Okay, then," I replied, and grabbed the dead guy by the ankles.

He left a red smear behind as I toted him out the rear exit. A few of the city's scavengers--those worse off than even the patrons of the Dripping Bucket--scattered from the alley. They left behind a smell like burning cow shit. Not their fault. Clean water didn't come cheap and thanks to Mane's policies, even use of a well carried a tax. I waited for them to scurry away and dropped the corpse on the cobblestones. I lit a cigar while I tried to decide if this constituted the lowest point of my life, or just a bump on the way down.

Sitting in an alley with a dead guy while you smoke your last cigar of the night, and his blood slowly seeps into the soles of your boots, makes you think. Not that I'm a big thinker on a normal day--I mean, I'm not stupid. I just tend to take things as they come. But if anything, that sort of situation makes you re-evaluate some life choices. When the dead guy sits up and takes a big fat breath, right after you've finished screaming, you make big decisions.

He coughed once, and something small and pink spattered from his lips against the cobbles. He smashed it with his heel, and then took a second, deeper breath.

"Got another one of those?" he asked, gesturing at my cigar.

I shrugged and handed him mine. He took a deep drag, then coughed, smoke puffing out of him like a blacksmith's forge at the bellows. He rubbed his throat, as if trying to massage away the soreness from the passage of the creature. He offered the cigar back, but I shook my head. The distinct taste of regret already lingered on my tongue.

"You okay?" he asked.

I nodded and swallowed, waiting for my heart to stop hammering.

"This happen a lot?" I asked.

"Not a lot, no. Enough. But not a lot." he eyed me up and down, and shrugged, as if coming to a decision. He offered me his hand. "I'm Cord."

I took it and gave it a little shake. "Nenn."

"You free this weekend?" he asked.

"That's a weird question."

"Why?"

"Well, you were just dead."

"I'm not now."

"I'm not really into necrophilia."

"Still not dead."

"Anymore. How do I know you won't die again?"

"You don't. So?"

"So what?"

"Are you free?"

I frowned at him. "I'm washing my hair."

"This isn't that kind of question. I had something better in mind."

"Mummer show? I'll be your beautiful assistant?"

He snorted. "How do you feel about a partnership?"

"Doing what?"

"Making money."

"Doing what?"

He explained, and I started to come around despite my misgivings. It already sounded better than another fourteen hours in the mill. Call me overcautious. I needed more before he convinced me this wasn't just another con. Granted, with the dying trick, an exceptional con, but at their core all cons reach for the same goal. You have something they want, they try to take it.

"That is really godsdamn specific. Also, why me?"

He gestured at the trail of blood. "Your first instinct was to hide the body, not call the guards."

"That was for free whiskey."

He shrugged. "Buy all the whiskey you want with our earnings."

"Nah."

"Nah?"

"Drinking got me into pulling a dead guy into an alley."

"But I was only temporarily dead."

"That's an incredibly weird technicality," I pointed out.

Silence fell between us.

"How'd you do that, anyway?" The question floated at the top of my mind like the vomit I barely kept down a few minutes ago.

He waved a hand. "Pissed off a Harrower."

I whistled low. "You poor bastard."

He nodded, and I felt bad for him despite myself. The word Harrower brought with it a nightmare wind that did its best to creep into your head. Wizards that powered their magic with the worst humanity is able to imagine, they worked for the highest bidder and flaunted their cruelty. You can imagine the unpleasantness.

"I thought you were gonna say it was a birth defect," I said.

"Pfft. Where's the mystery in that? The romance? The esoteric? Everyone's so rational. It's goddamn boring."

I rolled my eyes. "Fine."

"Okay."

A beat passed between us again.

"So?" Persistent, this one.

"So what?"

"The offer?"

"Oh, that." I thought about my decisions so far. A hard life and a short temper landed me on the nearest bar stool more often than not. I'd drug a dead guy into an alley. Working at the mill pissed me off more nights than not. I nodded.

"Sure."

"Great!" He stuck out one bloody hand. "Now, what do we call ourselves?"

"I'm Nenn."

"I know that. We need a name. Like the Dastardly Duo or the Bloody Two."

"How about no."

SOMETIMES I STILL ASKED MYSELF why I'd agreed to this new idea. I could have demanded my cut, walked away rich enough to afford a small home in a small village and shack up with a nice someone. Preferably someone who didn't fetishize knives and money. Opposites attract, after all. Maybe I'd woo a grandmother.

If I had to guess, I liked the company. I'd spent a good portion of my youth in an orphanage, and even then, I'd only had acquaintances, people I was familiar, but never friendly with. After, when they threw me out on the street, I floated. I found work as a gopher, running and fetching, and later, as a fixer of sorts. I'd become handy with a blade in the intervening years, thanks to a life in the alleys and low streets of the towns I drifted between.

That was the way of it though, wasn't it? Most men didn't need blades, even if they carried them. Their only real threat was other men. But women—you had to watch yourself. Men, boys, teens—they all wanted what you had, whether you willing to part with it or not, and that made for a dangerous world. So I picked up a knife, then another. And another. I practiced until my blisters became calluses and even those gave way to tough skin and scar tissue.

I'd never had formal training, but it doesn't take much to kill. And in the alleys and backstreets, you want a knife. You can swing a knife, or thrust with it, or any number of other wicked things you couldn't do with a sword or a pike, or even a mace. Knives will bleed a man out fast, and the right type of knife will punch through chain, find places not covered with armor.

Eventually, I landed at the mill. Cutting is lucrative, but the career outlook dimmer than most. Still, I'd missed my blades.

They're quick and they're wicked, and they've saved my life— and Cord's more than I could count. I couldn't account for his refusal to carry a weapon. Maybe it was because he had me. Maybe it was his past as a soldier—of which he never spoke, or his past as a prisoner, but it seemed directly killing was beyond his comfort zone.

Unfortunately, for the people he'd marked as enemies, he was already deft at engineering circumstances that meant he never had to lift a blade. That would scare some people. For me, it was part of why I liked him. He had principals. No matter what scam we pulled—he stuck to his ideals.

That's why our friendship worked. We played off one another's strengths, no matter what anyone else might have thought of them. When I was younger, I thought friends were just those people who you trusted to not stick a knife in your back, and now I knew better. Friends—true friends—were family, and they'd stab you right to your face.

Memory drifted away in tatters as Cord announced a detour in the usual way. By not telling anyone until we arrived at one of the early delta forks in the Lethe. Rek back-paddled so hard he nearly tipped the boat, flipping everyone's stomach as effectively as if someone showed us a pile of severed limbs. For a moment, we hung precariously on the edge of a cresting wave, Cord swearing, Rek wearing a grimace not out of place on a golem, and me hanging onto the gunwales. I tried not think about how quickly I'd drown between the weight of several crowns tucked in various places about my person and the knives. I thought briefly of stripping down, getting light so the water couldn't claim me. But that would have required letting go of the boat, and I couldn't convince my hands to obey me.

Finally, the boat righted, swinging about and barely missing a sharp outcrop of rock. We drifted peacefully up the northern tributary of the Lethe, frayed nerves settling in fits and twitches. Once a little way past the swirling current of the fork, we let the boat float a bit further before beaching it on a sandy shore, crawling out and stretching sore muscle and bone. Rek and Cord wandered off in one direction, I in another, to piss in the woods.

Cord speared a bass and fried it with soft potatoes and scallions. We watched the river roll by, unassuming in the mid-day sun, light fracturing and spraying across the tree line behind us. When we finished lunch, I leaned against a rock and lit a cigar—one of my last until we reached Tremaire—and watched fish jump and snatch at bugs skimming the surface of the water.

"What's the deal with Lux?" I asked.

"Not right," Rek said.

Cord grimaced. "Last we knew, she'd traveled back to Tremaire to take the exams at the Arcanum. Figured she'd learned enough in the world."

"Did she pass?"

"No idea."

"You can be sure she weirded out her professors. She's likely to be even weirder now. Messing with that kind of power, it changes people. And the tests don't help. No one really knows what goes on, but it tends to leave a mark," Rek said.

"She's not a Harrower, is she?" I asked, a knot of unease in my gut.

"Gods, no," Cord replied. "Just regular weird. Not freaky death cult nightmare weird."

"At least they've got the Leashmen," Rek said.

He made a good point. Nobody really liked the soldiers that hunted rogue wizards, but it kept the number of villages turned into pudding to a minimum.

We sat for a little longer, and then I stood, looking around. Cord nudged me as he passed, heading for the boat. When we'd landed, Rek still scowled to rival the black clouds of a plains storm. While I woolgathered, he and Rek talked for a good while. Now, the big man looked relaxed, almost happy. He climbed into the boat, and I pulled Cord to the side.

"What did you say to him?"

"Didn't say nothin'," Cord said.

He opened his jacket and pulled a small brown package from an inside pocket. I raised an eyebrow.

"Slipweed?" I asked.

"Put a little in with his fish."

"Why?"

"He's wound tighter than a leper's dick bandage."

I hissed a breath from between clenched teeth and looked over at Rek. He sat in the front of the boat, twirling the oar and making whooshing sounds.

"Have you considered the problem of drugging the person rowing the boat? Have you considered how we might end up crushed on the rocks, or maybe impaled on a stray log?"

Rek laughed, high and fast, and I glared at Cord. He shrugged and raised his hands in a gesture of innocence. I punched him in the chest.

"Unf," Cord said.

"Articulate as always," I snapped and made my way to the boat. "Just remember, if *we* die, it's for good, you dolt."

Cord sputtered out an apology and spent the next five minutes trying to wrestle the oar from Rek's over-muscled hands. When he finally grabbed it, he sighed in relief and pushed us off the bank, dipping the oar into the water. Rek flapped his hands in the air before him like birds. Cord started rowing, grumbling in complaint at the effort. I reached out, pushing him in the back with my boot. He rocked forward a little.

"Row, serf," I said.

He glared back, but did as asked, muttering darkly under his breath. I chuckled and watched the riverbank slip past.

———————

AS WE MOVED NORTH, the landscape changed, long grasses and gentle hills giving way to rocky soil quickly replaced by muddy fens and marshy landscape, cattails and reeds standing tall in brackish water. Moss clung to the river-bank, climbing up the black bark of pine and cypress, vying for space on their boles with insidious green vines that drooped and trailed in the water. The trees thickened, throwing our boat into the shadows of the setting sun. This part of the river was quiet. Most ships didn't take the time to travel to Tremaire, superstition and self-sufficiency keeping the bulk of traffic away.

Rek's euphoria lasted for a good portion of the trip, but as the sun slipped behind the trees and we hung a lantern from the bow, he grew quiet, head in his hands. He stared down at the bowsprit, watching his reflection just past. in the water.

"How's it going up there, buddy?" Cord asked.

I lifted a leg to tap him in the kidneys and instead let out a low groan as pain throbbed in my guts. Cord craned his neck at me.

"You okay?"

I grimaced and wrapped my arms around my stomach. It wasn't bad yet, but it promised to be. I dug a sliver of slipweed from my own private stash, and chewed furiously. Cord's face fell.

"Oh. Oh no."

"'Fraid so," I said through gritted teeth.

"If you could just not be a woman for a few more miles...?" Cord prompted.

I laid back on the boards of the boat and stared up at the stars. "Or you could go fuck yourself in the neck."

"I'm wounded," Cord said.

"You will be. Row faster, fathead."

Cord muttered to himself and the stars slipped by with renewed speed. Eventually, they blurred, and I found my eyelids heavier than forge hammers. I closed them and drifted with the night sky.

***

I WOKE some time later to a small package by my head. I felt the flow starting. Maybe it already had. Slipweed tended to unravel time for its users, hours, minutes, sometimes days passing by in a blink. I unwrapped the package and found a few kama—small absorbent bundles—and an envelope of slipweed. I eased my trousers down and slipped the kama in, then took another sliver of the slipweed. It took a few moments, but the cramps faded to a dull background ache, and my headache eased. Cord kept his back turned the entire time.

Now that I felt a little better, I looked around. The trees thinned as we approached Murkwater, the small lake that Tremaire and the Arcanum stood on. Rek resumed rowing duties, though silently, and the reason for Cord's quiet became apparent as he snored gently. A gentle mist sprung up in the forest, winding between trunk and undergrowth. Things moved in the fog, black and glistening, red and yellow eyes gleaming in the moonlight. I'd heard stories of failed experiments, summonings gone wrong, attempts at creating new life, released from the Arcanum. I hoped we needn't discover the truth.

Rek picked up the pace and I thanked small gods for the thin layer of protection the hull provided from the water. Any number of beasts likely lived there. Like most hungry creatures however, they needed to smell flesh or taste blood to want you. We considered that motivation enough to avoid stopping to sleep, or taking an overland route via horse.

As we rowed deeper into the forest, the mist pressed in from all sides. The atmosphere cloyed, and I felt the need to break it up. I remembered a story Cord mentioned once in passing about Rek and a horse.

"What's the deal with you and horses?" I asked Rek.

He shuddered, and Cord snorted awake.

"Horses?" Cord asked. "Oooh."

A sly grin crossed his face.

"Yeah, that's a great story."

"Please don't," Rek pleaded.

Cord waved it away. "Your dignity's fine. The horse isn't here."

"The story?" I prompted.

"Right. So, a few years back, this high muckity muck hires us for an expedition to the Hollow Hills. Some sort of artifact in the ruins down there. So, we gear up, and it's a bit of a trek down to there from the river, so we figure we'll do it proper. Besides, if we find a lot of loot, we'll need something to haul it all back with.

"We find a horse trader in this little town—Agresta? Anyway, he's got just what we need, nice mares for Lux and me. Beautiful horses, friendly, eat an apple right out of your hand. Rek however, needs a bigger horse."

"I can't help my size," Rek said.

"We know, buddy," Cord said, and patted him on the shoulder.

"Anyway, Rek isn't totally comfortable with things bigger than him, and this one was a great beast of a stallion. Hooves the size of dinner plates. So Rek's twice as nervous already."

"That thing was a monster."

"His name was Eugeen. He was as frightening as a cat."

"No cat could fit my entire arm in its mouth."

"So, Rek gets an idea. He disappears for a few hours, and when he comes back, he's smelly as shit, but confident. He grabs the saddle, puts a foot in a stirrup, and the wind shifts. This horse gets a whiff of him and rears. So here's Rek, suddenly dangling by a stirrup, tangled in the reins, and the horse is trying to bite him. Not little nips, either, but great big chomping bites.

"He starts screaming, the horse is kicking and biting, and finally Lux gets it to sleep with a little magic. We get Rek free, and when he's finally calmed down, ask him what happened. Turns out he'd doused himself in horse piss."

"For the love of fuck, why?" I asked.

"Thought he'd like me more if I smelled like a horse," Rek said.

"Yeah, but what kind of horse piss was it, Rek?" Cord asked.

"Stallion."

"And what kind of piss did you mean to use?"

He hung his head. "Mare."

"But that means..." I said.

Cord nodded. "Horse would've fucked him to death."

"Never again," Rek said.

"Just remember, coulda been worse," Cord said.

"How?"

"You could be pregnant with horse babies."

"I don't think that's how it works," I said.

Cord shrugged. "I'm not a chiurgeon."

Apparently, they considered Lux some sort of predator, bolting when she drew near. It's the animal kingdom's way of saying *fuck this, fuck that, and fuck you.* More importantly, even on the Veldt, horseflesh came at a premium. If you saw someone not in silk or velvet riding one, either they served as cavalry, or the horse belonged to someone else.

The trees thinned further, wide spaces cleared by brave workers, allowing the Arcanum's tower to view the landscape with some safety. The river widened out, and the tower came into view, a thick spire of brick thrusting toward the sky like a fat man's cock. I thought it perfectly indicative of the Arcanum's attitude. I don't know why anyone expected people capable of wielding godlike power to possess a shred of humility. They certainly didn't hold themselves to that standard.

We drifted into the Murkwater, and I shook Cord awake. He snorted and rubbed a hand over his face. The surface of the lake clouded over, like a storm roiling under the surface, and as we passed, lightning played in the depths. A small town surrounded the base of the tower ahead. Craftsmen, laborers, support staff, and magi who'd made the decision not to serve elsewhere made their homes there. Nearer the tower stood a hospital for those desperate for cures the chiurgeons, herbalists, and mundane alchemists couldn't provide.

A low wall surrounded it all, providing protection from the forest beasts with a combination of simple brick and sophisticated wards. Docks extended from the town into the water, footings plunging into the murky depths. Lights from Tremiare reflected in the lake, and as we approached, something black and huge roiled beneath the surface and swam deeper.

Rek pulled us up to a slip among several boats of varying size, tossing a dockhand a rope. We clambered out, stretching our legs, thankful to be on solid ground again. Cord placed his hands in the small of his back and bent, groaning, while I chewed another sliver of slipweed. At least on land and moving around, I'd have some relief from the cramps. When we'd recovered, Cord led us toward the dock gate, a swagger in his step. Damn him. How did he have a swagger after being still and uncomfortable for so long?

A bored-looking youth stood guard at the gate. He wore no

armor aside from a steel ring on a leather cord and a spear. He glanced blearily at us.

"Welcome to Tremaire. Mind yourself and we won't have to mind you," he intoned.

"Hex," Cord said.

The youth blinked.

"Hex, it's me."

"Cord?" Hex said.

"The one and only."

Hex smiled, and my stomach twisted in warning. His spear snapped out, impaling Cord's arm. He pulled it out with a grunt and tapped the end onto the flagstones, ignorant of the blood spilling down the tip. Cord shrieked, and then clapped a hand over the bleeding hole.

"Please proceed," Hex said, all business again.

Cord shot him a wounded look and walked through the gate, leaving a trail of red droplets. I caught up to him. He flexed a shoulder, trying to work the soreness out, and I saw the wound already bore a scab.

"You're the best at making friends," I said.

"He's just sore I didn't cut him in for more last time I was here."

"Uh huh. The best. Are there more friends of yours here? Because I feel like we should buy you some chainmail."

"He must be a friend. Cord's still alive," Rek said.

Cord muttered something under his breath and changed the subject. "If I remember right, Lux used to hang out at this little pub by the tower. Cosca's. You two up for a drink?"

I'd needed a drink since the start of my cycle. Since I'd just spent twelve hours sitting in a boat. Besides, I needed a privy so I could change my kama. I looked over at Rek to check his response, and noted his pale color. A drink might benefit him as well. He spent a good portion of our stroll among close buildings and lit alleys by shying away from the light. I suspected the slip-weed hangover of kicking in some time ago, his skull playing host to a variety of brain goblins. Amazing stuff, but the come-down could cripple a small bull, depending on how much you'd taken. From the size of him, I guessed Cord's dose close to enough to drop a battalion.

We fell into an easy pace, passing shops closed for the night, every manner of trinket and weapon in their windows. Some-where on the other side of the merchant district, a forge rang out. Deeper in, throaty laughter from a gathering. Cord chat-tered happily, and from the look on Rek's face, it seemed he might break that promise to wait to kill him again.

"Have you ever had the beer here? Oh, it's amazing, just the best. I think the wizards do something to it, but damn if it's ever had an ill side effect. And the potatoes! Just you wait—butter and onion and sausage and a touch of goat's cheese..."

Music and conversation overtopped him as Cosca's came into view. A large building and long, it took up one end of the street. Simple painted wood facade and a high thatched roof set it apart from the stone and glass buildings on the street. We stepped inside and the sensations nearly overwhelmed me. The smells of food, spiced and roasted, smelled amazing. All the bodies crammed into the small room did not. Other sensations crowded in alongside, fighting for attention. Music, conversa-tion, and bright bunting in the rafters. My mouth watered and I cursed Cord as he took his time finding us a table. When we finally sat, I snarled my order at the barmaid, and then made my way to the privy.

When I returned, a slight blonde with pale skin and cloudy eyes occupied a stage at one end of the room. I sat and watched while she put on a show, first pulling a bird from thin air, then transforming it into a lizard. She lifted the lizard from the stage, and with a sudden flourish, jammed it into her mouth, chewing furiously. The crowd let out cries of disgust. Someone retched when the woman swallowed. Silence filled the room, and she produced a dagger, holding it out for the crowd to see.

She plunged it into her stomach, opening her guts. Blood sprayed the front row of patrons, causing them to flinch in fear. One man scrambled to his feet from the front row, staggering away with his hands over his mouth. He couldn't seem to run fast enough and he vomited across the floorboards in a fat fan of lamb chunks and potato. She rummaged around in her insides with one hand, then, with a triumphant smile on her lips withdrew the bird, whole and undamaged. The crowd erupted into cheers, and she took a bow. When she straightened, her stomach was clean and unblemished, and she stepped from the stage. She headed our way and sat beside Cord.

"Nenn, meet Lux."

I nodded at her.

"I don't think I'm hungry anymore," Rek mumbled.

The waitress arrived, placing platters of meat and potato and tumblers of beer in front of us.

Rek took a deep breath, inhaling the scents. "Never mind, I'm still hungry," he corrected.

I agreed and reached over him, loading my plate. Cord hadn't exaggerated the quality of food at Cosca's. *Amazing* beer and potatoes made the world disappear while I tucked in. Lux's performance did nothing to put me off my appetite. For several minutes, I was unaware of anything else as I shoveled food into my mouth. When I finished, I pushed my chair back, and looked closer at Cord's guest.

Lux stared off into the distance, a slight glaze over her eyes. She turned her head my way, skin nearly parchment-thin, blue veins tracing their way across her cheeks and brow. She gave no indication she saw me or anything else in the room.

Cord looked up, noticed my empty plate. He gestured in my direction.

"Lux, meet Nenn. Nenn, meet Lux."

I nodded, and she favored me with a smile.

"Pleased to meet you. Where did you get that wonderful glow about your flesh? Your hair is wonderful. How do you keep the lice from it?" she asked.

I looked to Cord. He gave a slight shake of his head. It wasn't the weirdest introduction I'd experienced, but it counted among them. Cord changed the subject.

"So... Lux here was just telling me that she would love to join us—"

"Yes," Lux interrupted. "Yes, I would *love* to join your little ad-ven-ture, but you see, I have a condition, and I'm afraid the Arcanum won't let me go without a bit of a fight, or some extreme convincing."

"Condition?" I asked.

Cord groaned and banged his head into the table. I leaned in.

"What?" I asked.

"You can't just ask people why they're undead, Nenn."

Lux opened her mouth and sucked in a breath. I sat up and turned my attention back to her.

"I'm dead. Well, I mean I was, but now I'm not. It's more like a bad cold at this point, but no one's sure it's not catching, and they're worried if I bite someone they might accidentally die— oh, speaking of die, have you *seen* the Archmagus' robes? Heavenly. What was I saying? Oh yeah, I'm sorta dead, and we might need to kill some people to make them forget that."

"Whoa," Rek pushed his plate away and raised his hands, palms out. "I dunno about killing. Maybe we just rough them up?"

"See, the problem with that, is that wizards have long memories and bad tempers, and if you don't kill them and hide the bodies, they tend to hold a grudge," Cord said.

Lux nodded. The table fell silent, and I looked at Cord. He winked at me, so I looked at Lux. She shot me a smile, and I turned to Rek. He'd found something in his nails of great interest. I let out a long, drawn-out sigh. A grin spread across Cord's face.

"Relax, you'll love this plan," he said.

"Fuck. Who we gotta kill?" I said.

4

LET US NEVER SPEAK OF THIS AGAIN

I DID NOT LOVE this plan. Turned out the harbormaster needed killing. Because we also needed to steal a boat. Not a boat like we'd rowed in on, but a proper boat, with sails and a rudder and cabins. It also turned out that in addition to being a ranking member of the Council, the harbormaster moved about with two guards at all times. Leashmen who wouldn't hesitate to put a blade through any random neck they found themselves pointed at.

I excused myself to the privy to change my kama and seethe. I didn't know what Cord was dragging us into, but I felt the level of danger approaching lethal for everyone not named Cord. And maybe Lux. I didn't know if the undead could re-die, to be honest.

When I came out, he pulled me into a corner, a solemn look on his face.

"Wha-?" I said.

"We need to talk," he said.

"You couldn't wait until I came back to the table?"

He shook his head. "Not for this."

"So, you just ambush a person outside the privy? You are lucky I didn't have a knife. Or a full bladder."

"Isn't that why you went in there?"

"Yeah, but--I think we're getting sidetracked. What do you want?"

He nodded and took a deep breath through his nose. "Look, this could go bad for everyone. If we don't all make it out, I want you to run. Get as far away as you can."

"Shouldn't you be telling everyone this?"

He shook his head. "I need you to keep everyone together. Tell them I told you the whole plan, that you can pull it off without me, but you have to make a stop. Ditch them at the first dirtwater you come across and keep going."

"That seems... shitty."

He shook his head. "They can take care of themselves. Besides, splitting up will keep people off your back."

"Then what?"

"Find a man in Orlecht, name of Clane. He'll make sure you get your cut, no matter what."

I raised an eyebrow. "You have friends? In Orlecht?"

He shrugged. "You don't think I share everything with you, do you?"

I thought about it, shook my head. "No, you're not as dumb as you act."

"Good, Nenn. Good. Also, fuck you."

"Fuck you," I said, and he chucked me on the shoulder.

"Let's get back, shall we? Larceny and murder wait for no one."

I chuckled and followed him back to the table.

"FUCK FUCK FUCKITY FUCK," Cord said.

We sat in the second story of a netmaker's shop, looking out over the docks. It was little effort to convince the owner to let us rent the space. While nets are useful on a lake, they had to be made of special stuff in Tremaire, and it was expensive work. A little gold can grease a lot of palms, they say.

Boats bobbed in their berths, masts waving gently as they tossed a bit with the tide. Ours was a shallow draft tall ship just under forty feet named the Bough Mount, though none of us knew what that actually meant. Paint peeled from the hull, and the masts looked like they'd give you a splinter if you looked at them wrong. Still, it sat high in the water, and the sails looked to be in good condition.

Cord's string of profanity was due to a squat figure in robes surrounded by several men—far more than three—currently searching our boat. We watched them mill and huddle, some of the Leashmen taking up posts that effectively blocked off the dock and the berth, others poking around amidships. The harbormaster called something down into the cabin of the boat. Another figure in black robes with a flesh-enrobed skull tucked under his arm came up the stairs. Scarified skin in thick ridges of raised flesh marked out pale tracks on bare arms.

"Harrower," Cord said, voice low.

"How in the snowy hells did you manage to pick the one boat to steal that happens to be currently undergoing a rectal inspection?" I asked.

Rek leaned forward in his chair. "Cord could fuck up an erection if he was getting it stroked, that's how."

Lux giggled and Cord flipped them both the bird.

"Aw, Cordy, you know it's true. You remember that Ithian? What was his name? Yan? Had his hand in your trousers and you'd had too many? Dipped down to finish the job and you just puked right on his beautiful bald head. Never seen a man with skin that dark turn that red," Lux said.

Cord muttered something and turned to the window, watching the party on the dock. He fell quiet for several minutes, a stark counterpoint to Rek and Lux chatting behind us. Finally, he turned back, a slow grin spreading across his face.

"I have a plan," he said.

THE THING you have to understand about Cord's plans is this: they were usually very good. That was the upside. The downside meant that someone usually found themselves in mortal danger. There were better than even odds that thanks to the encounter with Hex, everyone already knew Cord had arrived. It flattened Cord's chances of strolling around without at least one Leashman trailing his shadow. We weren't usually so lucky though. There were probably three. A side effect of burning people on your deals meant they were inclined to no longer trust you, and ensure that no one else trusted you.

We suspected that was the reason for the boat search, though it wasn't a certainty. For one, we had no idea how they sussed out *which* boat Cord targeted. Wizards are wily, and sneaky, and generally not to be trusted. They might have pulled that information from the aether. They might have used a crystal ball. Maybe they threw a dart at a peasant until he squealed and pointed at the nearest thing that meant no one would throw darts at him. Between that and the disgruntled guard, it meant our plan to jump the harbormaster and steal the boat, or any boat at this point, was out of the question. In truth, I was a little relieved. I'd secretly agreed with Rek, but they'd forced me into a decision. Offing the Harbormaster seemed like a good way of sending up a 'please kill us' flare. I'd hoped they'd realize the insanity of it. I'd apparently hoped wrong.

Cord stared at the docks. "Can't you do your woman

thing, Nenn?"

"What the hell is the woman thing?"

"You know, boobs, butt, smile."

"That is really insulting."

"But it works, right?"

"Well, yeah. Men are stupid. But it's probably a bad idea in this case. Those men have swords, and in my experience, men who don't get what they want tend to try to take it."

"Yeah, they're shits like that," Rek agreed. "Think harder," he told Cord.

So, here we were. Ten Leashmen. One wizard. One Harrower. Even the wizard—a smile, an interest in his power and station—done. But the Harrower, that was a problem. They didn't think like men or women, didn't think of anything other than the dark and the things that lived there, and they could unleash it on you at any time. They were smart, and mean, and I suspected took joy in the combination. Gods forbid they ever gained significant power, and if it looked close that they might, gods willing, someone put them down.

<hr>

CORD AND LUX took a trip into the shopping district as soon as the sun lightened the horizon, leaving Rek and I to watch the dock. The coterie hadn't moved from their positions.

"They've been standing there for hours," Rek said. "We should probably come up with a new plan."

I was inclined to agree with him. I opened my mouth to say so when a new group of Leashmen arrived and relieved the others of duty. The Harbormaster left with them, though I noticed the Harrower still sat on crates nearby. Now and then, he raised the severed head he carried and spoke softly to it. I shuddered.

"Well, that's one down," I said, referring to the leaving wizard.

Rek nodded and crossed his arms over his chest, leaning back in his chair. "Whaddya think of Lux?"

"Creepy, but she's got a certain charm," I said.

Rek nodded. "She went through the trials here about three years back. It cracked her. She died and somehow came back. I don't know why they let her walk out of there. The Leashmen are paranoid about magic they don't understand."

"They don't understand necromancy?"

Rek shook his head. "From what they say, it wasn't necro. Whoever--or whatever--brought her back wasn't anywhere near."

"So why did they? Let her go, that is."

Rek shrugged. "Maybe she knew someone in the Circle. Maybe they took pity on her. Got to be hard, passing though the deadlands to the other side and then getting yanked back. Either way, she got real lucky."

"That's surprising, considering the Harrowers."

Rek shook his head. "Harrowers are scary, but they don't fuck with the Veil."

"Why *is* that?"

"Not sure. There's a rumor though that even touching the other side, just for a moment, can let all kinds of things into your head, let alone the world. Scares the hell out of the whitebeards, though."

"You think she brought something back?"

Rek waved a hand. "Could've. Might not have. Maybe she just woke something up."

"Like?"

"They say there are things sleeping beyond the Veil."

"What kind of things?"

"Dunno. Things. I'm just an interested observer, not a scholar."

"You're just full of interesting information."

Rek shrugged again. "I'm a freakin' font."

The door burst open and Cord and Lux swept in, bags in their hands.

"Darling!" Cord exclaimed. "You are going to love your new look!"

"Shit," I breathed.

They proceeded to pull robes, tunics, trousers, and all manner of accessories from the bags, tossing them into a pile on the floor. I spotted a number of earrings and chains, a femur; a gnarled stick carved with small faces I assumed was supposed to be a wand, and a stuffed squirrel. I picked it up out of morbid curiosity. The taxidermist had posed it with both paws raised, claws outspread, teeth bared. Buttons stood from its skull in place of eyes, and its tail was a dagger blade. I dropped it and wiped my hands on my trousers.

"What the fuck?" I asked.

Cord turned to me while emptying bags, a grin on his face. A shit-eating grin, in retrospect.

"You remember that idea I had?"

"Yeah?" I drew the word out, not liking where this was going.

"Well... you need a disguise."

My stomach sank. I looked at the accumulated accoutrements. Wands, robes, miscellaneous items for piercings... the squirrel. I looked at Cord in horror.

"You want me to pretend to be a Harrower!"

"Well, yeah."

"Why me?"

He sighed, as if long-suffering and I suppressed the urge to punch his nose into his sinus cavity.

"Lux is a student here. Rek looks like someone dug up a

boulder and taught it to talk, and I am well-known. Too much so. And that leaves you, my dear."

"Fuck," I muttered, and started to dig through the piles. I held up a hoop twisted to look like a barbed wire. "You know I don't have any piercings, right?"

Cord shrugged. "We'll improvise."

I sincerely hoped that didn't mean he'd find a way to pierce me. I sorted through the piles, trying to discern what a Harrower might wear. I needed to get in the right mindset. I took a deep breath, and tried to think scary thoughts. Spiders. Spiders made of dicks. Cord's dick. Yeah, that did it. I shuddered and picked out a sleeveless robe covered with scrawled writing, a necklace of teeth, and the squirrel. I slipped to the privy, changed my kama and my clothes, and chewed another sliver of slipweed. I'd been lucky, as it kept the worst of the cramps at bay so far.

I exited the privy to moderate applause, and grimaced.

"I feel like a troubled teen."

Cord laughed, then gestured that we should gather round.

THE SIMPLICITY of the plan both impressed and disappointed me. I love the beauty of a complex web of deception, but when it comes down to execution, simple is always better for the players. Unfortunately, it required two of us to put ourselves in the shit. Lux had the job of luring the Leashmen away. I needed to convince the Harrower to leave. If I couldn't talk him into it, I'd resort to plan B: stabbing him in the neck 'til he didn't live no more. I squirmed in the heavy robes while I waited for Lux to get into position. The wool scratched my skin into itchy redness, and I fought the urge to rip it off and throw it out the window, followed by a plunge directly into the lake.

The others waited closer to the boat. While Lux and I occupied the guards, they'd sneak aboard as soon as the coast was clear. I shifted again and blew an irritated breath. I didn't know how wizards did it. Cord claimed they were all naked underneath, but considering the small amount of now-inflamed skin mine touched, I sincerely fucking doubted it. Then again, maybe that explained all the latent evil.

Finally, a screech echoed down the street, breaking the waiting tension. A workman sprinted by, stopping only long enough to look behind him. Moments later, several more followed. Lux appeared soon after, running pell-mell at them, howling and growling the entire way. A siren sounded somewhere deeper in town, and an air of panic filled Tremaire like a haze as other groups popped into view and charged about in chaotic herds.

"Help! It's escaped! It's escaped!" A man in an apron yelled as he rounded a corner.

He carried a basket of baked goods, pelting Lux as she drew near. A pastry filled with custard exploded against her. She paused in her pursuit long enough to dip a finger in the dessert and bring it to her lips. She licked her lips and winked at the baker, sending him screaming as she loosed another roar.

He sprinted away in a panic, disappearing down a side street. I watched while the Leashmen's mild interest became alarm. The captain turned and said something to the Harrower, then readied squad arms and set off in a quick march down the street, filing away from the dock. I waited until the last disappeared around the corner, then straightened and sauntered onto the dock.

The harrower looked up as I approached. A pinched face held milky eyes, fat lips, and a shocking lack of eyebrows. It was a face built for cruelty. I halted a few feet from him. He spoke in a high, thin voice that set my teeth on edge.

"And what do you need? I supposed all our brothers and

sisters were in the Hive."

Oh good. They called it the Hive. That wasn't creepy at all. "The Harbormaster—"

"That fat shit? He couldn't find his cock in the dark with both hands and a glowlight."

"That's the one. He asked me to relieve you."

The Harrower frowned and turned his head to one side. "That seems unlikely. He knows what I've seen here. Death lurks," he lifted the severed skull and kissed its lips. "Yes, Raze knows it lurks. He has told me with his own dry lips."

I cleared my throat and gripped the squirrel dagger tighter. "Well, Biffy here says you're to leave."

"Really." The Harrower's not-eyebrows came together. "Interesting." He paused. "You know what I think? I think you're not a Harrower at all."

"I am too. I even have Biffy here." I waved the squirrel at him.

"Oh yeah? Then Harrow something."

"What?"

"You heard me. Bring forth a nightmare."

"You first."

He sighed, and stood. He was easily a foot taller than me; making me aware I stood alone on a dock with a half-mad wizard. He lifted the skull, and emitted a high-pitched squeal. I winced as it reached a peak, and the skull's eyes took on an unnatural glow. The air before him rippled and distorted, and I knew two things were about to happen. One, something very unpleasant was going to come out of that space, and two, he'd know I couldn't Harrow. I panicked.

I rushed him while he still held his eyes shut. I raised the squirrel, wicked tail blade glinting in the weird light from the skull's sockets. Just as the humming stopped in an abrupt squeal, I jammed the dagger end of the dead rodent into his throat and sawed sideways, spraying myself with blood. I left it as he toppled, all sound cutting off aside from a wet gurgle. I moved to push the body into the water, and a sound behind me made me spin.

Something fleshy came scuttling toward me, plump and pink.

"Oh gods." The words escaped me involuntarily.

It was a fucking dick spider. I cursed myself for imagining such a thing before facing a Harrower. It was worse than I'd pictured. My heart hammered in panic. I bravely screamed a battle cry that definitely wasn't a cry of disgust and stomped it to death with one steel-shod boot. The heel made the fleshy tubes burst and squish, spraying black ichor over the boards of the dock. As it died, it shuddered and chirped frantically. It stopped moving with one last horrifying squeal.

Heaving for breath, I pushed first it, and then the Harrower's body--still sporting a taxidermied squirrel protruding from the neck--into the lake. I imagined the wizard still squirming as he fell, and choked back a retch. He sank with a splash into the murky water, and even as his robes billowed under the surface, Cord and the rest came sprinting from their hiding places. Lux stopped long enough to give me a sideways look. They leaped over the side of the boat, and cast the ropes off.

"Fer fuck's sake, Nenn!" Cord hissed. "You gonna stand there in the fuckin' slop you made, or get on the godsdamned boat?"

I shook myself and fled, feet slipping for a moment in the gore. I pitched over the side of the dock, nearly joining the Harrower below, then a strong hand gripped my arm, and Rek hauled me aboard. The boat drifted away from the dock, and with a little help from Cord and Rek, was soon underway. I collapsed on the deck and watched the sky and clouds slip by as the sails unfurled and caught the wind.

5

DOESN'T THIS SHITHEAP GO ANY FASTER

WE CROSSED the lake at a good clip, the wind at our backs despite the tree cover when Cord shouted from the crow's nest.

"Masts!"

He slid down the rigging, moving as easily as a spider in its web, and the memory of the thing on the dock made me involuntarily scrape my boots on the deck. I suppressed a shudder of disgust. Cord jumped from the net of ropes and landed lightly on the deck. I was impressed. I hadn't expected him to move so nimbly. In the Veldt, knowing a ship or a boat was almost required education in your youth, and most of the common people did one stint or another aboard a fishing or farming trawler. Still, for a man of Cord's stature, his dexterity came as a small surprise.

He hurried up to the quarterdeck, where Rek manned the wheel. Cord pointed over his shoulder. I joined them, Lux climbing the stairs to the other side. We gathered at the aft, watching. For a moment, all we saw was the gentle curve of the horizon and the dwindling spire of the Arcanum. Then several tall masts appeared, breaking the line where water met sky.

They gained rapidly, churning up water behind them. And behind those, a massive shape breached the water, mottled skin absorbing the light.

"Mage engines," Cord spat. "They'll be on us in less than an hour."

"What's the thing following them?" I asked.

"Leviathan," Lux said.

"Fuck," Cord whispered.

"What do we do?" Rek asked. "This heap hasn't any weapons."

"We're not going to outrun them, either," Lux said. "I can whip up a wind that'll keep us ahead for a while, but we'll need another solution. Unless you can fly or breathe water, then you should probably start doing that."

Cord nodded. "Get us the wind."

Cord kept an eye on the ships behind us. Static built in the air nearby, then discharged with a whoosh, speeding our ship along at the head of our own private zephyr. I glanced once behind us and made my way down to the gallery. A privy sat amid our quarters, and I relieved myself, and then changed my kama. I sat for a short while, letting the roll of the water and the effect of the slipweed soothe my aches.

I curled and uncurled my toes, a trick taught me by an old constable. It was supposed to drive some of the stress away. All it did was make my feet cramp. The entire endeavor seemed cursed from the start. If I didn't know better, I'd think all the gods of the Veldt stood against us, arrayed like sentinels. The idea honestly made as much sense as humans interested in the affairs of ants.

I'm not much for religion, never really was. It's hard to believe in any deity that says 'This is your lot in life. You can't improve it, but if you worship me, I can make it not worse'.

That's not patronage, it's blackmail. It's a protection racket. I'd seen a million of them, growing up in the streets and the alleys. I could respect the hustle, but not the sentiment. Seemed to me those with power possessed a responsibility to those smaller than them. Had a *duty*. Don't be a shit, and don't make the world worse, and if you have the means, *make it better*. Life is already paved with a spiraling path toward entropy. We didn't need to add to it.

Not that Anaxos' priests knew anything about that. The churches were in on it. Tithe, donate, spend. Make the pews more comfortable, make the books more ornate, make the spire bigger so we can fuck the heavens with our giant phallic patriarchal metaphor. The only thing we shared was belief in Camor, patron of thieves. The difference was, we worshipped them in the open, and the priests sneered in public and knelt at the altar in secret. I honestly didn't know which would please Camor more. According to Cord, their sense of humor was only outweighed by their propensity for mischief.

A deep shuddering moan from the hold below interrupted my thoughts. I broke from the room and sprinted above deck, making for the aft. The others still gathered around the rail, watching the mage ships gain. I saw detail—naked steel masts crackling with energy, the hulls low and sleek. A crew of mundane sailors worked the decks, and three mages stood on the prow of each. At the near distance, power filled the air, thickening it.

"Gods, what did we steal?" I asked.

Cord shrugged. "Might be about who you killed."

I swallowed hard. The ship rocked slightly, and I tapped Cord on the shoulder. He looked away from our pursuers.

"There's something in the hold," I said.

He grimaced and nodded. "Hold the wheel," he said to Rek.

He motioned for Lux and me to follow and led us below deck. The stairs creaked as we descended. First past the middle decks, and then down to stowage. I halted when I saw the thing squatting in the middle of the floor.

"You knew about this?" I asked, suppressing the urge to punch Cord in the neck.

Cord nodded and Lux let out a low whistle.

"This is grotesque," Lux said. "Impressively so. I wonder how they managed this—I'd love to take it apart, see the tickings and the tockings and the little gristly bits."

I gave her side-eye. *This* was a Harrower engine. It followed the same principles of a mage engine—in design at least—black iron base above which a polished orb of obsidian floated. Around that, two bands of silver levitated and spun in opposition to one another. The difference was that mage engines ran on carefully grown and cultivated crystals. In the core of this one, someone had placed a human heart. It pumped away, as if it still in its owner's ribcage.

"Bleh," I said. My brain refused to find an articulate way to express my distaste.

I'd seen several gross things dealing with Cord's deaths, but this was in another room from that. Disturbing was the best I had at hand, but it felt a paltry description for the thing in front of me. Even as the silver hoops spun in lazy circles, a sort of dark light pulsed from the orb. My eyes ached looking at it.

"What's it do?" I asked.

"It uh..." Cord began.

"You don't know?" I asked, forcing my voice below the level of a scream.

Cord shrugged. "It's obviously very important."

"You stole the boat for *important*? To who?"

"To *whom*," he replied. I reached for my knives.

"It folds space," Lux said, interrupting us and keeping Cord from growing a new mouth in his neck.

"Explain that. How do you fold air?"

"If you've got two points, it brings them together by punching a hole in our reality and making a shortcut. Like cutting through a mountain instead of going around it. Super fast travel," she said.

I held up a hand. "Wait. Our reality? And a Harrower made it?" I shook my head. "No. Fuck no. No fuckin' way."

Cord chucked me on the shoulder, and for the third time that day I resisted the urge to break a part of him.

"C'mon, it'll be an adventure," he said.

"It'll be a disaster," I replied.

Cord opened his mouth to retort, but the ship shuddered and groaned, interrupting him. The boat listed for a moment before righting itself. His expression sobered.

"We were never going to outrun the mage engines without it."

My stomach knotted, then the ship shuddered again, and I heard the splinter of wood. Even from the hold, I heard Rek curse.

"We're gonna die here, Nenn," Cord said. "Or at least you will."

"I'm not a fan of death," Lux supplied. "Really, the once was enough."

I cursed and spat on the deck. "Fuck. Get it running. If we get out of this, I'm going to wear your balls for earrings, Cord."

He grinned, then saw my expression and let it drop. "You should get above deck," he said, then nodded to Lux.

I climbed the stairs as the air tightened around me. Up top, a gray hue crept into the world. Though I saw the mage ships nearby, they grew transparent as each second passed, sound leeching from their pursuit. A great sigh came from below, and then a scream, like someone caught in a spiked vice. The world shimmered, and then broke. Rek screamed at the transition, and I realized we'd forgotten to tell him about the engine. I ran to the quarterdeck to calm the big man as everything disappeared and we sailed into the black.

6

I KIND OF MISS THE DICK SPIDERS

"WOOBA. WOOBA. WOOBA," Rek repeated. He'd latched onto the nonsense word like a security blanket.

The first five minutes in the deadlands passed uneventfully for him. I even thought he might adjust. Then a five-foot worm wearing what he swore was his grandmother's face leapt from the water and exploded into a shower of living pork cutlets. He'd insisted on not talking since. I let him. We all had to cope.

"Well, shithead, how do we get back?" I asked Cord.

"Just..." he contorted his face as he thought. "Hm."

"*Hm* what?"

"Well, I thought we just turned it off, but I didn't see a lever."

"Oh good," I replied, and as the words left my mouth they materialized as three-inch words dripping ice. They hung in the air for a moment, and then burst into a spray of butterflies, scattering to the winds.

Lux giggled, and I shot her a look. "Not helping. You're the wizard. Go wiz something up."

"Wooba. Wooba," Rek agreed.

She giggled again, and I rolled my eyes. Of all of us, Lux

seemed unbothered by the strangeness of the place. She sat at the bow and stared out over the black water before us. I tried not to let her calm demeanor bother me, but the situation plus Cord's idiocy had my back up.

Lux's smile dropped, and she pointed to the starboard side of the ship. The banks of the river were little more than deeper black edges at the water, barely visible. We'd been lucky so far. Rek managed to keep us from running aground, but signs of stress showed in the big man as he did his best to keep us from wrecking on the shoals.

"How you doing, buddy?" I called up at him.

"WOOB," he replied.

Lux cleared her throat, and I followed her finger. The shore filled up with pale luminous bodies, strange even for the deadlands. Each held a conglomeration of bone and flesh, appendages not where you'd expect, mouths and eyes and teeth in rings and clusters, roaming like lost travelers on an unfamiliar sea.

"I'm sure that's fine," I said.

"Wooba," Rek agreed.

I checked the port side, and it was much the same, strange creatures gathering for some unknown reason. Lux grimaced.

"Life bleeders. They're drawn to us here. We need to get out now."

"Cord, Lux—get back down to the engine. Rek, find something to fight with."

"Wooba," Rek nodded.

They bustled about, following direction. I wondered at what point I'd become the de facto leader for our little band, and realized it was when Cord decided to launch us into the shit. Nearly as soon as I'd given the orders, the bleeders waded from the shore. We'd approached a narrow point in the river, and it wouldn't take them long to reach us.

I pulled the knives from my tunic and set myself at the starboard side, Rek taking port. He'd found a makeshift club, the end iron-shod, and readied himself. We didn't have long to wait. The first of the beasts climbed the hull, digging its claws into the wood, pulling itself up inch by inch. When it reached the rail, I severed its pale, grasping fingers and it fell soundless into the water. Behind me, I heard a thump, followed by two more as Rek repelled boarders from that side. Then they were on us en masse, and I fought with as much speed as I could muster, severing limbs and slitting throats, hamstringing opponents where possible. Each fell with that same eerie silence, and it started to unnerve me.

I heard Rek cry out and spared a glance I couldn't afford. Three of the beasts pinned him down, latching on with iron jaws, sawing through his flesh. I sprinted to him, but something else had me by the legs. I toppled to the deck, jarring my teeth and biting my tongue. I rolled and rammed a dagger through one massive eye. The thing recoiled as black ooze slid from the wound. I regained my feet in time for another two beasts to pile on, dragging me down again. They bit into my wrists with needle-sharp teeth. The skin parted like paper and I felt warm blood pool in my palms, trickle down my forearms. The deck shook, and I cried out. I squeezed my eyes shut, cursing Cord under my breath.

They dug deeper, and I felt cold seep into my fingers and toes as they drew something essential from me. Then Lux was there, white fire blazing from her hands. Each bleeder she touched collapsed into a puddle of empty flesh, and as she did, the light in her eyes grew, skin gaining pink radiance it hadn't held before. I gained my feet, as did Rek, each of us making a bloody mess of things. I swayed on my feet, but managed to rally. We pressed back to back to drive the tide of beasts away.

Still they came on, and I could tell Lux was at the end of her strength, corpsefire waning. I let one last scream of defiance as the bleeders closed in, and the world shook, shuddered, and shattered. I fell, and found myself staring up at blue skies and fluffy clouds. I blinked away the black spots gathering in my vision, then sat up. Greenery passed to either side and birdsong drifted on a pleasant breeze. Rek did the same, rubbing his head, and Lux wandered away, a sly smile on her face. I sank back down.

"Well, I'm wearing Cord's balls for earrings," I said.

"Wooba," Rek agreed.

7

EVERYTHING'S FINE, IGNORE THE CORPSES

THE HARROWER ENGINE dropped us somewhere down the eastern tributary of the Lethe. We found ourselves drifting alongside tall grasses topped with golden seeds and small wild-flowers nodding in the wind. Though summer still held sway, the breeze carried a crisp bite. Just a few miles north, and you'd run into the Bladesbacks, the range running practically the entire length of the Veldt, from the sea to the western kingdoms inland. From here, we saw the peaks, tall crags topped with a thick blanket of snow. Clouds crowded the tops, the black specks of birds wheeling above their tree-lined sides. Closer, green-blue lakes spread out in patchwork, waters shimmering under the sun.

Despite it being day, I yawned tremendously. I'd spent most of the night cleaning and binding wounds, cleaning myself and the deck—pushing pools of liquefied flesh into the river, and scrubbing dried blood from my skin. After, I'd fallen into bed. Pale many-limbed beasts stalked me across a black plain in my sleep, keeping me from falling too deep. I sat in the bow beside Lux, the two of us not talking—something Cord couldn't relate to—and let the brisk air slap me awake.

I'd had time to cool down, and my cramps and flow finally abated. Lux mentioned in an aside that time passed differently in the deadlands. I considered borrowing a Harrower engine on a regular basis on learning that little nugget. Hey, don't judge until that bitch, the Red Fairy, visits you.

I took in Lux while she stared out over the bow. Her skin gained a healthy hue since our encounter, and her hair looked fuller, less brittle. The milkiness in her eyes thinned, and her lips looked fuller.

"Cord hasn't noticed, has he?"

Lux turned toward me and smiled. She shook her head.

"No. Isn't that always the way?"

"What happened back there? In the deadlands?"

Lux shrugged. "I was able to steal some of their life."

"Is it permanent?"

"I don't know. But it feels good. Better than I've felt in a while. It hurts less. When I was dead..." she trailed off. I let her. You don't have to know everything, especially the things that hurt.

Cord called out from the crow's nest, interrupting our conversation.

"Village!"

We looked, and ahead, saw the telling signs of chimney smoke and a small berth for boats. Little more than fifteen or twenty homes, but it looked like heaven from where we sat. Rek spun the wheel, bringing us closer to shore. Cord slipped down the rigging and worked the windlass, dropping the anchor into the water. It landed on the riverbed with an audible clank, and a soft cheer went up from the boat.

"All ashore that's going ashore," Cord called, and loosed the rowboat from the side.

We climbed in and made our way into the village.

IT POSSESSED ONE INN, a largish affair for the size of the village that served both travelers on the Lethe and riders on the eastern road to Midian. None of us had eaten since Tremaire, and the slipped time in the deadlands did little to dull our hunger. We piled in and set the innkeeper to work frying potatoes and cutting thick slices of pig from a spit over the fire. While we waited, the group chatted. Cord remained oddly quiet for once. I waited a bit, ready for a quip or a set-up. Instead, he leaned in, strangely sober.

"What do you see here, Nenn?"

He'd slipped into teaching mode. I straightened a bit and looked around. The inn was cozy, at least near the fire, and men and women huddled over plates and bowls of food, or chatted in low tones over pints of ale. Serving women mingled through the crowd, aprons smudged with food residue and ash, or stained with beer spills. The longer I watched, the more I noticed how harried they looked. Hair in disarray, rouge and lip stain slightly blurred from the sweat they'd worked up. The edges of their clothing frayed in strings and ragged edges.

They spent more time at certain tables as well. Despite men with brash wandering hands and lewd mouths, if their clothes were finer, or if they wore the trappings of a soldier, their orders came quickly and more often. Next were tables with couples in regular clothing—nothing fancy, but still bought from a proper tailor. They too received fair service, though a bit slower. Like the soldiers and merchants, their plates groaned with piles of meat and cheese, rich potatoes.

Last and furthest from the fire sat the workers. Homespun clothes, tattered in some cases. They'd probably worked an entire week for the pleasure of stopping from the cold of the road for a warm meal, their fare lukewarm bowls of porridge. They spoke in low tones and did their best to avoid the attentions of the moneyed classes. If they saw a server more than once, it seemed unlikely.

When I'd been silent for a time, Cord leaned in again. "Doesn't seem right, does it?"

I shook my head.

"Seems like someone should do something."

Panic seized my chest, and I grabbed Cord's wrist. "Don't you dare burn this fucking village down."

Cord laughed, made a *psst* sound. "Wouldn't think of it. But sometimes people deserve a decent meal, don't they?"

I nodded. He worked himself free and approached the innkeeper, a fat bag appearing in his hand. They spoke in close, quiet tones, and the innkeeper took the bag with a smile. Cord returned to the table with a grin of his own.

"There. Not so bad, right? The innkeeper makes money; these people get a nice dinner and save some coin."

"All right," I admitted grudgingly. "You did a good thing."

He opened his mouth to gloat some more, but our plates arrived interrupting him. I stuffed a potato between his lips to shut him up. He made a muffled noise and set to chewing.

WE WALKED BACK to the boat to the sound of cheers. They dwindled behind us. Despite offers to bed down for the night and the promise of real food, leaving a Harrower engine unattended seemed like a terrible idea. Word got out that Cord paid for dinner and drinks and the people raised him up as hero of the day. The spirits in the room lifted immensely, and someone started a round of *My Lady Fanny*. Before long, almost the entire inn joined in, to the consternation of several of the more proper women in the room.

It wasn't until Rek pointed out that the soldiers looked less than happy that the local citizenry was anything but miserable that we made our goodbyes. We beat a hasty retreat down the country lane to the water, doing our best to appear unhurried.

"See, Nenn? Feels good to do good, right?" Cord said.

"I can't believe I'm saying this, but you managed to not fuck this up," Rek said.

"That was amazingly disaster-free," Lux said.

I opened my mouth to agree, and found myself staring at the business end of a short sword. My sentence changed of its own accord.

"Fuck," I said.

"Ever astute," Cord said.

Three men wearing chainmail and tabards blocked the path. The clink and chime of armor behind us alerted us to the presence of more arriving. I cursed again. The soldiers from the inn. The one with the blade pressed forward, pushing us back into a tight knot. He was thick and sturdy, chest like a barrel, arms the size of my thighs. I knew where my blades were, but wasn't sure I could get to them in time, let alone saw through that much muscle.

"Is there a problem, gentlemen?" Cord asked.

"Well, not as such," the big man replied. "But we noticed you seemed to have an overabundance of riches, and we being poor soldier types on poor soldier type salaries, thought you might like to redistribute the wealth."

Cord looked him up and down and winked at me. My stomach dropped. I knew the look of a man about to do something stupid. I knew it on Cord like the back of my hand. I moved my hands closer to my blades and shook my head.

"No," I mouthed. He ignored me.

"And why would I share with class traitors?" Cord asked.

The leader's brow beetled. It was obvious he didn't know the vagaries of socioeconomic policy, but he certainly knew an insult when he heard one. His men reached for their blades, and found ourselves confronted with a small hedge of steel.

"What'd you call me? We're as loyal to King Mane as anyone." he said.

"And that's the problem," Cord replied.

He pulled a knife free and launched himself onto the big man's blade, the steel ripping through his ribcage and punching out his back. The soldier had the good grace to look surprised before Cord rammed his knife into the man's eye. That done, Cord promptly died, dragging both men down into a floppy tangle. The street erupted into chaos.

A soldier charged Rek, but made a fatal mistake. He'd charged Rek. The big man possessed a surprising amount of speed. He sidestepped and grabbed his opponent's sword arm, then snapped it like a twig. Rek picked the blade up with a casual nonchalance and slammed it through the soldier's chest, chainmail parting like tissue. Two down.

Three came at Lux, then the night flashed bright white, leaving nothing but smoking piles of meat. That left the one facing me. I feinted, and he broke, turning tail down the path. I let him get a few yards away then tossed a dagger. It landed with a satisfying *thunk* in the back of his neck. He dropped like a sack of rocks.

We gathered our things, disentangling Cord's corpse from the mess, Rek carrying him like luggage back to the boat. Once aboard the Bough Mount, I raised the anchor while Rek unfurled the sails and got us running. Underway again, I joined him on the quarterdeck. Cord's body lay on the deck below us.

"Well, that was a fuckin' stain," Rek said.

"Isn't it always?"

"Yeah."

I looked up at the stars. "Nice night."

"Yeah."

We sailed on.

8

STORYTIME FOR WAYWARD ROGUES

WE MADE our slow way east by southeast, drifting down a wide branch of the Lethe that crawled its way toward Midian and the sea. We saw the ocean, a silver expanse to the east that brought with it the smells of salt and sand and the cries of gulls. Farther out, black shapes bobbed on the waves, trawlers and merchant ships at anchor.

Cord's body still lay on the deck. Rek wanted to put him below, but I'd argued against it, considering the strange things he vomited up when he revived. Gods only knew where they'd end up or what they'd become if they got loose in the hold. I couldn't understand why he'd thrown a life away so easily. Was he that committed to his crusade? Was he simply unhinged? Regardless, he was dead for now.

We kept watch in shifts, shooing the flies away and erecting a makeshift shelter that kept the worst of the sun from baking him like a roast pig. In the meantime, I took the chance to chat with Rek. I liked Lux, but let's be honest, she was pretty, but the kind of pretty that comes with roses. Hidden somewhere in all that were thorns, and they just waited to draw blood. To keep too-curious hands away from the blossom. This is a weird metaphor, right?

I wondered again at the lesson Cord tried to teach me in the village. The obvious takeaway was that things were hard, and inequality didn't make it better. There was more there though. I had the sinking feeling that he hadn't intended it as an admonishment to keep an eye on those less fortunate, to do a kindness for them. I saw the grim look in his eye, the disdain he had for the wealthy. I had the suspicion Cord meant to do for everyone. I only wondered what that entailed, and how much blood it required.

"You got that look in your eye," Rek said.

"What look?"

"That look that says you'd be better off if Cord wasn't causing trouble."

I didn't answer, and Rek shrugged. "We could toss him overboard, sail into the sunset."

When I still didn't answer, Rek chuckled. "Kidding. He'd pollute the river."

"I just keep thinking there's more to this. This isn't just a heist to him. I think Cord intends to go down in a big way, and that freaks me out a little. Where's that put the rest of us?"

Rek took a turn at thinking quietly. "I've known Cord a long time. He's a sonovabitch, but I'll be honest, he cares about his crew. Whatever happens, it'll happen for all of us."

"Did Cord tell you the plan?" I asked.

Cord had a habit of keeping his ideas close to the vest until the last minute. This one though, he'd deemed too important. He'd *needed* us to know, like it was a fire he couldn't control, and he needed to pass it on unless it burned him to a husk. He'd told me almost as soon as he'd decided.

Rek nodded and twitched the wheel, correcting for a sandbar. "Yeah, we're hitting the treasury."

"Does that seem insane to you?"

He shrugged. "No more than most of his ideas. But if I were pressed? I'd say it's way more dangerous than most of his ideas. He'd always been pretty content with small cons and knock-offs. If you ask me, that whole not-dying thing knocked those rocks in his head loose."

I thought of the tavern again. "Anaxos," I said.

"What about him?"

"Cord hates the rich. I think he'd eat them if he could. Who's richer than Anaxos?"

Rek thought for a minute. "A man with a lot of friends?"

"That doesn't sound right," I said.

"So he's gonna knock off the richest man in the world in order to what, teach him a lesson?"

The sound of retching interrupted us. I looked over to see Cord on his hands and knees, hacking his guts out. His throat distended, and a long worm, purple, with a shock of black hair spilled out. He punched it once, spattering its guts across the deck. He flopped back again, gasping.

"Yeah, we're gonna teach him a lesson," Cord said. His voice was a raw rasp. "To the tune of his money and his dignity. Fuck Anaxos Mane. He's an oleaginous sore on the face of the world, a pustule brimming with narcissism and contempt for simple human decency."

I looked at Rek. The big man shrugged. My stomach knotted, and I did my best to ignore the impending feeling of doom that threatened to creep up and beat me about the skull with a club.

EVENING DRIFTED IN, the clouds sliding from shades of pink to orange, then purple and black. We hung lanterns on the rails of the ship, and Rek retired to his cabin, with Lux not far behind. I'd had the opportunity to sleep a little during the day, and stayed up beside Cord as he took the wheel. His hands, though not particularly large, gripped the spokes with confidence.

Evening passed for an hour, maybe two, with each of us silent, enjoying the other's company. We might bicker, but Cord and I had ever been friends. Even then, I couldn't help shooting worried glances his way while he stared into the night, steering us away from sandbar and shoal.

Finally, he sighed. "You're too quiet."

I shrugged, though I knew he couldn't see it.

"You think I've cracked," he said.

It took me another minute to answer. "Wouldn't you worry?"

"About a friend that kept dying and resurrecting in increasingly horrible ways? Sure," he laughed. "But I'm not cracked."

He switched tracks, breaking the thread of the conversation.

"Have I ever told you the story of how Camor stole the sun?"

"You have not," I said.

"How do you know so little of the world, Nenn?"

"I'm like a babe in swaddling."

"A scary, stabby baby."

I chose to ignore that. "I'd never much taken to religion at the orphanage. I did the required, and little else. And Camor? Taboo among the nuns of Our Lady of Perpetual Weeping and Moaning."

He looked to the stars, peeking between cloud and strips of black above.

"You'll like this," he said.

He cleared his throat and began.

A LONG TIME ago - that's how these things always start, anyways - there was the dark, and man, and man was afraid of the dark.

So many stories start in the dark. That's because for a long time, man didn't have light. They huddled together, in their caves and their secret places, away from the beasts. They held sharpened sticks and fended off the night when it came for them. They weren't always successful. Men died. Women died. Children died. Or worse.

Worse?

Sometimes the dark didn't kill them, but got inside. Some, it made sick. Others, it took. It brought them into the fold and changed them, made them crave the flesh of families, made them hunt their own children. Others, it made generals, great leaders of beasts that had never seen the light. They fought for so long, but the thing about fighting for so long in the dark, with no light at the end, is that you get tired. You just want to sleep. Some gave up. They walked into the long night and never looked back.

So it went, generation after generation, until one day, all the people that ever were at that point huddled together in one cave. They were sore and weary, and began to argue.

"We should fight until the end," some said.

"We should walk out," others said, "let the dark take us."

"We should lie down and sleep until the end," said the third group.

It was then that a voice, younger than the others, but still strong, spoke up. "We should fight with something they've never seen before."

"And what is that?

"Light."

They shook their heads in bewilderment and scratched their pates and wondered if the young man had gone mad. He held up his hands for quiet, and then told them of a dream he'd had, of a glittering thing that shone in a way that the dark couldn't stop. Of the way the things in the night were afraid of it. The way beasts feared it. When they asked where it came from, he told them it was a thing of the gods.

So, the young man told them his story. And they laughed at him. Until he went to the mouth of the cave and stared into the dark. Then, they no longer laughed. They begged and pleaded, and wheedled and cried and finally cursed, saying that if he was going to throw away the future of the clan, then he could rot in the dark with the rest of them.

Their warnings and curses went unheeded though, and he walked out.

What happened next?

He found the light.

How?

Tests, trials, labors. There are always three.

Three is sacred to one deity or another - the Goddess, God, Camor - it's all very mathematical and proper, as things are with their sort.

So, what happened?

Well, he walked. For a long time. And it was dull. There was very little to see at that time, due to the darkness. Not many things could live in it, though somehow man did. I suspect resourcefulness was a gift from the gods, because man could find food in the dark - mushrooms and lichen from the caves, water from the grottos, meat from the occasional lizard that wandered through - though, let me tell you, raw lizard tastes awful. Sure, it's a delicacy some places, but not for me. They also found wood from trees that grew in the caves where a lizard carried a seed, though it grew hard and leafless and completely inflammable. A joke of the dark, I think.

He walked for three days, somehow avoiding the eyes of the

dark, and on the third day, came to a stream. A bird--ravens were common even then--had landed on a rock in the stream after some beast or other wounded its wing, and stood trapped atop the small piece of shale. While the water wasn't deep for a man, it was deadly to a bird not made for swimming, so the boy decided he would wade in and rescue the raven. When he reached the edge of the stream, the bird spoke.

"Look out!" It called. "The water is thick with the teeth of the dead!"

The boy looked down and saw it to be true. Beneath the surface of the water, bone-white teeth glinted in the moonlight.

I thought you said there wasn't any light.

Moonlight is not the same as light. You know that. Could you grow a tree by moonlight? Frighten a predator?

Sorry.

The boy paused at the edge of the water and looked. He had his spear with him, and thought "maybe...," so he laid it across the stream, and it reached the rock. The raven hopped across, holding its broken wing out. Just before the end, it dipped its beak into the water and grabbed a tooth, holding it up as it hopped onto the shore. The boy held his hand out and the raven spat the smooth white canine into his hand. It was long and sharp, and he felt it ready to bite.

"Thank you," said the raven. "Fasten this to your spear, and you will be able to pierce even the sky."

"Will you be okay?" The boy asked.

The raven bobbed its head. "I will be fine. Now go."

The boy strapped the tooth to the point of his spear and went on his way, leaving the raven behind. He walked another three days, until he came to a great forest, one older than even the darkness, and worked his way through.

Wait. I thought you just said trees couldn't grow in moonlight.

You're right - they can't. I did say this place was older than the dark. Such things did - still do - exist.

The boy came to the center of the forest, and there he saw a bear, leg stuck fast in one of the night's traps. He went to the bear and knelt beside him, inspecting his leg.

"I think I can get it off," the boy said.

The bear shook his head. "Do not. It is a strong tar. Even touching it would stick you hopelessly."

The boy thought for a moment, then used his spear to pry the jaws of the trap apart. The mechanism snapped open, and the bear pulled his leg free. The tar clung to the tip of the spear.

"Thank you, boy," the bear said. "With that tar, you can catch the most cunning of prey."

He wandered into the woods, leaving the boy alone. After a time, the boy continued. He walked for three more days, leaving the forest behind. By now, his stomach was growling, and his step was unsure. He had come so far, and been lucky in that the dark seemed not to see him. Finally, he came to an arch set in a plain countryside. It had no house, nor any frame, but you could not see the other side through it. He stepped though, and screamed in horror.

The light was more than he'd expected, more than he'd dreamt. It seared his skin, made his eyes burn. He cowered before it, and flung his hands over his face. He lay that way for some time, his hands over his eyes. He cursed the gods and their tricks, and cursed the dark and its cruelty. He trembled, part in fear, part in rage. He could not die here! He could not let the gods have their joke!

Slowly, he stood, and through squinting eyes, he picked up his spear. He aimed with a trembling hand. Sweat covered his skin, and his grip was unsure. Still, he pulled back, and let fly. The spear flew like an arrow, like a hawk at its prey. It struck the sun, and with a *thunk*, sliced off a piece that stuck to the tar. The spear fell away and landed to earth, the tip still burning.

The boy picked up the torch, and marveling at its light weight and heat, returned the way he'd come. He decided if he couldn't destroy the thing in the sky, he would steal a piece for his people. Let the gods have their joke - he would use it to his advantage. He walked, back through the arch and through the forest, beside the stream, and finally, back to his cave. Where he went, the light spread, driving back the dark things, making greenery bloom around him. He called out to his people.

"Come and see what I have brought!"

They came, tempted by the light, and though they shielded their eyes, they rejoiced at the new sights, at the fleeing darkness.

"What do we do with it?" They asked the boy.

In answer, he flung the spear into the sky, and there it stuck.

And that's how we got the sun.

CORD'S VOICE drifted off over the water.

"I thought you said Camor had no gender?" I asked, genuinely curious.

"Ah, but that is a story for another time. Did you learn anything from this one?"

I thought. "Aye. Sometimes you have to steal, even from the gods. For the good of all."

Cord nodded. "That's Camor's first rule. Do for others as you'd do for yourself. Everything else is fair game."

9

DOLPHIN ORGY

DAWN SPLIT THE NIGHT, spilling the light's guts across the land. It bled pinks and golds that leached from the clouds as the sun rose higher, lighting the end of the Veldt and the start of the sea. I blinked the sleep from my eyes and dipped my head into a bucket at the rail, blowing water from my nose, and then visited the privy. When I re-emerged, Rek was back at the wheel, and Cord laid out a small feast—little silver fish and dried seaweed. We ate in silence and watched as the ship passed the outskirts of Midian.

Traffic had picked up again, and we joined a steady stream of ships and smaller scullers and boats approaching the city. A sound off the port side drew me, and I peered into the water. Orcas by groups of two thrashed together, churning it to froth. I called to Cord.

"What are they doing?" I asked.

He sauntered over and leaned across the rail, watching. A crooked grin crept onto his face.

"Fucking. Geez Nenn, you've never seen fucking?"

He went back to his meal, leaving me to stare down at the orgy going on below.

"I've seen fucking," I muttered. "Not *fish*, but..."

I wandered away from the rail, my interest lost in the mating habits of fish. If I was honest, too much time had passed since I'd had anything between my legs that didn't belong to me. I squashed the thought and wandered back to the meal.

The city loomed in the distance, a smudge on the near horizon. At this distance clouds of smoke rose from the districts as if the city burned. Closer, massive farms dominated wide expanses of the alluvial plain, dim shapes walking among the rows or guiding mounts with plows. They picked and weeded, guided irrigation ditches, or slopped pails of night soil exported from the city onto the crops. As we passed, snatches of song and shouts came to us, and once, a small group of children ran along the bank, their clothing dull but well kept. They waved at the ship as it passed and shouted in half-heard nonsense. We waved back and threw them small candies Cord had produced from somewhere, and then we moved on.

"All of this," Cord said, after the children passed. "All of this could have belonged to these people. They should be rich. They should be fat and happy. But you see their spun clothing, the bird bones of their shoulders."

He fell silent and spat into the water, then sat looking across the fields.

I SHOULD HAVE SEEN it then. At the time, I'd thought it was the job. There's a lot of stress in getting a heist together. Assembling your team, planning, avoiding notice, pulling it off, and not getting killed by the guards. And the bigger the heist, the bigger all of these risks. And this was the mother of all heists.

Yeah, I should have known. But part of me, the part that was Cord's friend and not his partner, the part that wanted to ease his hurt and soothe his trouble, only saw the surface. I missed the rot beneath. The black canker that ached and throbbed even from the heart of Midian. That was the true weight on Cord's mind. That was the truth of his sudden furtiveness, his mood swings. Maybe it was fallout from his deaths, the corrupt magic that burned through his veins. Regardless, the darkness there called to him. Not in any way that spoke of kinship, but as anathema to his own, and he felt the urge to take a chiurgeon's tools and cut it free.

But you can never really diagnose the fatal stuff until its got its hooks good and deep in your guts.

THE APPEARANCE of sheds along the river heralded our approach to Midian. Small ramshackle things built from cast-off wood and cloth, they clustered together as if huddling against a cold that didn't come to this part of the world. They leaned on one another for support, drunken companions in the shadow of walls that dwarfed them in every aspect. The main tributary of the Lethe ran through the city, a water gate allowing ships passage through and to the sea. The walls themselves were thirty feet tall, sold gray brick cut from the clay of the delta.

Shapes stood watch between crenellations, figures wielding spear and crossbow. They clustered thicker toward the shanty-town side of the wall, though they guarded lazily, chatting among one another, spears leaning against the stonework. Someone feared this side of the city, even from inside the walls, though it appeared the common soldiers did not.

Cord took the wheel from Rek and guided us deeper into the shantytown, Up a side path on the delta. We moved away from the docks proper.

"Uh, docks are that way," Rek said.

"Yep," Cord replied.

"Okay, so why are we going this way?" Rek asked.

"Because they don't care who docks here. They care who docks in the city. What do you think *they'll* think of this shitheap?"

Lux nodded. "They also won't stab us. That's pretty good."

"I didn't say that," Cord said.

"What?" Lux replied.

"Well, I mean. Shantytown. You think they won't stab us for this boat?"

"I uh," Lux stammered. Panic lit her eyes for a brief moment, and then she reasserted control.

"We're going to trade it," Cord said.

"For what?" I asked.

"Safe passage. And information."

"But how do we leave?" Rek asked.

Cord shrugged. "Ownership is such a temporary thing. Better not to get bound up in impermanence."

"We're going to steal it back," I said.

"Potato, larceny," he said.

He steered us between two leaning shanties larger than the others. The builders here in the shadow of the wall had grown brave, and some of the buildings reached two, three stories, leaning and wobbling in the wind. These were slightly different. Sturdy and square, they formed a gate of their own, and as we passed under, I glanced up. Eyes and the glinting points of crossbow bolts stared back. They watched our passage for a tense moment. I felt my shoulders try to climb, and forced them down.

Then we were through, and I let out a breath as we came to a wide area of the river where ramshackle docks stood in crooked blocks against one another. Cord steered us into a berth and Rek spun the windlass, dropping the anchor. It hit the bottom with a clang and clank of chain, and I helped Lux shove a board over to the docks as men in rough clothing tied the boat off.

We disembarked, Cord hopping lightly from the board. A man, fat as any I'd ever seen and wearing clothes much finer than his own retinue, grabbed Cord in a bear hug. The lifted him from his feet with a deep roar, laughing as he did so. Lux and Rek looked at me. I shrugged. I saw their point. This one hadn't tried to stab him. He was either worse than Cord, or actually liked him, a deeply weird concept.

The big man set Cord on his feet and looked at the rest of us. He nodded to himself, and then turned, motioning we were to follow. We shared another look, and walked after.

I caught up to Cord as we walked and leaned in.

"Who is this?"

"Torlc. Merchant, fence, and information broker."

"He's taking the boat?"

Cord nodded.

"Do you trust him?"

"Fuck no."

"Then what are we doing here?"

"Misdirection," he said, and waggled his eyebrows.

I opened my mouth to ask another question, but it seemed we'd arrived at our destination. We stood before another solid building, this one with a door and two guards posted. They wore simple mail and wielded short blades. The one to my left, with a florid face, nodded in greeting. Torlc turned and bowed, hand sweeping out.

"Welcome to my humble abode," he said, and led the way in.

Torlc's 'humble abode' was anything but. Gilt-framed paintings, some I recognized by the styles—masters all—jostled one another alongside statuary painted in garish colors. Burgundy and gold crowded the place like too many people shouting, and the flooring consisted of thick carpet unmarred by piss or wine spills.

He led us to a room deeper in, wide and tall, a long table of rare hardwood shining in the center, tall chairs arrayed around it. A feast occupied the table, more than fifteen families could ever afford in a year, heaping plates of pork and beef, roast poultry and rice, and such a variety of breads the commingling scents made my head spin. He entreated us to eat, and we fell to, subsisting on nothing more than small fish and hard biscuits over the past weeks.

When we were satiated, we pushed our chairs back, and Torlc called for pipes, offering each of us one from a fine wooden tray. I could not fathom the wealth in this place, and I refused on principle. It is one thing to eat another man's already prepared meat, but the things here that could feed and clothe families—it made the food turn in my guts. I wondered how Cord could stand it.

He sat back with Torlc, and the sweet smells of slipweed and tobacco filled the air. Silence passed between them for a time, until the big man finally spoke.

"You have something for me?" Torlc asked.

Cord nodded, pointed with the pipe stem toward the dock. "She's all yours."

"And how can I help you?"

"I need information."

"What kind?"

"Guard movements, dispositions, and the name of a good key maker."

Torlc raised an eyebrow, and then turned his head, nodding to a guard standing in the shadows. I tensed, hands going to my daggers, but the man held only a small chest. He presented it to the fence. Torlc lifted the lid, revealing several small scrolls, tightly rolled and nestled into individual compartments. He lifted three and passed them to Cord, who secreted them into his jerkin. The guard withdrew at a wave from one of Torlc's pudgy many-ringed hands, and he and Cord resumed talking.

"It's all very ceremonial, isn't it?"

Lux was at my elbow, her breath smelling of beef and wine.

"Wizards just pull it from your head, you know," she held out a hand, like someone gathering wool, then snatched at the air, drawing it back, "If they want it enough." Her face fell. "Sorry."

I strained to hear her whisper.

"I've not been right since the trials," she said.

"They killed you," I said.

She turned a cold eye on me and I felt I'd overstepped. But she let it lie.

"It's something I had to do. You would not understand." I frowned at that, but she continued. "No, I mean no offence. There is pain, and then there is... what I have endured. What I do."

I nodded, and placed a hand on hers. "I spoke out of line. My apologies."

She squeezed my hand and something warm kindled in my stomach. I ignored it until I could sort it out later, and then looked to Rek for some indication of normalcy. He gave me an apologetic look and shrugged. He knew as well as I did that normalcy was a thing left far behind. The scraping of chairs across the wooden floor caught my attention, and I turned back to Torlc and Cord. They set their pipes aside and stood, embracing. When they separated, Cord turned to us.

"Ready?"

We stood, filing from the room. Torlc stayed behind, his guards guiding us to the exit. We stepped from the door, sea air cool and refreshing after the close heat of Torlc's home. Cord led us down rickety boardwalks that snaked between shanties.

Fearful faces peered out, of all color and gender, adults and children. I could see the hunger in their eyes, the dirt smudged across their cheeks, yellow irises, painfully thin arms and legs.

We moved deeper into the shantytown, the delta wet below the boardwalks. We crossed an open area, where the walk fell away but for a simple bridge, and Cord pulled the papers from his jerkin, letting them fall into the water and sink. When they'd disappeared, he pulled us into the shadow of the city walls, until we were against the brick itself. A simple grate stood before us, knocked into the masonry in a haphazard way.

"Thank the gods for government work, eh?" Cord smirked, and motioned to Rek.

The big man grabbed the sides of the grate and ripped it from the bricks with a grunt and a tumble of masonry, exposing a tunnel that ran into the city proper. Cord waved us through, and the afternoon light and as we punctured Midian, the passage temporarily eclipsed the afternoon light.

10

STUFF THIS IN YOUR KEYHOLE

MIDIAN WAS... well, Midian was a shithole. How else do you describe a city outgrowing its walls with little interest in improving on anything other than the lives of the wealthy? It was a teeming shithole though, and we exited the tunnel into a crowd of citizens wandering the craftsman's district. The guards above had no more noticed our entrance than a cow notices a fly, and we walked among the people as if we belonged there.

The shops and workshops were middling-sized brick buildings, the sounds of hammer and awl, saw and rasp echoing from their walls. The smoke was thicker here, and the city smelled even worse up close—sweat from the press of bodies, smoke and chemical from tannery and blacksmith, tobacco from shoppers, and fish and spices from the inns scattered up and down the district. More guards walked the street, though most had a lazy attitude, weapons held in a desultory manner, armor ill-fitting or sloppy. Posters of Anaxos covered nearly every flat surface, likenesses rendered by someone with a flattering eye, and enumerating the king's every good deed.

Cord led us down a side street and up a set of stairs attached to a two-story stone building set just a little way from the road, tearing down posters as he passed them. Squatters eyed us as we entered, Cord pushing the heavy wood door aside, then shutting them and the majority of the scents of the city out. The place was spacious and furnished, if sparse, and clean. An unlit fireplace stood against one wall, but we had no need to light it. Thankfully, it was still summer, but it always summer in the Veldt, some effect of an unseen enchantment, and one the kingdom exploited for years.

"Vacation home?" I asked Cord.

He smirked and plopped down on an overstuffed couch, setting his feet on a long table before it.

"Why'd you throw away the papers?" Rek asked.

"Ah, that's a good question," Cord said.

Lux wandered over to a similar couch and flopped into the cushions.

"You didn't trust him, you cheeky devil," Lux said.

Cord nodded. "He would've had the guards on us in an hour. He's not just a fence, he's the most dishonest crook I've ever known. This'll keep 'em running for a bit. Besides, I know a couple of groups looking for that boat. He'll be tied up for days."

I grinned. "You set the mages and the soldiers on him."

Cord shrugged. "He's a fucker. They'll be here in a couple days, rough him up, piss in his wine. You know what they say—rats get uh..."

"Stitches?" Rek supplied.

Cord frowned. "I was gonna say dead, but you've always been a softy."

"Now what?" I asked, breaking the conversation.

"We need supplies. Various and sundry. Marvelous and wondrous."

"How much of that slipweed did you smoke?" I asked.

Cord held his hands apart about a foot. "Just a little."

"Shit. Okay, you need to sober up."

"Fuck sober. We need to move. Midian doesn't wait, and neither should we. We'll split into two groups. Lux—go with Rek. I need you to visit a woman on the south side. She's a genius with chemicals. Her name's Mere. Ask for the Hollow Hills special, but do not let her talk you into eating anything in the shop. She loves to experiment. Nenn, you're with me. We're going to visit a key maker just down the street."

We left the building, splitting up when we hit merchant's row. We waited a bit for the other group to disappear down a side street before Cord led us down another alley. The walls narrow, the spaces empty but for the occasional vagrant. Some called out to Cord, and he stooped to talk to them, slipping them a coin here or some morsel of food he hid in his pockets. In their hands, they held scraps of paper, and as I passed, one slipped one into my hand. It was a likeness of Cord, or at least I thought it was supposed to be.

"You're famous," I said.

Cord grinned. "Yeah, that's got to bug the shit out of Mane. I hope his chicken tastes like chicken assholes every time he thinks of me."

"You ever think you're helping him?"

"How's that now?"

"Men in power need boogeymen. They need people to be pissed at something so they don't notice the robbery at home."

Cord held up the flyer. "Backfired, didn't it? What this idiot did was let his fear get the better of him. He's made me a hero."

"Hero doesn't sound right."

"I'm a legend, Nenn. It's only a matter of time before someone builds a statue."

I snorted.

"I just hope they get the cock right," he muttered.

As we moved among the denizens of the alley, he glad-handed and coddled, smiled and cajoled, and they responded like moths to a flame. Cord might have been a bastard, but he was a likeable one.

Still, the closeness of the walls made me nervous. We couldn't afford a death here. The plan had a timeline, and in order to pull it off, we needed to meet it without distraction. Even Cord dying could set us back up to a week. Cord would have cursed me for putting that out there, so when the men with knives showed up at the end of the alley, I cursed myself and pulled my blades free.

I shoved Cord behind me, and he disappeared behind a wall of the dispossessed. I was glad for their protectiveness toward their savior. I turned my attention to our would-be assailants, and gave them a grin. One on three isn't even close to fair. At least, for them.

Two knives left my hands as soon as Cord was clear, sinking into tender throats, spraying the walls with crimson as the men fell, choking on their own blood. The third man, lurking behind the other two, stepped forward, and I saw why he'd lurked. It looked like someone piled muscle on top of muscle, making a small mountain of meat. Beady eyes peered from beneath a floppy haircut. He held a longsword, telling me he wasn't a genius, at least. Big blades are hard to swing in small spaces. I counted the advantage as mine.

I stepped back, waiting for him to come to me. He stared for a moment, chest heaving. Maybe he wasn't completely dumb. I decided to test that theory.

"Hey lumpy, this blade's pretty hungry. Looks like you could feed it for days. I mean, your buddies there are already sating my other knives."

He looked down, face reddening, and back up. One leg moved forward ponderously, then he pushed off, and was moving faster than his bulk would seem to allow for. I waited, and he swung the sword. I slipped back, letting it hit the bricks to one side, and ran at him in a sudden rush, feet finding purchase on the wall. He looked up in time to see my blade come down, digging into his shoulder. He screamed and I used it to spin myself around, my last blade snapping out and coming across his throat, ripping windpipe and carotid. His sword dropped from nerveless fingers, and I landed on his back as he fell, riding him to the ground. I hopped off and sheathed my daggers.

Cord emerged from the crowd, which melted back into the shadows. He chuckled.

"My blades are hungry," he said, mocking me.

"Hey."

"Where did you learn that?"

"I read," I said defensively.

"Okay," he said, and pushed past me, stepping over the bodies.

I stopped long enough to check them for sigils or markings. On each, I found an eagle tattoo on their right shoulder. I caught up to Cord.

"Eagle tattoos."

"Oh good," Cord said. "That was quicker than I'd expected."

"What was?"

"Mane knows we're here. Or suspects it. Those are his mercenary guard."

"This is bad, right?"

"Normally I'd say yes, but in this case, it means he's already paranoid."

"How is that good?"

"Paranoid people do stupid things."

"Ah."

He nodded and stopped walking. We'd arrived at the back door to a small shop. Cord rapped on it three times, then waited.

After a moment, the door opened a crack, and a thin dark face peered out.

"Cord," the man said.

"Leck," Cord replied.

"Cord."

"Leck."

"Cord," Leck was becoming agitated.

"Lec-"

"Sonovabitch. Do you have it or not?" Leck finally sighed.

Cord rummaged around in his jerkin and produced a carved pipe.

"Where'd you get that?" I asked.

"Hm? Oh, Torlc had extras."

"That's impressive. I didn't even see you steal it."

"I *am* impressive. You hear that, Leck?"

Leck sighed, and held his hand out the door. Cord stuck the pipe in it, and the hand pulled back, the door opening gently. We stepped into the dim shop. Every manner of mechanism and carving decorated the walls, the space filled with a vaguely persistent and annoying ticking. He led us to a set of benches where moulds and scraps of metal took up nearly as much space as carved birds, pipes, and flowers.

"Your turn." Cord said.

Leck held up a key—though unlike any I'd seen before. Four-sided, and each head had a different configuration of teeth. Cord took it and slipped it into his jerkin.

"Whaddya need that for, anyway?" Leck asked.

Cord shrugged. "You collect pipes, I collect keys."

"Weird, but okay."

A bell in the front of the shop jingled, and I peeked through the separating curtain. Two men, wearing simple leather armor entered. They carried short blades on their hips, and an eagle crest emblazoned across their chests.

"Coming," Leck called.

I moved to Cord's elbow. He was picking up various keys and slipping them into his jerkin beside the other.

"What are you doing?" I hissed.

"Lotta doors out there."

"Okay, but we need to use one right now."

"Ah. Guards?"

"Two, in the front."

"Then out the back it is. Like—"

"Don't," I warned, as we made our way to the door.

"Like poo," Cord finished.

"Gods damn it," I swore as we slipped out the back.

11

CAMOR'S PUCKERED ASSHOLE HAS A NICE RING TO IT

CORD LED us down the alley apace, juking left and pulling me after him into a space where the intersection of three similar-looking buildings formed an optical illusion of a wall. We sunk deeper into the craftsman district, and the sounds of running feet passed us by. We leaned against a wall, holding our breath until they'd faded, then continued on via a snakelike route that skirted, but never left, the quarter.

For a short while, the sounds of shouting and citizens calling for help drifted to us. Cord clenched his jaw at the noise, but said nothing. He knew as well as I did to get involved now would just get us killed. When it finally stopped, we made our way back to the safe house. These alleys were empty, dirtier than the ones we'd passed through before. Foul-smelling puddles congealed on the cobbles and even the birds that scavenged the city found little of interest here. The walls were crumbling, and the whole area smelled of mold and disrepair. It seemed Anaxos was more concerned with keeping up appearances than keeping the city from collapsing on itself.

As we walked, I stayed a rough step behind Cord, eyes on the dark places where anyone could just pop out and gut us.

Anxiety balled up my stomach, and a sullen silence filled alleys. Finally, I broke the quiet, just hoping to dispel the bleak curtain.

"Do you trust Leck?" I asked.

Cord shrugged, the motion twitching his jerkin. "As much as I trust anyone."

"What if they put him to the question?"

"They won't."

"Why's that?"

"He knows where the bodies are buried. Who do you think designs most of the city's locks? Besides, he's got a small fortune in that collection of his, and it's not all licit. Giving me up means casting light in his own closet."

We turned a corner and passed into the craftsman's quarter once again, some distance from our safe house, but unnoticed. The street cleared of guards, and though some of the passersby still looked fearful, the general atmosphere had relaxed. As we walked through the crowd, Cord winked at a young lady with dark hair and almond eyes, her cheeks lighting in a blush. I opened my mouth to chastise him when he did the same to a man with a barrel chest and thick forearms. I watched, bemused, as the man blinked and looked away, and then we were past them.

"You ever been in love, Cord?"

"Of course. I usually fall in love at least once per city."

"Not what I meant."

"Oh, you mean the real thing," he was quiet for a moment, then shook his head. "No, I don't think so. Not enough time for all that. Besides, I'd be a terrible father."

"Okay, then why all this? In the stories, when someone wants to teach someone a lesson, it's because they've been broken or betrayed, or their true love was killed."

Cord made a face. "Anyone that needs an inciting incident

to do the right thing probably wasn't all that good of a person to begin with, I'd think. What kind of books are you reading, anyway?"

"Adventures."

"Don't have enough of your own?"

We turned another corner, coming on the safe house. My retort died on my lips. Rek and Lux stood around the stairs, waiting for us. Blood covered the front of Rek's torso, and Lux's tunic had several tears in it outlined in crimson, none of which seemed to bother her.

"What in Camor's puckered asshole happened here?" I asked.

Lux looked paler than normal. "We were jumped outside the chemist's. Barely got away."

"But you got the acid?" Cord asked.

Rek grunted and handed over a small lead vial he'd produced from his belt. Cord grinned and climbed the stairs into the safe house.

"A thanks would be nice!" Rek called up after.

"Thanks for not breaking this!" Cord yelled back.

Rek growled, and we followed him into the house.

CORD HAD his feet up on the table again, turning the vial of acid over and over, a pipe in his mouth. The others made their way to their rooms, the afternoon fight having worn them out. In truth, I was exhausted as well, but Cord had other ideas.

"Someone knew we were here," he said.

"Seems obvious now. How long you think we've got in the house here?"

"Few hours. We're gonna move as soon as we can."

"How do you think they found out?"

"I suspect Torlc ratted on us. At least that's what I'm gonna tell myself for now. The other possibility is a bit depressing—that one of us is leaking info."

"Why would anyone do that?"

Cord sighed and set the vial down. "Why would anyone do anything, Nenn? Greed, self-preservation, revenge?"

"They don't hate you that much, do they?"

He looked at the door, contemplating. Finally, he shook his head. "No, I don't think so. But we've got history, and history is complicated, all knotted up like a skein drawn out too far."

"So what's next?"

"We'll move into the Citizen district."

"Aren't those houses all occupied? No one actually leaves a Citizen home empty if they've got the means, right?"

"Right," he grinned around the pipe stem. "We're gonna 'borrow' one. Now go wake up the others. We've got to get moving."

THE TRIP from shop to residential districts was short, and as we had a strict policy of not even breathing the same air as the guards, uneventful. A low wall ran around the Citizen district, creating the illusion of safety. In reality, it wasn't much higher than four feet, and though composed of brick, it looked like a stiff wind might blow it down. Cord had an opinion about this, as he did most things—locks and walls only kept honest people out. The determined would still get in. We hopped the wall with that same determination—not even enough to break a sweat really—and crept across neat lawns and carefully tended gardens.

Guards patrolled the streets here, and though lanterns lined the road proper, they did little to light the hedges and garden walls we hid behind. The houses were tall and straight here, fresh paint covering them in bright colors, the stones of the walls neat and unbroken. Some lawns held swings and slides, and others outdoor grills for entertaining. We wound our way across the neighborhood until we reached a neat blue home, its windows clean, its lawn clipped to precision. Cord approached the backdoor and pulled a key from his jerkin, slipping it into the lock. It popped with a gentle *click*, and we were through.

The home was austere but tasteful, simple wooden floors and plaster walls hung with little more than decorative blankets. An armor stand stood in one corner of the living area, a blade propped against it, black boots shining in the moonlight. A set of stairs leading to the second level and three bedrooms stood in one corner. In the kitchen, a simple wooden table stood beside a basin for food preparation, and a trapdoor leading to a cellar. In the privy, a pile of one-sheets beside a raised stool with a hole in the seat. Cord held us in the living room, talking in a low whisper.

"Nenn, get the cellar open. Rek, come upstairs with me. Lux —keep an ear out."

We split, and I moved to the kitchen. The trapdoor was set with a simple brass ring, and I gave it a tug, revealing a set of wooden stairs. They led to a storage area, jars of preserved food on the shelves, and dried herbs hanging from the ceiling. It smelled of dill and dry earth. I found a lantern hanging from a beam and lit it for a break from the near-blackness. It revealed an area a little deeper from storage, shelves of papers and a table, and supporting posts. I checked over a few of the papers and noted they were names and ranks beside payment numbers and posts. My stomach started to knot.

A banging from the stairs pulled me away, and I spun, blades in my hand. I half-relaxed, seeing it was Cord and Rek leading a bound and muffled man down the stairs. His eyes were wide, and he wore a nightshirt stained with sweat, his black hair plastered to his forehead. He struggled, but against the two men could not free himself, and finally slumped as they bound him to the desk. He watched us, still fearful.

I pulled Cord to the side.

"Watch him," he told Rek, then turned to me. "Yes?" he asked, a grin on his face.

"Cord," I seethed, "is that the fucking captain of the guard?"

"Well, you know, titles are tricky. One guy gets promoted over another, and then-"

"Cord."

"Yeah, that's him."

"Why are we in his fucking house?"

"We're going to have a conversation with him."

I glared at him.

"Okay, an interrogation."

"Abso-fucking-lutely not. I will not torture anyone."

"A mental interrogation," he tapped his head. "You're going to torture me."

I fingered my blades, squinting in suspicion.

"I've been smoking slipweed all night. I can't die, and I heal fast. I need him to see that if you'll hurt me, you'll hurt him worse."

I thought about it, then nodded. It was Cord's turn to squint.

"You didn't have to agree so quickly," he said.

"I'm a team player."

We walked over to the captain, who was regarding us with a mixture of fear, annoyance, and curiosity.

"Captain," Cord said, "we need information. Give it to us, and my friend here won't vivisect you."

I grinned and picked at a nail with a knife. His eyes flicked from me to Cord.

"We need to know where the vault is, and what the guard disposition is like there."

The captain's eyebrows came together and he shook his head, droplets of sweat spraying the table. He tried to rise, and Rek put a heavy hand on his shoulder, slamming him back into his chair, teeth coming together with a *clack*.

"Nenn?" Cord said.

I slipped the knife back into its sheath and moved. My fist caught Cord across the jaw, and I heard his teeth rattle, a single white molar popping out of his lips and skittering across the table. He spat blood. The captain stared, eyes again the size of saucers.

"Captain? You gotta help, or she's gonna kill me."

He shook his head a second time, and I hammered my knee into Cord's balls, and when he doubled over, brought my fist down again. His head rocked, and Cord swayed, but he kept his feet.

"You gotta help me man, this bitch is crazy!" Cord shouted at him.

The captain flicked his eyes back and forth, and sweat redoubled its efforts on his forehead. I grabbed Cord's hand and snapped his pinky, the sound like a small branch breaking. Rek winced, and the captain made a muffled sound of horror.

Cord leaned on the table, pale and sweating himself now. He loomed over the captain. "You believe in law and order, right? Justice? Are you gonna let her kill me? What do you think she's gonna do to you?"

The captain lowered his lids, and I did the thing I'd been saving up. I grabbed Cord's hand and flattened it against the table. He fixed me with a panicked look, then one of agony as I brought my blade down, severing the broken pinky. The stump sprayed blood across the table, marring the captain's nightshirt. His eyes went wide as Cord collapsed and I approached the bound man, blade held low. I pressed it against the inside of his thigh, and the stink of urine filled the air.

Muffled sounds of protest issued from below the gag, and I nodded at Rek. He pulled the gag down.

"Gret's balls, please don't cut my dick off please don't cut my dick off."

"You have an answer for me?"

"It's in the low town. Anaxos knew no one would ever look there. Four guards, plainclothes, and a Harrower."

"Thanks," I patted his cheek.

Cord popped back up, grinning. He held a bloody rag to the stump of his finger. The captain cursed.

"Okay, Rek," he said.

Rek nodded, and punched the man, once. The captain slumped, unconscious. The room returned to quiet.

"Really Nenn, my finger?" Cord asked.

I shrugged. "You said you heal fast."

"Yeah, but I don't regrow limbs. That was my favorite finger. It fit places."

"Stop whining, you have two."

He showed me another finger, and I climbed the stairs to get some rest.

12

BAD TIMING AND GOOD LOVIN'

DREAMS ARE RIGHT in that weird country between home and a city you've never visited before. The ground feels familiar —here a tree you used to play under, there an old dog, his one ear tattered from too many fights—and wrong, as if the walk-ways developed hillocks you didn't remember. In this one, I'm seven, maybe eight, in the yard of Our Lady of the Constant Weeping and Moaning, or some such thing.

Kids played in the dirt, fenced with sticks, or just beat one another to a pulp over a bit they'd squirreled away, a piece of fruit saved up from lunch. We were the orphaned ones. Sure, some of us had dead family—flux, war, robbery—but a good portion of us were there because our parents couldn't afford us anymore. So they sold us for a few silvers or a crown, and they got to eat for a few months. Some turned it into a job. And before you start to judge, don't. The state kept us alive, and selling us kept them alive. You did what you could. Survival for most people isn't an optional instinct, and when it kicks in, you fight like a rabid dog to keep what's yours.

So there I was, playing in the dirt when I hear a shout, and a big kid—probably only weeks from shipping out to the state laundries—steps over to a girl. She's got some sort of bauble, probably just a single copper bit, but in my dream, it's a glass sphere, and in that sphere, lives we could have lived. He knocks her over, and before I can think, I'm on him. Biting, clawing, spitting. He goes down crying, his head suddenly that of a donkey, braying into the hot sun.

The kids, they raise me up, chant 'Nenn, Nenn, Nenn', and the girl hands me her bauble. I see a beach. I see tanned flesh and cold drinks, and I see white sand and blue surf. Something on my face is wet, and when I wipe it away, the dream breaks.

I GROPED AROUND in the dark and pulled a cigar from my pack, lighting it and savoring the thick heady smoke. It had been a while—I'd learned a long time ago that a woman smoking a cigar in public was like a man with a dick on his forehead. People remembered that shit.

Something outside caught my attention, and I crept to the window, peering out. The street was dim, lit only by a single lantern from my vantage point, but I could make out two shapes. One, a hunched man in a cloak, stood near to another with wild hair. I couldn't make out their speech, but could tell they were deep in conversation, gestures and hand bobs marking it a lively one. Finally, they split, the man in the cloak drifting away into the dark, and the other turning. The light caught her face and Lux glanced over her shoulder before heading back toward the house.

My brain tried to stitch together any scenario where this made sense. Maybe she was buying info. Maybe she needed a fix. Maybe she was selling us out. This went on for a while until my door opened. I turned, light from the hall outlining Lux's slim form. She hesitated a moment, then closed it, padding to me, sitting on my bedroll.

"Can't sleep," she whispered.

I decided to keep what I'd just seen to myself, until I'd sorted my thoughts. Truth was, loneliness and the dream ended up working me into knots, and I didn't trust myself to make a decision untainted by emotion.

"Wanna talk about it?"

She turned her head, gave me a smile. Her breath was sweet, like late roses, her skin lovely.

"It's lonely, death," she said. "You can't imagine—you'd think there would be all of these people on the other side, waiting for you—family—but it's just another land like this one. You have to make your own way. And maybe they're out there, waiting. Maybe that land is just another test, but it leaves you cold. And if you come back—it comes back with you, that emptiness."

I didn't know how to respond to that. Instead, I set the cigar down and wrapped my arms around her. She smelled of autumn leaves, and placed her head on my shoulder, then turned until she faced me. She leaned in and kissed me on the lips, and I hesitated only for a moment. Then I returned it. Her skin was softer than I'd expected, her body warmer than I'd anticipated, her lips sweeter than I thought possible.

I WOKE ALONE and padded down the stairs to find Lux at the kitchen table, working on a plate of simple wheat cakes. Another sat to the side for me, and I dug in, glancing once or twice at her. She did little to return the notice, and I mentally shrugged. Of all the times to get entangled, this wasn't the best. I filed away the talk I'd wanted to have with her for after we were done, and finished my breakfast, pushing the plate away when done.

"Where are the others?" I asked.

I wanted to talk to Cord about Lux sneaking around the night before. Despite what we'd shared, it hooked barbs into my gut, and I knew she wasn't ready to share whatever secret she kept. Rek would wax philosophical about morality, or tell me a story about the time the four of them fell into a pile of pig shit and discovered a rose. I needed someone who wouldn't bullshit me.

"Downstairs," Lux said. She looked tired, dark circles under her eyes. Whatever happened the night before kept her up, even after our entanglement.

I shoved away from the table, and took the cellar stairs down. I paused at the bottom. Four wooden planks standing upright occupied the storeroom floor, each holding a lock. The captain was gone, and in his place was a makeshift map. Rek sat in the chair, looking it over, and Cord leaned against a post, a smug look on his face.

"Where's the captain?" I asked.

"Dumped him in the shantytown after a nice dose of nepe."

"Wow," I said, "Well, if he remembers his name by next week, I'll be impressed."

"That *would* be good timing," Cord said.

"So what's all this?" I asked.

"Practice," Rek rumbled without looking up.

"Each of these is an approximation of the lock on the vault," Cord said.

I leaned in, taking the locks in. They were solid steel, four bolts coming from the edge of the door, the keyhole in the shape of a clover. I assumed Cord's key would fit that hole. Several sigils surrounded the doorplate in concentric circles. I ran my hand over them.

"What are these?"

"Wards. Strengthening for the wood and iron, alarm for the lock, pain for anyone trying to crack it. These aren't as strong as what we'll encounter at the vault, but they still bite."

"I thought you had a key."

"Yeah, but if something happens to me, you'll need to know how to crack this."

"Why not Lux? She's the mage."

"By the time we get to the vault, she'll be restricted. The mages are bringing their Leashmen."

"How do you know this?"

"She told me."

That must have been what I'd seen the night before, then. Lux paid for information. I let relief loosen my shoulders a little, then looked at the locks and sighed. I wasn't tickled with being the sacrificial lamb here.

"Okay, where do I start?"

THE DOOR SPARKED, and the chalk in my hand popped out and skittered across the floor, electricity seizing my muscles. I screamed through clenched teeth, and Lux sighed behind me.

"No, NO! You've got to bisect the first orbital, then trisect the second, not the other way around! You're going to get us all killed." She turned to Cord. "She's going to get us all killed."

I flipped her the bird and picked up the chalk. I couldn't wrap my head around the damn sigils on the door. Every time I looked at them, they seemed to crawl across the wood, and I couldn't make out where one circular set started and the other ended.

"What if we just scrape them off the door?" I asked.

"They they'll be scraping you off the wall," Lux said.

"Cord, tell her to relax, or I'm going to use blood to bisect these orbitals."

"That'll never work," Lux said.

"She means yours," Cord said.

Lux shut her jaw with a snap, and I turned back to the door, studying the runes again. They were simple constructions, ones Lux claimed most fledgling mages learned in their first couple of years at the Arcanum. The trick was, every time I cut a circle, the second actually did move, making the sequence I needed to part there harder to suss out. It was a simple but maddening countermeasure.

I thought of those puzzles they sold at the carnival, sliding bits of wood where you moved pieces one way, then the other, back and forth until you had the picture they made. I put the chalk to the wood, crossing out the first set of symbols. A snap, and the second set rotated, putting them out of alignment with the first.

I stepped back and looked, trying to see the picture, where the pieces should be, instead of where they were.

"You admiring your squiggle?" Cord asked.

I ignored him and made quick motions with the chalk, splitting the second line. It cracked, and the third spun, but by then I had the trick of it, and worked my way down, cracking the lines like they were children's' puzzles. The last snapped, and I stepped back.

"Gret's balls, she did it," Lux said. "We might not all die."

Cord grinned and handed me a set of picks.

"Now the lock."

I grinned back and took to it. It was complex, but not impossible. I set two of the picks, using a third to hold tension, then the other two in the same configuration. Then, I worked a bar across the entire set, twisting them at the same time. It resisted. I gave it a bit more torsion, and the lock snapped open. Cord clapped me on the back.

"Holy shit, I think the weird one's right. We might not die."

Rek called me over to the map they'd laid out on the desk. I didn't recognize the districts, but red highlighted one area, and another encircled.

"Lowtown and the vault?" I asked.

Rek nodded. "Way I see it, we're gonna need a distraction. A bloody big one."

"I got that," Cord said. "I have a plan."

We groaned in unison.

13

DOES THIS MEAN YOU WANT YOUR SHIRT BACK

THERE ARE few things as maddening as trying to figure out why someone slept with you when they would rather not talk about it. I looked at Lux, reclined on the captain's couch, head tilted back, eyes half-lidded. I wanted to yell at her, to shake her, to throw cutlery. Instead, I sat on my couch and brooded, staring at the knots and whorls in the wall like they offended me, and I had pledged a blood oath against their families.

I knew it was nerves. There were other women, other men, other cities. This wasn't the first, wouldn't be the last. The problem was proximity. Lux was close, annoyingly so for someone who wouldn't talk, so I couldn't just move on, shake the feeling. As for her silence—well, she was half-dead. And maybe she just needed release. Maybe she just needed to spend the night with someone who wouldn't make a big deal of it, and I was fucking it up.

I let out a long sigh, and she finally tilted her head forward, glanced at me. A slow smile spread across her face, and I returned it. Too quickly, probably. I tried to squash it, and it turned into a grimace. Her eyebrows came together gently, and I shook my head. Lux chuckled and walked to window, pushing the drapes aside. After a moment, she let them drop. When she turned back, her skin somehow became paler.

"Leashmen are here," she said.

Cord entered from the kitchen. "What, this street?"

Lux turned, an ugly sneer on her lip. "No, you dolt. This room. Yes, this street."

Cord joined her at the window, cursing under his breath. "How in the seven snowy hells did they find us?"

I glanced at Lux, remembering her late-night encounter. She moved across the room, sitting beside me. Her weight settled into my leg, the point of her hip in mine. I shifted, sparing her a glance. Her eyes were wide, her hands clenched.

"What now?" Rek asked.

"Something they'll never expect," Cord said. "We attack."

"What?" Lux's voice rose three registers.

"Well, I can't come up with all the damn plans," Cord growled. "Nenn?"

"Let's burn the place down," I said.

"That... that doesn't seem better," Cord said.

Lux nodded. "Yeah... no. That's better. Better than being stabbed, anyway."

WE WATCHED the house burn from two gardens away, the guard and fire brigade arriving to keep it from spreading. It's amazing how fast some things burn. Well, not as amazing when you consider how much lamp oil and fire we applied to the place, but still. It was a lot of fire. The shouts of the Leashmen and their wizards echoed down the stone streets. We'd kicked a hornets' nest, but it was localized.

"That poor bastard," Rek said. "He's gonna wake up in the

shants, finally remember who he is, and come home to wet ashes."

Cord led us away from the chaos. "Serves him right," he called over his shoulder.

"How so?"

"Anyone working for Anaxos at this point has to know how complicit they are in this nightmare. A few burnt belongings should be the least punishment for them."

The statement, unusually flat for Cord, dropped a blanket of silence on us, and we followed him for a while between garden walls and over hedges, the green of the residential lawns dazzling in the aftereffects of the blaze. We rounded a corner, ready to leap the wall and move deeper into the city when a cry sounded out above the others.

"Rogue!"

I turned to see a Leashman in their deep blue chain armor, whip and chains free. He spotted Lux, and advanced. It was only a matter of time before his cry alerted the others.

"Nenn," Cord said.

I split from the group and circled around, slipping between a pair of rosebushes grown wild enough to belong in the fae court, loosening my knives in their sheaths. I caught glimpses of the Leashman as he moved past me, but he was too deep into his pursuit of Lux to notice any sound I made.

As soon as he passed, I slipped from between the bushes, blades out. He was at half a run now, whip uncoiling with a grace I hadn't expected. He lashed out, catching Lux around the ankle as the wizard tried to escape.

Lux cried out, raising one arm and flicking a lance of fire at the mage hunter. It raged across the open space, then simply died, snuffed out like a candle flame. The Leashman wrenched on the whip, dragging her closer, and I moved in, blades out.

Something heavy and impossibly hard collided with my

skull and the world went sideways. Then dark. I found myself on my side in the cool grass while the rest of the squad appeared, whips coiling around Lux.

The Leashmen reeled her in as I lay prone. Lux gave one last desperate struggle, the bonds of the whips leaving her skin red and raw. She shouted something, a word that made my stomach clench. The air around her began to ripple, opening on —somewhere—and then a Leashman's blade was through her, ripping into ribcage and spine.

She slumped and I cried out as her body went still. Strong hands grabbed me, pulling me from the path, dragging me out of sight. I heard whispered words, though they meant nothing, and felt the heat of tears on my cheeks.

14

PARTY CRASHING AND INSURRECTION
FOR FUN AND PROFIT

I WOKE TO CORD SINGING.

"Dun dun dun. 'Nother one bites the dust."

I groaned and sat up. My head ached like someone hired a dwarf to hammer on my skull with a femur. I rubbed eyes filled with sand, and my mouth tasted like seven days' worth of rotgut poured down my throat.

"What are you singing, and why do I have a hangover?" I asked.

Cord stopped humming. "Rek figured you might be sad if you woke up too soon. I was worried about your concussion."

"That doesn't sound right."

"Right. Other way around."

"The song?"

Cord resumed humming. "And another one down and—" he shrugged. "Just popped into my head."

I opened my mouth to make a remark about things that should stay in his head when I felt the weight of the quiet in the room. The memory of Lux impaled flashed into my mind, and I choked back a sob.

"You still crying over her?"

I glared at Cord, and heard Rek shift in his seat. My hand crept to my blade.

"Uh, Cord. Watch your mouth now," Rek warned.

Cord held his hands up in placation. "It's—sorry. We found out who the rats were."

"Who?"

"Lux," Rek rumbled.

I sat all the way up, a frown across my face. "That can't—there's no way—"

Cord interrupted. "We found a note in her room. Lux was so desperate to reverse whatever had been done to her that she was willing to sell us out to Anaxos in return for a cure."

"That doesn't explain the Leashmen."

"Anaxos double-crossed her. She told the bastard where we were, and the King, long may he shit his trousers, thought he'd get rid of all of his problems and turned Lux into the Leashmen."

"Well, fuck me sideways with a sharp stick."

Cord screwed up his face. "That sounds not fun."

"None of this is fun, Cord."

"Give me a day. It'll be fun."

My head started aching again and I groaned, leaning back into the cushions.

THE SECOND TIME I WOKE, my head reduced itself to a dull background ache, though my throat and my body cried out for water. I picked up a mug sitting next to the couch I laid on and drank deeply. I had no doubt Rek set it there for me, and added it to the list of debts I felt I owed him. All the bells of St. Bastard's cathedral finally stopped ringing in my head and I took in the room, noticing details for the first time.

Gray was a good descriptor. The walls and floors were nondescript wood, and though it wasn't cramped or filthy, it was plain. A simple sitting room, privy, and kitchen made up the whole of the apartment. Equally simple furniture filled the space, the only luxury afforded comfortable cushions on the couch and chairs. Someone—probably Rek—had left a plate of bread and cheese along with a carafe of water, and I set to, filling up. It did little to snuff the grief, but it made me feel better anyway, and when I finished, I felt full, and a little pissed. Betrayal is a hard meal to swallow.

I wondered what I would have done in that situation, and realized I didn't know. My family never cared enough for me to care back, and Cord was a big boy. He could take care of himself. I guess if I found myself in that situation though, I'd cut throat and shit fire to fix what was broken. The thought cooled my rage a little, and I sank into the couch and wished for a cigar.

Cord swept in at that moment, and as if he'd read my mind, dumped a paper bag into my lap. It smelled of tobacco. It smelled of heaven. I opened it and pulled out a cigar, fishing around inside until I managed to find a box of lightsticks. I struck one, lit the cigar, and puffed contentedly.

"What's this for?" I asked.

"We're celebrating."

"What's there to celebrate?"

Rek bustled in the door behind Cord, slamming it behind him.

"St. Cruciatus Day," he said.

"Wazzat?"

"It's the day the rich people celebrate being rich by throwing extravagant parties. It's usually a shitshow by the end as they try to outdo each other, and everyone gets so fuckin' drunk you could light the fumes coming off their tongues," Cord said.

"Okay, but what is it?" I asked. Partly because I knew Rek would tell me. Partly to annoy Cord.

"It's the day we celebrate Arn Cruciatus, the Savior of the Hollow Hills. He single-handedly held back a wight invasion. Died horribly, but if he hadn't, he wouldn't be a martyr, would he?"

"What do the rich have to do with it, then?"

"The same thing the rich always have to do with it. If it's not about them, they make it about them," Cord said.

"What do we have to do with it, then?" I was enjoying poking Cord.

He sighed. "We are going to use the opportunity to..."

"Don't say it," I said.

"Have some fucking fun," he finished.

WHILE I'D BEEN OUT, Midian put on its party shoes. Rek picked out a dress that surprisingly, wasn't awful. A whalebone corset with ruffled skirts, and a white mask that showed only my eyes. Graceful curls suggesting cheekbones, leading up to a pair of short horns, decorated the mask.

I'd fought a little bit at the idea of getting dressed up to go out, but the men insisted, saying part of the celebration was dressing up. Everyone dressed as wights, a reminder of what would have happened if Cruciatus failed. The men wore tight breeches and long embroidered waistcoats, high boots and masks similar to mine, white with embellishments, leading to horns.

When we stepped out, the city had transformed. Bright pennants and bunting hung from every rooftop, and rose petals fluttered in scattered rows through the streets. Citizens mingled regardless of class, though for some the quality of their costumes made that evident enough. Beer and wine casks sat on wagons at every corner, the crowd gathering in choke points around them.

I watched the people milling about, chatter filling the air. They pressed in close, the crowd warm and breathing. My hand went to the blade strapped to my thigh. Cord appeared from the crowd and pressed a cup into it instead.

"Relax," he said, sipping from his own cup.

"Hard to. Cord without an angle is like a rat without a tail."

Rek snorted from behind me. He moved to Cord's side, the crowd parting naturally for the big man. I took a sip from the mug. It was cool and sweet, the grapes strong enough to make my lips pucker a little.

"Good, right?" Cord asked.

In answer, I drained my cup and handed it back to him. "I'm going to enjoy myself now," I said. "And I swear by Gret's balls that if you fuck this up for me, Cord, they'll never find your meat."

He laughed, then choked on it. "Wait. What about my bones?"

"I'll use them for earrings."

He blinked. "Noted."

He waved to Rek, and they disappeared into the crowd, leaving me alone for the first time in days.

BY THE TIME the moon reached its peak, we were all quite drunk. Someone started a round of Rena's Skirts, and someone else steered it into bawdy territory.

Oh Rena's skirts
Climb the knee
I wish she'd do the same for me
Oh Rena's skirts

Oft do tangle
But her chest
They let dangle!

I was about to lead the next verse with a clever cross rhyme involving hussy, but someone grabbed my arm and pulled me from the crowd. I rounded on them, a scowl on my face. Or what I hoped was a scowl. One eyebrow was up, the other down. No matter what I tried, the rogue wouldn't follow the other.

"Who in the frozen blue fuck do you think you are?" I asked.

The newcomer swept the wide-brimmed feather hat he wore off and bowed low. "Lord Chanterry, Second in the Circle, my lady. It seemed you had fallen in with ruffians, and I thought only to rescue you."

In response, I brought one boot up in a swift motion, catching him in the chest. He flailed back, arms pinwheeling. As he arced backward, I brought the other foot up, stumbling only a little, and smashed his balls. He screamed, spinning arms forgetting they were attempting to maintain his balance, and clutched his groin as he crunched backwards into the stones. He lay there, groaning, and I stood over him.

"I'm no lady, my Lord."

A pair of strong arms grabbed me, yanking me into the crowd, and I found myself running beside Rek, breathless and laughing as we displaced noble and wretch, tipping cups from hands and pies from teeth. We collapsed against an alley wall, Rek peering back into the crowd. Despite their indignation at our flight, they closed ranks, chatting and laughing again as if nothing happened. It occurred to me that there is no manner of small ills that alcohol cannot soothe.

Rek took hold of my arm again, a light touch, and pointed down the street. "Look there, here's something."

I peered from the alley to see the crowd parting. They made neat aisles to each side, making way for a figure approaching. It stepped from further down the street, teetering on legs extended by stilts. It wore all black, the mask on its face painted into a fearsome warrior visage, charms and wards sewn into the cloth of its costume. It wielded a giant mock sword, and where it swept it, the crowd fell prone. I watched as it approached, laying the crowd low, silence falling wherever it walked.

For a moment, it seemed even the bright pennants and the blazing lanterns dimmed as it passed and silence descended. A chill swept across my skin as though a cool wind kicked up. As the caricature of St. Cruciatus loomed past the alley, I felt the world tilt. I gasped and grabbed at Rek's arm for support, steadying myself. Then it passed, and the figure was down another street. We stood in silence accompanied only by the sound of rustling finery as people began to rise at its passing. I looked at Rek.

"It happens," he said. "The weakness. There is nothing supernatural about the mummery here, but it affects everyone differently. Some say it is because they are haunted, and the spirit of the saint rides the actor, driving away ghosts as they walk."

"Is that why they still celebrate this?"

Rek shrugged and we picked our way through the crowd, heading toward the apartment. The revelers were beginning to disperse, the merriment broken by the somber play that swept through the streets.

"Could be. Superstition is powerful," he said. "Could be people need to believe the plague that calls itself Anaxos can eventually be banished."

"Isn't that dangerous?" I asked. "Seditious, even?"

Rek shrugged again. "Maybe. But imagine the disaster the king would have on his hands should he ban the celebration. He weathers it for a night because to do so otherwise would be to light a fire he couldn't possibly contain. At least not without quenching it in a lake of blood."

The roar of a crowd nearby interrupted Rek. He changed directions, leading us toward it.

"That didn't sound like a happy cheer," I said.

"What's a happy cheer sound like?"

"Yay!"

"What'd this sound like?"

"Yarg!"

We turned another corner into an open square. A crowd gathered at the edges, holding back. An effigy of Anaxos Mane stood in the center of the plaza, and the St. Cruciatus actor circled it, raising his arms and waving his blade around. With each wave, the crowd roared, that *yarg* I heard earlier. He completed two more passes, the crowd's volume increasing, until it was nearly an unintelligible scream.

The actor closed the distance to the effigy, his mask set in grim determination, and swept the head off the king's likeness with a swift motion. The crowd exploded, and I feared for our lives. Rek pulled me close and used himself as a shield, plowing our way back to the apartment.

We burst through the door, shaking and sweating, fear energy coursing through our veins. I collapsed on the couch, trying to even out my breathing.

"Cord?" I asked.

"Cord," Rek nodded.

I breathed a curse and lit a cigar.

15

YOU REALLY SHOULDN'T DRINK THAT

CORD DIDN'T RETURN that night. I slept on the well-stuffed couch, and when he crept through the door in the morning, I sat up, pushing my hair back and wiping sleep from my eyes. My head ached from the wine, but once again, Rek provided, and I grabbed a stuffed pastry from the table. It was warm and savory, and I chewed while I watched Cord in silence. He put on a lopsided grin and flopped opposite me.

"Good night?" I asked.

"Nice enough."

"Cause any trouble?"

He shrugged. "A certain man and his wife will be a little tender today. A bit sore myself, if I'm honest. Blacksmiths are resilient. But fun."

"So, you didn't, I don't know—kill the king in effigy last night?"

He opened his eyes in an approximation of innocence and grabbed the last of the meat pie from my hand, popping it in his mouth and chewing. "I wouldn't know anything about that, madam. Heard there was quite a ruckus, though."

"A ruckus."

"Aye, a ruckus," he swallowed his bite and dusted his hands off, then gave me a wink.

"Anyway," he continued, "we've a busy day today."

"How so?"

"We're breaking into the vault."

"Without our wizard? With the Leashmen in town?"

Cord waved a hand. "Leashmen have already left. Fucked off to Tremaire. They got what they came for. Besides, you can crack the runes."

"And the soldiers you pissed off in that backwater?"

"Busy. Or they will be."

A crash sounded outside the apartment, followed by shouting, and the sounds of feet pounding on cobblestones. I shot Cord a glance.

"Distraction?"

He shrugged. "The start of one. C'mon. We need to get up top so we can avoid the worst of it."

He led me to a side room, a ladder leading to a trapdoor in the roof. We climbed up, Rek already waiting. The morning air had a chill, and Rek handed me a light cloak. I took it gratefully, and followed them to the edge of the roof. The streets were already a low form of chaos. Mobs pushed down avenues like murders of crows, tearing down posters of the king, waving effigies. Where a hapless barrel or cart stood in their way, they rolled over it like a fleshy tide, smashing it to flinders and moving on.

Cord guided us to the other side of the roof, where a plank sat, bridging the gap between buildings. I could see other boards marking the whole of the area, leading to the high street and the King's Avenue. Cord led us across the first plank, and we followed, moving low and fast, trying to avoid the gaze of guards that were currently trying to contain the mobs.

"How'd you get all this done?" I asked as we crossed the first plank.

"I have my ways," Cord said.

"He means he hired someone to do it, then dosed them with nepe," Rek said.

"You don't know," Cord said. "I am very mysterious."

"Like mushrooms that grow in shit," Rek said.

"What?" Cord said.

"I mean, how do they even get there? Why do they only grow in shit? Would you eat one?" Rek said.

"I wouldn't eat Cord," I said. "No idea where he's been."

"That's hurtfu... okay, that's fair," Cord said.

The path to the Avenue was long and circuitous, the streets below chaos. As we moved, something occurred to me.

"Why do we need a distraction this big?" I asked Cord. "I thought there were only a few guards and a Harrower. Surely we could have drawn them away with a warehouse fire, or something."

Cord shook his head. "Elite guard. They're fanatical. The only thing that's going to pull them away is a direct threat to the king."

"All this is so we can rob a bank?"

Cord stopped and spun on me, finger in the air. "Not just any bank. *The* bank."

"Why?" It hadn't occurred to me before to ask, but now curiosity scratched at my brain like a caterpillar on the skin. "There are a hundred banks in the Veldt. Any one of them could bring us more money than we could spend in a lifetime."

Cord turned and started moving again. "If you're going to teach a rich and powerful dickhead a lesson, you stick to what you know. Because my dear, we're not just thieves. We're *exceptional* thieves."

We reached the edge of a roof and stopped, Cord dropping

to his stomach. Rek and I followed suit, edging out over the ledge. We'd set up on the roof of a galleria across from the palace. It crazed into the sky, each spire vying for space beside the others, a riot of phallic contention that threatened to beat one another to death for the right to be the one to cast its shadow over the land. A thick wall surrounded the plaza below us, a solid iron gate blocking the road to Anaxos' manse. More walls stood to each side, blocking alleys and shop entrances, and as we watched, another rolled into place and braced behind the seething crowd.

I looked at the rippling mass of humanity below, their discontent plain even from our vantage point. They were on the verge of tipping, a spark threatening conflagration. Fists were raised, chants were chanted, and we saw bags of produce being passed about, their current state of ripeness evident from the clouds of flies that followed. Occasionally, a tomato or a thick ripe squash spattered against the gate, a case of premature protestation.

"You really riled 'em up, Cord," Rek said. I thought I detected a hint of grudging respect finally.

Cord just grinned and pointed, marking out the space where a figure climbed the gate battlements. The grin dropped a second later as the figure resolved itself, a man in tattered robes, a severed hand clutched in his own as if he were holding the hand of his lover. The crowd surged, pressing against the walls and the gate, the entrance groaning as the unexpected weight of a thousand bodies exerted pressure. Fruit and vegetables flew, though most missed the mark by a wide margin, coming to sail over the Harrower's head, or spattering against the wall.

The Harrower raised an arm for silence, but the crowd continued to shout their complaints. He shrugged and raised the other arm. He spoke, his voice amplified by magic.

"You were given the chance to disperse. You ignored it.

Surely, you cannot think yourselves wounded by these policies, these things we do for your own welfare? Wealth for Anaxos means wealth for the kingdom. Your children, conscripted for Anaxos, means strength for the kingdom. The rite of first choice —yes, the right to bed your brides—means more children, for the kingdom. Anaxos gives and gives, and what do you do? You protest. You throw his gifts in his face. You are ungrateful piss-babies, and thus shall be treated as such."

Even as the words cut off, a high-pitched whine issued from the Harrower's mouth. Above the now penned-in protestors, the sky rippled and threatened to split. We watched in horror. Cord set his jaw as the sky ripped open, body tensed like a spring. Rek and I did the same, the tension on the rooftop palpable. Each of us had reasons, but we knew this was the moment to commit to memory. This was the moment that the world tilted on its axis and poured poison into our ears.

Yellow liquid spilled from the rip in the sky, a vast torrent, and with it the smells of ammonia and protein. The deluge filled the enclosed street, rising in moments from ankle-deep to waist. It surged, and the protestor's screams ended abruptly as the vast lake of piss closed over their heads. Shadow and shape flailed in the murky yellow, and for a moment, all was quiet. I heard Rek crying, the sound ripping small chunks from my heart. The crowd stopped struggling as it filled their lungs, weighted their clothing. Soon, the street was a lagoon of floating corpses. Cord turned to me, tendons on his neck taut.

"This is why, Nenn," he said, his voice cold fury. "We'll take his fortune, and break this bastard's back. Let's go."

He led us down another set of planks, the rooftops descending until we passed the street level and found ourselves in a part of town lower than the rest. At one point, canals flowed across Midian, allowing traffic and trade to flow freely. But as the city grew, they drained the canals and built homes, as ramshackle as they were.

We landed on the street, the city quiet around us, a preternatural stillness that crept up my spine. Cord led us down one alley, past two warehouses long disused, and finally to a house so broken and rotting it was a wonder the city had not pulled it down, or that fire hadn't claimed it long ago. Cord glanced around, pushed the door open, and stepped inside. We followed.

The inside was a shock. I'd expected rot and stench, maybe tattered and abandoned furniture, a nest of rats or insects. Instead, the interior was solid stone, carved from one massive block. Someone spent some time crafting the illusion and making it permanent. Another bonus of insane wealth. Nothing else occupied the ten by ten space, and at its end stood a tall door with a clover lock, glyphs carved in concentric circles around it. Cord handed me a piece of chalk.

"Your turn," he said.

WE OPENED THE DOOR. Some things just don't go the way you expect. Your info is old, an added layer of complexity you didn't plan for, any number of things. This wasn't that. For once, it went smoothly, and I held my breath as I worked, waiting for the other shoe to drop.

The runes slipped through my brain, lighting up like lanternflies on a summer night, and Cord's key worked perfectly. My heart hammered at the prospect of that much money in our hands, and I have to admit, I was sweating a little, hands shaky as the door swung open. I looked inside. And swore.

16

NICE CODPIECE, JARETH

"IS THAT A FOREST?" I asked.

Cord nodded. "Either that, or someone's garden has really gotten out of hand."

The forest beyond the vault door held little color—gray earth from which white trees reached toward a leaden sky with skeletal limbs. The trees formed a convenient path, a packed-earth lane that led toward a tower that lorded over the land like the hilt of a blade thrust into the earth.

"Ready?" Rek rumbled from beside us.

I looked over. At some point, he donned a leather cuirass and bracers, and a massive greatsword hung from his hip, though at his size, even the tip hung free from the floor.

"Where did you get that?" I asked.

He shrugged. Cord patted me on the shoulder and slipped through the door.

"Rek is large and mysterious. Let's leave it at that."

Rek shouldered past me, shooting me a grin. I hesitated at the entrance, then stepped through. I paused just past the threshold, waiting for the worst to happen. A rush of guards, a blaring alarm. When nothing came, I moved forward hesitantly. Cord glanced over his shoulder.

"You coming, or you think maybe you'll set up a cabin here, have a nice vacation home?"

I flipped him the bird and jogged to catch up. The silence of the place was eerie. Not even the crunch of leaf or twig disturbed our passage, and it seemed even normal sound came muffled to us. The trees flanked us, guardians to a dead land, and I realized where we were.

"Deadlands," I said.

"Then we'd better hurry," Cord said.

We ran down the lane, the only sound that of our footfalls and heavy breathing. The tower grew closer, and though it threw no shadow, a chill emanated from it. We halted to catch our breath and I took in the structure. The stone was smooth and white, a tall arch cut into the base. Inside, a simple pedestal stood in the entry.

"Trap?" I asked.

"Trap," Rek said.

"If this were any trappier, it would be named Trap Trap-person and have a tunic someone embroidered the word *trap* on," Cord said.

"So what do we do?" I asked.

Cord shrugged. "Do it anyway."

He entered the tower, and we followed suit. The interior was hollow, and I found it fitting. Like most things Anaxos claimed, it was all show and no substance. He had little use for anything that didn't lend itself to his own aggrandizement. The more I saw, the more I realized Cord had the right of it. The man was a menace. He cared only about himself, his image, and his wealth. If we could take even one of those things away, it would be a well-deserved wound.

The pedestal was empty. Behind it was a door of ivory, the surface carved in intricate design.

"What in the snowy hells is this?" I asked.

"The trap," Cord said. He leaned on the pedestal and turned to me. "You asked why St. Cruciatus was so important."

"Yeah, but I don't see what that has to do with this."

He gestured to the door, and I took a closer look. Carvings of wraiths adorned its outer edges, and in the center in bas-relief stood a likeness of Cruciatus. I turned back.

"There are seven gods, Nenn. Hesh and Vesh, Kerr and Murr, Gret and Gren, and Camor. Have you ever noticed only those of wealth have long names and surnames? Have you ever wondered who Cruciatus really was?"

I shook my head.

"He was one of us. His true name was Crux. A simple blacksmith from one of the nameless villages on the Veldt. They stole that from us by renaming him. But they couldn't steal what he did. They'd steal the gods' names too, if they could. Nothing is sacred when you've got more wealth than most families see in several lifetimes."

"What's that got to do with the door?"

"Here's the clever part. Crux would never allow one of *them* through that door."

"So..."

"Well, Rek's too big. And I'm too befouled by sorcery. So that leaves you."

I glanced at the door. "Fuck."

I stepped to it, grasping the carved handle. Cord called out.

"He's going to show you things, Nenn. Don't let them dig too deeply into you."

I took a breath, squared my shoulders, and stepped through.

THE GOBLIN KING sat atop an outcrop of stone perched on a hill, his narrow blade planted point-first in the earth between his booted feet, the edge dripping crimson. Carrion birds wheeled and called above him, a cacophony of misery echoing from ribbed throats, an eyeball pierced on the end of a gore-encrusted beak, its optic nerve fluttering in the breeze with the flap of ebon wings. Arrayed around him, the remains of a once-grand army as though a whirlwind swept through their ranks, bodies broken, severed, exsanguinated.

He held his head as one who has suffered a loss, as one who has come to the end of a long road of exhaustion, and there, found only more road. He did not weep though the ground doubled and trebled before him and the carmine drops on his blade blurred to the point of blossoming into petals.

And yet, and yet, the sound of footfalls, of a light step avoiding rigid steel and limp flesh. Of breath held to keep out the scents of offal and shit and the coppery tang of blood spilled by the liter, by the gallon, by the barrel. The rasp of breath sucked in, the stifled cry as vision met the cloudy eyes of the dead and saw only the uncertainty of an eternity not promised. Then, the end of the approach. A stillness in the air, the screaming quiet of anticipation as the visitor screwed up his courage to speak.

"Speak," the king commanded, for command was his province, the land he had always known.

The voice atop the blackened boots, boots that had seen summers and winters in the ash of many a hearth, spoke low and hesitant, a thing from the underbrush that fears the sun.

"H... How?"

The goblin king gestured to a stone similar to the one he sat on. The stranger settled, not comfortably, but as well as one can afford when perched on granite and faced with an embodied force of nature. When he settled, the king looked up and regarded the man. Plain face, a dusting of whiskers across a straight jaw. Thick nose, bright eyes that shone with, if not intelligence, curiosity.

"I would ask you the same," the king replied. "How is it you've survived..." he gestured to the surrounding carnage. An indication. An indictment.

The man shrugged. "I wasn't here. I saw it though. The light. Heard it. The sound."

The goblin king nodded and shifted on his stone. "Then, let me ask - are you mad?"

"How do you mean?"

"You saw what happened here and decided to investigate?"

"I'm a curious sort. Besides, it seemed to be over." He looked around, though not at the dead. Instead, his gaze sought the abstract. The silence in the aftermath. "Was I wrong?"

The king shook his head and looked up, past the avian storm that gathered. The sun still stood high, a vast unblinking eye. He addressed the man.

"I have time."

"For?"

"Questions. You have curiosity, no? Let me sate it."

"And then?"

The king shrugged. "We shall see."

The man nodded and pulled a case from his side, unrolling a sheaf of parchment, tipping free an inkpot and a quill. He looked around, and with a demeanor that practically vibrated with unease, pulled a board shield from under a dead man, the body squelching with movement. He grimaced, and then moved quicker, needing to distance himself. He stretched the parchment out and laid it across the dry side of the board. He dipped the quill and glanced up at the king.

"Tell me a story."

"What kind of story?"

"Yours."

"Why?"

"People will want to read it. To know you. To know this."

The king sighed and tilted his head back, trying to remember. Memory floated at the edge, vagaries, a chiaroscuro of thought. He tilted his head back, gaze rolling down his nose at the scribe like water off a hill. Quizzical, concerned. The emotions roiled and mingled, dripping from his lips.

"Do you remember your mother?"

The scribe blinked, confusion writ on his face plain as the ink on his fingertips. "Yes, a stout woman. Severe at times. Then, who wouldn't be, with muddy boots on rushes, six children, and a gruff husband. She was a wonderful cook. Sweetbreads, stew..." he trailed off.

"Interesting. I remember nothing. Well, not *nothing*. Perhaps... I don't know that she was ever *there* in the traditional sense. Nor that she was stern. But I have mementos of her. The scent of bog peat in the summer. The whine of gnats in heat. The green throat of bull rushes pulling toward one another, reeds rubbing, chirping a symphony in time to the creak and croak of toad and frog."

The scribe frowned even as his quill nib scratched against the parchment. *Scritch scritch scritch.* The utterance of print, the lexicon of language, each moment measured in quarts and distance. He reflected on that thought, and decided if he tried to write something worse, he couldn't. This was it. Purple prose shitting itself against the wall, letting the words drip down like fly-ridden effluvia. He grunted once and scribbled, letting the ink blot out the words, obliterate the ephemeral bullshit. He could do better. He began again.

His mother was a swamp.

Fuck no. Another blot. This one nearly tearing the paper.

He looked up apologetically, then motioned for the king to continue.

"My father? Very well. My father. Dry. Distant. Harsh. Hot. Rough. A hundred, a thousand adjectives, all too small or too large to fit him. Too wrong, and yet almost right."

Better, the scribe thought. Filter out the frippery. He thought back to the beginning, thinking he would need to revise. He kept writing, the quill a small blur. He raised his free hand and spun his fingers, insisting the king go on, insisting on the continuance of story, the uninterrupted flow of idea.

"My childhood?" The king harrumphed, a sound of discontent. "What of yours?"

The scribe looked up, blinked. "I spent the majority of my early days weeding plots and cutting thatch. Sometimes, when the harvest finished, grain stacked and milled, and it was too soon to hang meat to dry, I played with the farm dogs. Sometimes I ran to the market and spent what few coins I had on paper and charcoal. My father nearly took my head off when he found them. He'd taught us letters, but not that they were much use beyond knowing how to read the proclamations and keep our heads down. He was determined that we would be thatchers, herds, row workers. I was not."

The king nodded, the great white mane of his hair bobbing. "I played. In caves and trees, in stone labyrinth and mossed battlefield. It wasn't for lack of work, but lack of guidance. It was there I learned my first scraps of sorcery - how to bleed a man from his pores, how to twist his bones so he looked like a dog when viewed in the right light. How to chase the small dragonflies when they came near, and the way their thoraxes crunched under your molars."

He leaned closer, the hilt of his blade tipping to one side, coming to rest against his thigh. "Do you wonder, dear man, how you and I diverged so?"

The scribe shrugged. "The fae are what they are."

The king waved it away. "A useless tautology. I assumed a man of words would know better. We diverged because we wished it so. Would you have the strength to survive in my world? A wildling even among wild things? I would have withered in your world. Survived, yes, but never lived. You make your own reality, scribe."

"You're suggesting I wanted to be... normal?"

The king shrugged. "I'm suggesting you survived. Whether you lived or not is of your own mind to make up."

"Interesting." The scribe took a breath and frowned at the words he'd written. Clearer, cleaner. The king's words stuck with him. *Had he lived? Would he have touched magic and brought it into his breast in lieu of meat or love?* He shrugged, muscle playing with its own landscape, and put quill to parchment.

"How did you become king?"

"How does anyone become king? Deceit, divine right, and inbreeding."

The scribe raised an eyebrow, giving the king a look that said *perhaps you've shared too much.* The king moved on, head tilted toward the sun. Perhaps he gauged the hour, perhaps trying to remember something once important, now relegated to insignificance in the face of time.

"We have little time left. You may ask me one more," he said.

The look in his eyes was predatory, the glint of light in the pupils like that of a hawk ready to strike, anticipation a hooked talon. The scribe screwed up his face, chewed on the tip of the quill. It had to be good. Lachlan's press would pay by the word for the account of the stranger who laid waste to Renfen's entire army.

The scribe looked around, at bodies bloating in the sun, fat toadstools of flesh putrefying, ready to spill red and glistening spoor. His gorge rose, a thick tide of boiled oats and greasy sausage, and he choked it back, looking away. *How does someone do this?* He glanced again, just from the corner of his eye, the look of a man who has seen a dangerous thought, and wonders if he looks at it full, would it cut his mind? Would it hollow his thoughts and lay him out in the sun with all these others, gibbering, until the gravediggers came and found him playing with himself in the blood-dewed grass?

His eyes flicked back to the king, to the perfectly coiffed hair, the perfect vest and leggings, the codpiece that exaggerated more than just words. The king quirked a smile at the scribe as he caught him looking, and the scribe blushed. *How?*

No, the voice in his head answered, that part that when looking over the words later, corrected the incorrect, *no. Why?*

"Why?" The scribe echoed the word, letting it tumble from his lips in place of the vomit, and the king smiled this time.

"Finally, the heart of the matter. The marrow of the bone. *Why.*" He sat back, and the blade slipped to the ground, unnoticed. "Because. Because I can."

"Surely there's more?"

"Does there have to be?"

"For a sane man, for a man who wants to make sense of the words written here, of the world he describes, yes."

"Then write this: there was a girl. Or maybe a boy. A promise. A lie. There was a death, and vengeance. There was a love unrequited. There was a dragon, and a sorcerer, and a crone. There was a fairy and a goblin, one pure, one corrupt. There was a labyrinth and a child. There was a battle. A kingdom lost, and an empire found. I was a king. I am a king. And I will do what I gods. Damn. Well. Please."

While he spoke, dread wormed its way into the scribe's heart, moving deeper and deeper until it sat entrenched like a barbed arrow. His eyes darted to the goblin king's blade, and as every dismissal dripped from his lips, he forgot to write, forgot to put down the truth he saw. These were the words of a tyrant. He leaned forward, the king seemingly forgetting him in his rant. His fingers trembled, his arm ached, and then, the sword was in his hand, the grip both cool and gritty with dried blood and sand.

He raised the blade, intending to stab it into the king's heart, to end the coming horror. Words tumbled from his lips, a short squall in the blazing heat of the king's conviction.

"You're mad. Madder than any who came before. A coming terror."

And then the king stood above him, hand outstretched, and he saw the truth. Reality is what you make it, and the king made his own. No simple warrior stood before the scribe, but a being that encompassed all things and rejected his. Neither and both. Terrible and frightening, powerful and irresistible. The scribe trembled, and the tip of the blade faltered, dipped, dipped... and ended in the dirt. The king took the blade from him, not ungently. He knelt next to the scribe, whose eyes filled with tears. He spoke soft, his voice honeyed mead in the scribe's ears.

"You can call me mad, a terror. I suppose those are true things in a way. Mercy for those who need it may seem like madness from the outside to those who do not desire succor. But I have sat to the side for so, so many years while men ground others to dirt, while they subjugated others at a whim, for money, for the color of their skin, for the way they speak, or the things they worship. You have letters and fine food and the strength of conviction. You have *absolute* conviction that what you do in the now is right, and yet cannot see past the horizon.

"And yes, I provide mercy. I feel the question trembling on your lips. I relieve you of your burdens, of your convictions. I bring you the clarity of freedom.

"You can write this, then, if it eases your heart: I do this for love. Love drives us all, and even love led these men to this field. Love led *you* here, did it not?"

The scribe, turning the words over in his head, nodded in agreement. He loved few things as he loved words. It led him down paths both bright and dim, from under his family's sheltering arms, from the beds of others who would have him as his own. He wandered still, searching for a specific love, and in wandering, found it - a country where rivers of ink flowed across a vellum landscape.

He picked up the scribe's quill and pressed it into his hand. "Love will make or break a man. Love may shatter hearts and mend souls. Love can raise a people up or cast them into the gutter. Nothing worth doing is worth doing without it. I do this *because* I love."

He leaned in and kissed the scribe just behind the ear, his lips soft and warm, and his breath smelling of sweet clover. Then he straightened and sauntered away, leaving the scribe alone. He listened to the buzz of flies on the dead, a symphony of one-string violins. He crumpled the paper, tossing it to the side, where it came to rest in a pool of clotting blood. The parchment pulled in the red until it blossomed like carnations across the rumpled surface. He watched it bloom, and then pulled a new sheet from his case, dipped his quill, and wrote:

The goblin king sat atop an outcrop of stone perched on a hill, his heart full of love.

THE VISION FADED, and I stood with the handle in my hand. I blinked, and turned back.

"What the hells was that?" I asked.

Cord and Rek still stood there, though now a box appeared

on the pedestal. Cord's hand hovered it. He leaned in, looking at it closely, then glanced up.

"A story. Maybe a lesson. Maybe just a glimpse at history. Be glad. Had the saint decided you were anything but worthy, the things you might have seen would have torn your mind to shreds."

"And you thought it was okay to send me through there?"

Cord shrugged. "I was never really worried. You're good people, Nenn. Now Rek, he probably would have had to ride a horse. If you know what I mean."

Rek muttered something and turned to keep an eye on the entrance. I swallowed and looked at the door, then backed away a little. I turned my attention to the box.

"Is this it?" I asked. "Seems small."

Cord lifted the lid of the box, revealing a jewel the size of Rek's fist. It was the color of summer grass, carved in the shape of a heart, and when he held it to the meager light, it hummed softly. I smelled ocean air and heard the call of gulls, and thought I spied summer glades in its depths.

"What is that?" Rek asked.

"The heart of Crux," Cord said.

"I thought the wealth of a kingdom would be more... golden?" I said.

Cord nodded, and slipped the stone into a bag at his side. A little of the light in the room seemed to dim.

"The heart is worth a kingdom's fortune," he said. "We can get gold anywhere, but this—Anaxos has abused his power and no longer deserves it. Let some other kingdom have their endless summer."

We left the tower, trotting down the forest path. As we went, I caught glimpses of shadows in the trees, stalking our movements. Rek said nothing, but freed his blade, and I pulled my knives from their sheaths. The exit loomed ahead, the threshold closer with each step. Cord picked up the pace, and we were soon sprinting as the trees shook with the force of the things following us.

A cry from in front, and I skidded to a halt beside the others as three of the things following burst from the tree line. They were tall and thin, pale with red eyes. Their faces were bone masks from which all manner of horns protruded. Long black claws sprouted from ice-white hands. The lead swiped at Cord, and came up short two hands as Rek's blade split them from its wrists. A quick backswing severed it in two, and its halves toppled. I spun around Cord and planted both my blades in another wraith's eyes. It tumbled back, and Cord slipped between the legs of another, thick hands grasping its skull and twisting with a satisfying *snap*.

As soon as the body hit the ground, we resumed running. One of the monsters pulled Rek down, and he cried out, a great bellow of rage and pain. I moved back, driving my knives into the wraith's spine. Rek shot me a look of gratitude, and we moved again. We burst into the vault room, the wraiths on our heels, and Rek spun to face them, blade in hand.

"Shut the door!" I shouted.

"No time," Cord said, and pointed out the door facing the street. Guards marched in single file, boots ringing on the stone.

Rek set his shoulders. "Go. I'll hold them off."

I shook my head and set myself. Cord grabbed my arm, whispering fiercely into my ear.

"If we all die here, there was no point to this."

He pulled me to the door and pushed the bag into my arms, then pulled a knife from my hip.

"Run. I'll catch up," he said, and set himself to meet the guards coming from the other direction.

I hesitated, fear and guilt warring within me. An arrow embedded itself into the doorframe. I unfroze and ran down the street at a sprint, disappearing into alley after alley. I found the first of the planks, scrambling upward and moving across the rooftops again, until the sounds of battle faded with each building I crossed.

When I felt I was a safe distance, I slowed, trying to avoid alerting the patrols that crept below. Fires blazed in the city, and mobs of citizens still clashed with guards. Finally, the moon high in the night sky, I found the apartment and slipped in under cover of darkness. I hid the jewel under the couch, and when an hour passed, let myself cry until I fell asleep.

17

THAT GUY'S NOT GONNA SHIT RIGHT FOR A WEEK

I SPENT three days in a haze, a bottle of Juarin whiskey and a tin of slipweed helping to numb the pain. A part of me knew Cord couldn't die, that there was always the possibility he'd walk through the door. But he could be captured, thrown in chains, dropped at the bottom of the Lethe, clubbed, dismembered, or set on fire. Functional immortality didn't mean freedom from suffering.

I wondered what the gods were thinking. If they were thinking. What kind of deity allows the kind of suffering I'd seen in the Veldt? What kind of deity allows beings like the Harrowers to exist, for creatures like Mane to exist? I thought about what Cord would say. He'd probably tell me the gods were disinterested, that they'd made the world for themselves, and that we were the intruders here. He'd probably say that Camor was the only one who really cared about us, and that was because we amused them.

If that was the case, I had no use for any of them. They let the living suffer and from what I'd seen, even the dead had no peace. Maybe beyond the deadlands there was a hallowed hall of peace and contentment, but no sage wrote of it, no wizard spoke of it. That left us to fend for ourselves. I could do that. I'd been doing that since my parents sold me, since the women at the orphanage turned me out onto the street at sixteen, and I had to cut my way through the alleys to survive.

I missed my friends. I missed Cord. He'd become a part of my life, like an old dog that hangs around. I realized that wasn't fair though. I busted his balls, but it was because I knew deep down that Cord was the big brother I'd never had. Self-pity wasn't going to bring him back. In the meantime, I had to shake my torpor.

I rolled from the couch and into the street. It was quiet but for the destitute and sick, clotting the alleys and resting sore feet on street corners. Others, dealers and prostitute, were just trying to survive. I took a little time to explore the alleys and warrens of Lowtown. We'd not spent much time doing just that since we'd arrived, and now I walked among the tumbledown buildings and dirty streets.

Most of it was in disrepair, and even the merchants that set up shop here looked to be nearly as destitute as its denizens were. Shops carried threadbare clothing, food on the verge of rotting, and medicine as likely to kill as cure. For every chirugeon with a bloody floor and dirty instruments there was an apothecary willing to sell you things that would take the pain away, and a pawn broker willing to take your possessions so you could afford either.

No posters of Anaxos hung here, no guards patrolled the area. Instead, gangs of tough-looking teens with curved blades skulked in the shadows, and men with gapped teeth and scars lounged in bars and pubs, looking for the next piece of work to wet their blades. If Anaxos wanted the whole of Lowtown to sink into the Lethe, ignoring it couldn't have been a better plan.

I found a prostitute and her brother on a corner by a rundown pub. They were both pretty, maybe too much so for

Lowtown, and I wondered how long until the city stole that from them also. We negotiated, and I brought them back to the apartment, soothing their worried looks by leaving my blades on the table. I wanted to honor Cord one last time before I left this stinking city for good, and if Cord would have done anything, it was fuck his way through the local stable.

The girl had high breasts with dark nipples, her brother a pretty cock. We spent the night with one another, with slip-weed, and with the sounds of our moans keeping us company. When we were done, I kissed each, slipped them five crowns apiece, and the sack holding the heart. I didn't need it. I gave them advice. It was simple. Get out. Don't look back. And don't open the sack until you're a world away. When the door closed, I slipped into a blissful sleep, too tired to worry for a time.

THE SOUND of hammering brought me around, and I slipped from bed. I gathered my things and crept out the door, knives in their sheathes. I thought I could hire a crew at the docks, get them to sail the Bough Mount out of the shantytown. I passed a workman with a hammer and paused to see where the sound that woke me came from.

The poster he'd hung laid me on my ass as sure as if someone told me they wanted me to have their children, or that everyone was expected, without delay, to fuck a duck. The headline screamed from the one-sheet, bold as brass:

**NOTORIOUS THIEF FOUND
BODY TO BE DISPLAYED**

That was the thing with Mane. Whenever someone pissed in his gruel, he liked to put them up front and center, dead or alive, to show the little people the consequences of screwing with His Royal Personage. I read on. Turned out, the places we'd hit hit in the past couple years hadn't been small-time. Or rather, they had, but on purpose. Misdirection by the elite. Hide a lot of money in a lot of little places, so no one notices you've got half the economy tied up. Cord somehow knew and took every single one of the king's bookmakers to the wash. Combine that with the theft of Crux's heart, and he'd really pissed off Mane. The paper said he'd enraged the bastard to the point the old miser planned on showing up personally to judge the corpse as the head of the criminal organization that plagued the kingdom for so long.

I wasn't sure what that meant. They'd hang the body? Quarter it? Feed it to a manticore? The first wasn't so bad. Cord would come back; we'd take a break and do it all over again somewhere else. Or maybe we'd just retire. The other two options, though – I didn't know much about magic and resurrection, but I'm pretty sure once you're manticore shit, that's it.

I had to do *something*. I checked my things, and made my way to the square. Maybe I could convince them I was his poor sister. Maybe I could convince them to spare the body and punish him in spirit. Maybe they'd spit-roast me, too. Either way, I had to try. I left the apartment behind and went to town.

THEY'D HELD the gathering in the market square, the vendors cleared out, the stalls and booths taken down, and in their place, a tall wooden platform hung with colorful banners, each bearing the king's livery. Guards stood watch at each entrance, and in the crowd. They'd quelled the mobs, for now.

The place teemed with people, noble and peasant alike jostling for position in order to view the mastermind that foiled King Mane. Vendors mingled in the crowd, trays heaped with small mincemeat pies and cups of mulled wine that spiced the air and made my stomach rumble. The whole place took on the air of a festival.

I looked up and saw Cord's body propped against a short wooden wall. Someone, no doubt the king's chief propagandist, had placed a jester's hat on his head and drawn a crude caricature next to him, of a bloated Cord holding bags of money.; His smile leered, X's painted over his eyes. The king towered over him in the drawing, a flaming sword in one hand, a speech bubble above with the word 'Cad!' printed within. It looked like a child did the work, or a very dumb adult. I thought Cord would have gotten a good laugh.

I pressed my way into the crowd, for the most part getting as much notice as a beggar on the low street. A waiter passed, and I snagged a pie and a cup of wine. He stopped to sneer at me, but found other things to do when a noble with more money than sense, if his haircut was any indication, snapped his smarmy little fingers. The waiter disappeared into the crowd and I found a spot on the wall to chew on the pie and sip the wine. My appetite had fled though, and I tossed the food to the side. I craned my neck to see what they'd planned on doing with Cord.

A round of trumpets blaring knocked me from my near-coma, and I started, standing up straight. The crowd shuffled and slithered closer together, making way for a troop of knights in bright chainmail, their iron-shod boots ringing against the cobbles. They stomped to a halt at the base of the platform, spaced arm-length apart, turning their backs to the crowd. A page in a haircut that made me wonder if an official hair-cutting bowl existed in the castle came next, a scroll in his hands. He, too, stopped at the base of the platform and unrolled the parchment, cleared his throat, and read.

"Hear ye! The illustrious King Mane, Herald of the Gods, Protector of the Realm, Divinely Chosen of the Four Duchies,

Holder of the Sixteen Names, and Wielder of His Divine Manhood, commands that you shall attend and witness the judgment he pronounces on this thief, scoundrel, and traitor to the throne!"

For a moment I was afraid I had sprained something rolling my eyes. I blinked and looked up at Cord. Now would be a good time for him to wake the fuck up and run. Barring that, now would be a good time for him to be dead for good. I cast about - no way was I getting him down from there. I resigned myself to watching and idly wondered if I could recover his body after. I could probably use our savings to give him a nice burial and then retire to some nation that didn't have a treaty with these assholes.

The trumpets blared again and the crowd grew silent. The king, resplendent in crimson and gold, a shining peaked crown on his head, walked between his knights with utter confidence. His Harrower lurked behind, generally creeping the crowd out. Mane climbed the steps to the platform. His pinched face and bald pate gleamed in the noon sun. He raised his arms.

"Silence!"

Never mind that no one had been talking. He lowered his arms and smiled to the crowd. I slipped through it, little notice paid to me as Mane commanded the attention of the attendees.

"I am so glad you all could come. This is what it means to be a Midianite. Men and women, commoner and noble. You all know I rose to the throne from humble beginnings, my own father little more than a duke, not much land to his name other than several million crowns, a forest, and a few thousand acres. You know how I worked hard, donated my men and my time to the wars of my predecessors. You know how I care about you. I made being a smith, a farmer, a cobbler - I made all of these great again in the eyes of the gods!"

He paused for the polite smattering of applause. Someone

jingled a bell. When it died out, he continued. I found myself only a couple feet away from his Harrower, the man still holding the severed hand in his own.

"And now"—His mien turned sad, his voice downcast—"And now, one of your own, a commoner, a citizen of the kingdom, decided to steal from us. Yes, he stole from me, but in turn all of you, for is not my wealth your wealth? Is not my fortune your own?"

More applause, the jingling of bells louder, though the king did not seem to notice it.

"So, it saddens me. I hate to hurt the little people."

He didn't seem to notice or care he was talking about a corpse. I wondered how this didn't bother anyone else the way it made my skin creep across my bones.

"But, everyone must be treated equally. So, I proclaim that this traitor, this loser, this *scum* be purged with fire."

He leaned in and kissed Cord on the cheek. Then the other. Cord's eyes popped open, and his hands shot up, grabbing the king by his face and kissing him full on the mouth. Something squirmed between them, Cord's throat bulging, passing from his mouth to the king. When it finished, Cord let him go. The king fell back, clutching his stomach as Cord staggered to his feet and threw himself off the far end of the stage.

For a moment, silence held the crowd. The knights stood as though they had shit their armor and feared to leave a trail. Bells jingled merrily. I assumed that meant Cord was fleeing. I stood rooted in place though, and for a split second, it looked like nothing else would happen. Then, with a sound like a ripping sail and a geyser of blood and bone, something the size of a small dog ripped from the king's guts. It savaged him on the way out, his wails of pain ending as though someone had hit him in the face with a hammer.

The Harrower lifted his arms, as if to perform some act of

horrific magic, and I slammed both blades into his spine. The high hum died on his lips, blood bursting from between his teeth. He collapsed into a heap, and I slipped back into the crowd. They'd begun to riot, alternately cheering and screaming as they took down first the knights, then the herald, ripping chunks of hair from his scalp.

One by one, nobles were borne down and beaten or torn apart. Someone recovered the king's flaming sword and set the platform aflame, then ran the blade through at least three other nobles. They pinwheeled through the crowd like meat torches, dripping molten flesh like candle wax. I edged my way out and fled the carnage, narrowly avoiding the grasping arms of a waiter beaten with his own tray and a wild milliner with an eight-inch hatpin.

I ran down the street as fast as I could, not looking back, heading for the cottage. Screw Cord; screw Midian. There wasn't time for niceties like Camor's first rule, or even hiring a crew to get out of town. Hook, crook, or carved flesh, I was leaving. My new plan was to get out so fast I left a Nenn-shaped hole in the wall.

18

BANDIT LETTUCE TOMATO

I'D JUST ABOUT HIT the craftsman quarter when a roar went up from the northern part of the city. I turned back to see the glow of flames, great plumes of smoke rising into the sky like black serpents. Terrified guards and townspeople rushed past, and more than once, I heard cries of *wights*. I supposed Rek hadn't shut that door after all.

I made my way to the breach in the wall we'd entered in, plunging through the tunnel and out the other side. I burst onto the boardwalk of the shantytown to find its citizens already fleeing, loading up small boats and larger skiffs with belongings, crowding one another as they all vied to fit. I fought my way through the crowds, running down planks that already beginning to sink into the river.

Torlc's place still stood, but the door hung on broken hinges. Torlc's body hung impaled on a long pike. I wondered at the strength it had taken to do that, and thought it better not to find out. A figure stood beside the pike, weeping, and curiosity seized me. I approached.

The stranger's head was the size of a large pumpkin, the skin smooth and crimson, taut and shining. He turned at the sound of my footsteps and I found myself looking into eyes red with weeping, a yellowish ooze dripping from them, seeds marking the liquid.

"What happened here?" I asked.

"The Leashmen. They killed him. And their Harrower cursed me. I'm a tomato!"

"A... tomato?"

He nodded his bulbous head and more of the yellow stuff dripped from his eyes. He flicked out a tongue to clear it away.

"Oh gods, I'm so delicious!" he wailed.

I backed away until I was a safe distance and sprinted to the Bough Mount. It still bobbed in its berth, untouched. I wondered why the wizards left it, and got my answer when four hooded figures stepped from below decks. I skidded to a halt. One of them held a blade, and another lifted a hand, energy crackling between their fingers. They seemed to consider me for a moment, then the third, smaller than the others, raised a hand and beckoned me aboard. I hesitated only for a moment. The smell of the city burning, the cries of the citizens, and the howls of the wights came to me on the wind. It was all the motivation I needed. When the world rears up and says *get the fuck out of the way*, you listen.

I hopped aboard, and in a matter of moments, the ship began to move, the crewmen navigating away with perfect efficiency. I flopped onto the deck, watching as the city dwindled. The mainsail was let down, and we picked up speed. Midian drew further and further away. Clouds gathered above, a chill sweeping across the water. We rounded a bend and the city disappeared. The first flakes of snow fell.

I heaved a sigh, and laid on the deck. The shorter stranger sat beside me.

"The Kingkillers?"

He tipped his hood back, as did the others. Lux, Rek, and Cord, all grinning.

"You didn't think that Harrower cursed only me, did you?" Cord said.

I punched him in the face, and he reeled back, the others bursting into laughter. He held his nose for a moment, letting blood trickle between his fingers. When he pulled them away, he was still grinning.

"Hell of a plan, huh?" he asked.

"Yeah, hell of a plan. Did Rek finally get to kill you?"

He nodded. "Right after you left. Blade through the lung. Really hurt."

"Good," I said and leaned in to hug him. "Where to now?"

He shrugged, looked around at the snow falling in fat flakes. "Someplace warmer, I think."

19

THIS IS THE CHAPTER ABOUT AN ASSHOLE

HE SANK BENEATH THE WAVES, spilling a viscous cloud of red. Blood ballooned out from the wound in his neck like ribbon pulled from a child's stuffed toy. Had it been any other time, any other place, any other person, he'd think it beautiful. Instead, he gagged on the taste of sewage runoff, fish, and blood. His lungs burst for air, and despite himself, he sucked in a breath, trying desperately to breathe. All he got for his trouble was a lungful of brackish water and a parasite that thought to itself *what the fuck*, but quickly settled in.

The waters around Tremaire were frightening, even to a Harrower. The wizards in the tower dumped failed experiments there, the Harrowers sometimes using the lake as a testing ground for horrors they dared not unleash on land. Flakes of white silt and the loose scales of something floated by him, and he thrashed to escape. He wanted to reach out to his brothers and sisters in the Hive, to let them know he was dying, to avenge his death. He knew it didn't matter. Harrowers were by nature solitary creatures. If by some miracle you managed to get them to work together, by hook or crook, it was always a short partnership. No, a Harrower was about a Harrower, and little else.

He thrashed again, sending little fish scattering in his wake, and reached toward the surface. His gift burned just below his chest, trapped now, as he was, and he knew even if he tried screaming the Sorrow, there would be no escape. He would simply bleed out and die, sinking to the bottom like a whale, more chum for the deep dwellers, bones bleached and alone.

His vision flickered. They say your whole life flashes before your eyes before death. Each flicker of darkness came to him with a crackle and a snap. His lungs burned, and his ribs threatened to shatter with the effort of holding the lake out. He had little strength left. He screamed into the water as the dark claimed him, the sound causing the wound in his neck to pulse like a mouth, vomiting crimson threads into the gray water. In his last moments of conscious thought, he supposed it was true. Everyone's like a book. When we're opened, we're red.

HIS NAME, before the Change, was Qualinast Aurelian. He had been a good child. Dull, perhaps, but studious. He remembered that. Before. Before the box had come to him, unassuming in its simplicity, unadorned in any way. Simple pine, like the Gentian forests he'd grown up near. He'd questioned his father and the servants as to what it might be, or who'd delivered it, but no one had answers for him. Included was a note, the hand spidery, the prose rhyming.

Inner sight
Outer eyes
From the dark
The dead ones rise
Beyond the gate
The blackened sun
Will you look

Little one

He'd set the box on the mantle in his room, the card beside it. Truth be told, the card sent a chill up his spine. For a time he forgot about it. You know how it is with young boys--sunshine and grass, warm chaff in the air and trimmed branches for swords. Days with friends, chasing bright motes of sunlight across creek beds, shoving in line with friends at the bakers. Early morning smell of pastries in the oven, afternoon smell of roast pig. Music at night. Finally, his head in his mother's lap as he drifted to sleep, her fingers tangled in his hair.

Still, no summer lasts forever, and the rains came. Holed up in a castle once comfortable, chill drafts blew between the stones of the walls, the ceilings dripped. Exploring only left you cold and dirty. Friends and adults found important things to do, leaving him wandering the dusty library, or to his own devices in his room. Outside, thunder rippled across the forest, the wind bending the trees back like supple spines.

Boredom fossilized him, turned his thoughts to mud and rubbish. He imagined the rain outside falling in his head, slicking the normally bright pathways of his mind. He glanced around his room, at the discarded toys. Wooden soldiers and brightly-painted nobles, animals and beasts carved and smoothed, and tin swords cut and hammered to his size. His eyes fell on the box on the mantle, and he padded over and took it down. He flopped back on the bed and ran his fingers over it.

The wood was cool to the touch--almost cold--and smooth. A simple clasp held it shut. He held it up to his ear and shook it. Something inside rattled. He wondered what it could hold. A pair of dice? Perhaps little bones, gathered and bleached and carved into interesting shapes? He'd seen something similar once at a mummer's show, the actor wearing a necklace of them. Maybe it was sweets. Candies from far-off Ilicia, delicate lace-

chocolate from Yaro, maybe those hard but sweet dried meats from Midian.

At the thought, his stomach rumbled, and he shook it once more, listening to the rattle. There was no embargo on opening the box. He'd simply not found it interesting in the summer. His mouth watered at the idea of sugar melting on his tongue, the sweet rush of chocolate as it filled his senses. Unable to wait any longer, he popped the clasp and flipped the lid open, peering inside.

Eyes. Two disembodied eyes lay inside, milky-white and dried. He almost dropped the box, but the curiosity of youth made him grip it tighter, pull it close to his face. He watched with morbid fascination as spider legs sprouted from each, and they began to move. At first, a sort of dark wonder held him, and he watched as the legs kicked and floundered, righted the eyes. They climbed the sides of the box, then hopped out, onto his hand.

Instinct caused him to loosen his grip on the wood, but by then, it was too late. The eyes scrambled up his arms, clawed their way up his neck. They pinched as they crossed his cheeks, and though he clawed and fought and wept, they kept coming. With precise motions, they thrust their legs into his eyes and wrenched the orbs out.

His screams attracted his mother. She burst into the room in time to see his eyes settle into his head. He felt the hot stream of blood covering his cheeks from the pair that had once occupied his sockets. He turned to her, jaws clenched in a rictus of agony, and screamed through his teeth.

Where Florinima Aurelian had once stood, he saw only a naked mass of raw flesh. He screamed and went to the window, hoping it had been an illusion. Below, in the stableyards, horses milled together under the lessening rain. Their black carapaces glinted in the gloaming, their manes of braided intestines shone wetly.

He opened his mouth and screamed again, this time bright and high, and in his mind, a door opened. The horror that stood on the other side reached out welcoming arms, and Qualinast fell into them gratefully.

Oros loves you, child, the god said.

PART II

Ladies and Gentleman, step right up and
See the man who told the truth

Metallica, Bad Seed

20

WAY TO GO, FUCKBRAIN

MIDIAN BURNED AT OUR BACKS, and we sped west. Behind us, a ramshackle fleet of scows and tall ships jostled for position between the banks of the Lethe. They fled the ruins of Mane's kingdom as surely as cockroaches flee a burning house. The future lay ahead in murky vagaries. What of the magi that pursued us, or their Leashmen? No sign. Would our passage stir the ire of anyone watching? We didn't know that either. Cord suspected it would remain unremarked upon for some time, at least until they cleaned up the mess we'd made. Then in all likelihood, they'd start looking for someone to blame. He planned to be nowhere near when the hammer came down.

We spent three days outrunning the refugees. When their sails finally dwindled on the horizon, the masts like a broken forest behind us, Cord called us to the deck. He looked at the encroaching mountains ahead, and the sere edges of the Veldt, where the plains met the stony hills before the range thrust into the sky.

"We're broke," he announced.

"Surprise," Rek rumbled.

"How?" Lux asked.

Cord shrugged. "Takes a lot of money to bring down a city."

"So now what?" I asked. "Back to the same old?"

He looked toward the hills again and shook his head. "Nah, I think I've got something better in mind. This whole area was used as a resting place for some ancient bigwigs."

I turned down my mouth in distaste. "Grave robbing? Really?"

"Hey, they don't need it," he said.

"They *are* dead," Rek said, Lux nodding in agreement.

"Aren't you worried about curses, or... or... something?" I finished lamely.

Cord snorted a laugh and patted me on the shoulder as he passed. Rek made his way back to the wheel. I was left alone with Lux. I looked around at the still-calm day, the blue sky. The snow hadn't reached this far yet.

"Nice day, huh?"

She gave me a sideways glance and left me alone on the deck. I huffed out a sigh of annoyance and went to watch the river pass by. Nothing was ever easy. If it was, and you had a head on your shoulders, you knew damn well not to trust it.

"YEAH, THIS IS THE DEAD GUY," Cord said.

"How can you tell?" I asked, peering over his shoulder.

The body in question was wizened and gray, wisps of hair trailing from a mostly bald and peeling scalp, nails the length of small knives, and flesh like leathered parchment. His lips had long ago pulled back from yellowing teeth, eyes milky and staring at the ceiling of the barrow. He had been entombed naked, and Cord pointed at the enormous member hanging between his legs.

"Akkalon the Gifted, they called him."

I grimaced. "Akkalon the Destroyer seems more fitting."

Cord snorted. "It's not the size of the boat, Nenn. It's how many people are rowing it." He frowned. "Or something like that."

He reached down and shifted the body to the side, kicking up a small puff of dust and what I imagined was dried flesh. I pulled back and covered my mouth while he rummaged around. Finally, he came up with a cry of triumph, a glittering blade in his hand.

"A sword?" I didn't try to keep the incredulity from my voice. "We trekked through nearly a half-mile of stinking earth and bones for a fucking sword?"

Cord looked hurt. "It's a magic sword."

I narrowed my eyes and set my jaw. "Cord, I swear to Gret's balls if you're jerking me around..."

He waved it around, muttering. Movement over his shoulder caught my eye, and I stepped to the side to see better. These old tombs were full of drafty corridors that could stir up dust and make cobwebs wave like flags. I felt no breeze however, and stared, trying to figure out where the movement came from. I lifted the torch, lighting the alcoves in the walls.

"Cord..."

"Hold on just a godsdamned minute... *alakaham*! Fuck, no. Hmm... *riesling*! No..."

"Cord!" I nearly shouted, backing away.

He finally turned to look, the sword drooping in his hand. The dead trudged from the alcoves, eyes blazing with yellow light. A sound nearby caught our attention, and we looked in time to see Akkalon rising from his tomb, clawed hands gripping the lip of the stone.

"Run!" Cord said.

I didn't' really need an invitation, as I was already several paces ahead of him. We slipped past the chamber entrance, feet pounding as the moans of the dead followed us. Once in the straightaway that was the antechamber hall, I risked a glance back.

Akkalon took the lead, his massive dick flopping side-to-side, beating dust from ancient thighs. I screamed and put on more speed, leaving Cord behind. I should have felt bad about it. I did not. I reached the door to the hall, where Rek posted up as a guard. The big man looked at me, then down the hall, and started to close the door.

"Hold the door!" Cord called, barely ahead of the dead. "Hold the fucking door!"

Rek stopped pushing the massive slab, waiting impatiently. It seemed like hours before Cord burst through the gap, the dead close and loud.

"Close the door! Close the fucking door!" He shouted.

Rek put his shoulder into it, and the door slammed shut just as a trio of clutching hands reached through. The heavy stone crushed the bones and tore the skin free, dropping the limbs to the ground where they lay, unmoving. Cord stood panting, hands on his knees. We could hear the frustrated dead on the other side, clawing, scratching, and moaning.

"They can't get through, right?" I asked.

Rek shrugged. "They'd have to be stronger than me." He turned to Cord. "What'd you get?"

"A sword," I said.

"A *magic* sword," Cord said.

We started the long walk back to the surface.

"What's it do?" Rek asked.

"I have no fuckin' idea," Cord said.

The tunnel slanted upward, and soon we exited the barrow into bright sunlight and a summer breeze. The hills around us— some other burial sites, some natural hills—glowed a verdant green with the growth of a good season. The sky above was a sharp blue, the clouds white and fluffy in the sky. Lux leaned beside the barrow entrance, staring off across the landscape and contemplating whatever inner life the resurrected held in their breast.

Cord tossed the sword to Lux as he passed, the wizard catching the blade deftly.

"What's this?" she asked.

"Sword," I said.

"*Magic* sword," Cord said.

"No idea what it fuckin' does," Rek rumbled as he passed.

"That's... useful," Lux said.

We made our way to the campsite. The river was about two miles south, where our boat, the Codfather, sat at anchor. Cord renamed it. None of us got the joke. I'd complained a little about not having mounts to move us and our gear back and forth, but the truth of the matter was that we didn't have room on the ship, and most horses would have little to nothing to do with our little group.

We'd camped at the edge of a small copse, the trees providing welcome shade. It was nice, but it was hot, and I'd begun to sweat in places I'd rather not chafe. I collapsed onto my bedroll and rummaged around, finally digging out a piece of jerky and a waterskin. I drank deeply and chewed the meat while the others settled in.

I wasn't in love with this idea, grave robbing. Easy money, he'd said. After all, who was gonna fight back? Turns out the dead. The old bastards—part of the former Tevint Imperium—had been spiteful and pretty damn possessive in death. Booby-traps, curses, undead guards, and a litany of other nastiness. Even the ones too poor to afford the standard 'fuck everybody' package were fortunate enough to have some nasty beasties crawl into their tombs and breed.

They settled in, Cord finding his own jerky to chew while

Rek polished the big axe he'd started carrying. He'd lugged a greatsword for a while, but decided against it in the long run. Said it took too much finesse for a guy his size. The axe was easier, he said. You could clear whole hallways with it. Lux sat further out, poring over the new sword.

So here we were, our little band of outlaws, on a summer day, in the land of the dead. That's when the sword started screaming. Lux jumped and flipped the sword into the air. It arced over and over, spinning, then plunged straight down, into Cord's foot.

"Sonofamotherfuck!" he shouted.

The sword was saying something, one word repeatedly, and I leaned in, waving at Cord to shush. He shot me an outraged look, but clamped his lips shut.

"OrosOrosOrosOrosOrosOros," the sword babbled.

"Satisfied?" Cord snapped.

I nodded.

"Then pull it the fuck out," he said.

I gripped the hilt and smirked at him. "That's what she said," I replied, and yanked the blade from his foot.

He sighed and grabbed the wounded limb, squeezing it to stop the blood flow. In a few moments, it stopped entirely, and he lowered it to the ground. One bonus to the curse—when he doesn't die, he heals fast.

The sword grew quiet again, and I looked around.

"Oros?" I asked.

Rek shrugged. I looked to Lux, her face paler than normal, eyes wide.

"No," she said.

I walked over, sat beside her. "Who is it, Lux?"

"It's not... it's not possible."

"That's not vague at all," Cord groused. I shot him a look and he snapped his mouth shut.

"Lux?" I prompted.

"When we were in the Academy, we had a lot of classes," she said, then blushed, as if embarrassed about stating the obvious. "Anyway, history was my favorite. I loved the deep knowledge—where we came from, how things happened. I especially loved the stories about the Tevint Imperium—mage-kings who used their magic to better the land and the people."

"So what caused their collapse?" Rek asked, leaning in.

"Unlike a lot of lost history, there was another kingdom nearby, a fledgling thing, but its historians were already interested in how the Imperium got where they had. They recorded it all. The kings of Tevint decided that they could do better—be better—they joined their power, and tried to bring heaven to earth. As punishment, the gods sent one of their own, Oros, to end their folly."

"So why would the sword be concerned with this Oros now?" Cord asked.

"Because. They couldn't win. They were obliterated to the last, but as revenge, they managed to cast one final enchantment. They crafted a prison for Oros, trapping them, and with the last of their strength, set guards about the prison."

"And that prison?"

"I think we just cracked it," I said.

"Fffff...," Cord said.

"Yes, fuck," I agreed.

21

PIRATES ARE JUST THIEVES WITH MORE SYPHILIS

NATURALLY, we did what any self-respecting group of thieves would do. We ran. I won't bog you down with particulars, but we packed camp, moved two miles, and got on the boat so fast we would have left scorch marks across the plain if possible. Once underway, we watched the far banks of the former Tevint Imperium dwindle. Cord spat in the water as they disappeared from sight.

"So what now?" I asked.

We leaned against the rail, watching the banks of the Lethe pass as the boat traveled westward. Rek stood at the helm, a rock against the wind, Lux below, stowing the sword and our gear.

"I've been this way a long time back," Cord said.

"When was this?"

"Another life. I was a young man."

"You mean you didn't spring from your mother like this?"

"I've always been devastatingly handsome, if that's what you mean."

"Sure. Anyway, you were saying?"

"There's a little city in a valley just on the other side of the Godsteeth. It should take about a day, maybe two to get there.

We can stop, regroup, maybe think about sailing all the way to Orlecht."

"That's in the Western Kingdoms."

"Yeah."

"You looking for a new start, or just trying to outrun a god?"

Cord sighed, a heavy thing. "I wish I knew, Nenn."

He grew quiet then, and I left him alone with his thoughts, climbing the stairs to the wheel, and taking a seat at the bench behind Rek. His cats wandered this part of the deck, mewing and pawing at one another, or lazing in the late sun.

"How is he?" Rek asked.

"Different. The same. I think something in Midian changed him. Marked him a little. He's been taking bigger risks, sometimes for little to no reward. I'm not sure what he's trying to work out, but I wish he'd do it soon."

Rek stared off toward the setting sun, quiet for a few minutes. Finally, he spoke. "You ever hear the phrase Bancroft's Bones, Nenn?"

I shook my head. "Not that I recall."

He nodded. "It comes from out west. There's a story that goes with it."

I watched a fat orange tabby swat at a playful black who'd decided the tabby's tail was a spritely bit of prey. "I've got some time."

"Jeseh Bancroft was a king... four? Five? Centuries ago. By all accounts, he was a good king, or if not good, at least competent. He'd kept his kingdom at peace for his reign, even managing to unite some of the disparate tribes around him and bring them into the fold. His people were well-fed, happy, and for the most part, unbothered by most of the things that bother any kingdom.

"As for Bancroft, he had a wife—Maryska—who he doted on. By all accounts, the things he did for the kingdom, he did for her. For fifteen years, they loved one another as no one another thing. Then one morning, Jeseh woke, and Maryska was gone. At first, he assumed she left for the gardens, or the hunt. She had a great falcon she would take on rides, and in the early morning, have it snatch up hare and fox.

"But morning moved to afternoon, and afternoon to night, and she still had not returned. Jeseh sent his guard out to find her, and they too, did not return. He spent his armies and then mercenaries, and each time, they vanished without a trace.

"A year passed. The kingdom crumbled, outside forces seeing it ripe for predation. In time, Bancroft abandoned the throne, taking up his once-shining sword and donning his mail. He walked out in the morning, and by afternoon was... gone.

"In time, those who remembered his kingdom said that Bancroft still stalked the plains, looking for Maryska. They speak of his fleshless form, clattering across the grasses. Bancroft's Bones. A reminder that if you focus only on one thing your entire life, when it's gone, you'll likely have nothing left.

"That's what eats at Cord. What if he's only found this one thing? What will be left of him if he loses it?"

"But Cord's always been Cord. He'll always be Cord."

"Not all of us are content with that. He's touched greatness, and now he's chasing that high."

I grimaced. "Grim."

"We live in a land of undead, Harrowers, and machines driven by flesh. Grim is a good day."

"But we also have sweetrolls."

"Ahh, sweetrolls. You know, I'll be happy when we get a break from fish."

"What's wrong with fish? The cats love it."

"So do seals, Nenn. I am not a seal. Or a cat for that matter."

"Fair enough."

We sank back into silence, and as the stars lit themselves

like lanternflies, I listened to the waters roll beneath us, and hoped I'd not hear Bancroft clattering his way across the plain.

DAWN BROKE. Rather, Cord broke it with a cry of *sail!* He slid down the rigging and came to a halt on the forecastle. We'd been fortunate in that the river had been empty since our flight from Midian. Anyone who might have pursued us was currently stuck in a hopeless jumble between the plains and the mountains. Traffic was sparse between Midian and Orlecht at the moment, most of the weekly trading vessels having already passed through or berthed at a halfway point further west. Though the river was wide for two ships abreast in most places, it narrowed between the ranges, and at times deck would narrowly miss scraping deck.

Cord pointed toward where the river spilled from the mountains. A ship, comparable in size to the *Codfather* swept up the waters, its prow splitting the waves. Black sails hung from its masts, and a skull and crossbones flew just above the crow's nest.

"Ah, fuck," Rek said.

"What?" I asked. I hadn't seen those particular colors flying before, but I had sense enough to know they were bad.

"Pirates," Lux said.

"Like thieves, with less style," Cord said.

"What do we do?"

"We can try to look poor," Rek said.

Cord snorted. "Has that ever stopped us?"

Rek shook his head.

"Get your knives," Cord said to me. "Lux--"

"On it," she said.

She stepped to the prow and widened her stance, moving with the waves.

"Outrun them?" I asked.

Cord shook his head. "Normally, I'd say yeah. But I don't want to use the Harrower engine here if I can help it."

"That's a first."

He nodded and took the wheel, leaving Rek free to step to the deck, axe in hand. We waited another minute.

"Why doesn't he want to use the engine?" I asked Rek.

The big man shrugged. "Maybe he's got a score to settle."

Something tugged at my guts and I shouted at Cord over my shoulder.

"Do you know these assholes? Because I am not dying for a grudge."

"No, of course not."

"Cord."

"How well can you ever really *know* anyone anyway?"

"Fuck," I muttered.

The other boat's prow came even with ours and then slid past, until the decks were side by side. Without warning, ropes were slung over the rails, hooks at the end. The other captain made a motion with his wheel, and the hulls crashed together. The squeal of oiled planks and the splintering of wood filled the air. On the deck opposite us, men waited, blades in hand, eyes alight. A big man, nearly matching Rek for size, shirtless and rippling with muscle called out.

"Avast, ye dogs!"

"Dogs?" Cord called out. "That's hurtful! Nenn can't help the way she looks."

"Remind me to stab him if we survive this," I said to Rek.

The big man grunted and started hacking at the ropes that bound the ships together. They separated with a snap and a twang, but even with my help, there were too many, and sailors scrambled across. I gave up on the ties and started in on the intruders.

The first man, a thin thing wielding a rapier flung himself at me. His blade scored a mark on my arm, drawing a line of blood. He stepped back, hoping to finish me with a lunge, and I stepped back as he moved forward. He overbalanced in his eagerness. His feet tangled and he tripped, bringing the nape of his neck in range, and I rammed a blade into his spine. His body collapsed, spilling blood onto the deck.

I heard Rek grunt and saw two men accosting him, one with matched daggers, another with a cutlass. They came at him in tandem, but only for a moment. He swept the axe out, and felled them both like trees. Intestines joined the mess on the deck, and we struggled to keep our footing.

I snapped my attention back to the next boarder, a man with a hook hand and an eyepatch. He swung the hook at my head and missed by a mile. I planted my other blade in his good eye and drew two new ones as he fell to the deck like a net full of fish.

The rails had fully met, and more men swarmed over, the big man who'd shouted at Cord following.

"Get off my boat, Ked!" Cord shouted.

The big man engaged Rek, shouting back. "Make me!"

I strained to see the outcome, but already men swarmed me, and I had my hands full. As many as I dropped, another seemed to take their place, and soon I was sweating and breathing hard, leaking blood from a dozen small wounds and at least one good one. Thankfully, my blood was up, and I didn't feel them yet.

Rek roared from the deck, and Ked swore in return. A clash of steel, and Rek shouted, "Cord!"

"Lux!" Cord shouted in reply.

A concussive blast echoed a second later, flattening everyone on deck. My head swam, but I managed to sit up. I saw men scattered like autumn leaves, Rek and Ked included. Lux stepped down from the prow, the wind blowing her robes behind her like wings, her hair out in a halo. Power crackled from her fingertips. I noticed the way her hips swung. For a moment, I could only see the red of her lips, the pale beauty of her face. Then the first of the pirates exploded as eldritch power lashed from her hands and enveloped him.

Blood, innards, and limbs rained down on the men. For a moment, only shocked silence reigned. Then a second man exploded, and chaos replaced the quiet as they scrambled to regain their ship. The ones who made the deck hacked at the ropes frantically, trying to disentangle the boats.

Lux continued down the deck, lashing out with power, the air filled with red mist. She reached Ked and placed a hand on his head. His eyes bulged, then with a sound like a sack ripping, his skeleton burst from his flesh, his remains pouring muck like a torn sausage.

The last of the sailors had fled the *Codfather*, and Lux turned to them, watching. With a gesture from her, the ropes burned, and the other ship began to drift away. A cheer went up. Lux quirked an eyebrow, raised her other hand, and the ship imploded, timber and rope and flesh collapsing in on itself like crumpled paper. The *Codfather* began to move under its own power again, leaving the sinking wreckage behind. Lux let a long sigh and sank to the deck. We sat silent for a long moment.

Finally, Cord broke it.

"Yo ho ho, bitches."

WE'D BEEN on the boat for a while, navigation through the western ridge of mountains taking longer than we'd planned or liked. We'd been recuperating and cooped up for a while, and Cord kept telling me this joke—it goes something like this:

Thief walks into a bar

Bartender says "What'll you have?"
Thief says "Gimme all you got"
Bartender drops his pants
Thief looks disappointed, points to the lockbox and says "I'm gonna need change"

I was convinced he did it out of some misguided attempt to lighten the mood, or maybe to alleviate his own boredom. Whatever the case, I'd threatened to stab him in places that would itch when they healed.

If you'd asked me four years ago what my life plan was, I probably would have told you that I was going to work in the mill until I died, it burned down, or I drank so much my brain jumped out of my ear to its death. Now—I still wasn't sure what the long-term plan was, but here, in the moment? I was going to enjoy our ragtag group of rogues. We did a good thing in Midian. We stopped a tyrant, and we taught the people a lesson. They'd never thank us for it, but in time, they certainly wouldn't allow another despot to press a boot against their neck.

I lit a cigar and drifted over to Rek, the big man standing still as stone, eyes locked on the horizon. The stones and the cliffs of the Teeth stood over us in mute grays, moss and lichen clinging to the rock faces and trailing in the water of the Lethe. The river twisted and turned between the outcrops, rushing to rapids in some places, but still wide enough for our boat to make the passage. Lux suggested we just use the Harrower engine below deck—a machine of steel and flesh that let us skip entire sections of the journey—but none of us wanted a repeat jaunt to the Deadlands since our escape from Tremaire, and after some inspection, it seemed the power driving it had gone out. Well enough, we made good time under sail and current. That's the thing about thieves. Even when you've the best of intentions, you often find yourself on the run. Appreciation was harder to come by than a lice-free bedroll.

Rek looked down. "Cord telling that joke again?"

I nodded. "Did he make that up?"

Rek sighed. "Yeah. Proud of it, isn't he?"

"Like a kid showing you the pile he made in a chamber pot."

Rek snorted a laugh. I made my way to the bench set across the bow and watched our wake. Cord finally gave me a break— he hung from above in the mainmast, watching for land. I glanced over at Lux. I'd thought I had little love left in me. The world will bleed it out of you if you let it, the sharp blade of reality an edge that leaves cuts that refuse to heal. Still—she'd said nothing since, and I'd been gracious in keeping my infatuation to a minimum. Cord often said love was like the strikers I used to light my cigars. Bright, hot, and dangerous as fuck. He was full of aphorisms and bullshit, and didn't usually bother sorting one from another.

We rounded a bend, and Cord called out, sliding down the netting and mast to land on his feet like a cat. He pointed ahead and I followed the line of his finger to a mass of scaffolding erected against the rocks. As we drew closer, we saw bodies hanging from each, signs dangling from bloated feet.

SORCERER

We passed beneath, the bodies twisting in our wake, flies and crows dislodged in black clouds from their stinking prizes

"Remember," Cord called out. "If anyone asks, Lux is an arcane manipulator."

"Isn't that just a fancy way of saying wizard?" I asked.

He shrugged. "I prefer to think of myself as eloquent."

"Most of your vocabulary consists of how to say 'Let's fuck' in different languages."

"I am a worldly man."

"You're full of shit."

He opened his mouth to reply and closed it again as the ship rounded another bend and came into a straightaway that opened into a wide lagoon. Neat docks lined up in the water, clean berths held clean ships, and waited for others scattered around the lake. Their hulls were fresh-painted, their sails impossibly white. Further in from the waterfront, the city was laid out in clean lines and well-kept homes and stores, even a temple at one end of the area, looking as though its stones had just endured a fresh scrubbing. As we neared, we saw people walking the streets in simple but well-kept clothing, gathering in conversation while holding simple wicker baskets, or chatting in a park that bordered the water.

"Holy shit," Rek said. "It's..." words failed him.

"It's like no one here has ever been licked in the—"

I shot Cord an elbow. The last of the sentence came out a grunt. He wasn't wrong. This place had repression written all over it.

Rek guided the boat in with a skillful hand, the flaking paint and filthy sails drawing stares from nearby onlookers. Lux and Cord threw the dockhands ropes. They tied off the boat with some reluctance while Rek spun the windlass, dropping anchor, and I pushed a plank out over the rail. We disembarked to silence, most of the town staring or moving out of our way in harried fashion. A young man stood nearby, one of those that helped tie off the ship.

Cord clapped him on the back. "Hey kid, any idea where I can get a good meal? I've eaten naught but fish for a week. You know the saying—give a man a fish, and he eats for a day, teach a man to fish, and he's likely to cut his own tongue out? No?"

The youth stood, staring opened-mouthed.

"Ah, I see you've had the fish."

Then, in an aside to me, "Poor lad's mute. An admirable quality in a politician, but completely useless in a tour guide." He smiled at the hapless dockworker. "No worries, we'll find our way."

He slapped the young man on the ass, making him jump, and we continued on, Rek making apologies as he passed.

WE WALKED UP THE THOROUGHFARE, neat shops with clean glass and fresh-painted stucco facades lining the street like waiting suitors. Shoppers kept to themselves, giving us a wide berth. They shot us furtive glances that Cord returned with beaming smiles and winks, sending them scurrying down the street or stepping into shops in search of shelter.

"Are you going to annoy everyone in town?" I asked Cord.

He shrugged. "The gods made me friendly. Clearly these people just need to warm to me."

"Friendly or creepy?" Rek asked.

"Creepy," Lux conceded.

"Mutiny," Cord muttered.

"We're on land. It's treason now," Rek said.

Cord caught sight of a young woman who hadn't scurried away at our appearance. He approached and leaned against the wall.

"We're looking for an inn." he wore a smarmy grin, and I rolled my eyes.

She made a complex symbol across her body, hand traversing from shoulder to shoulder, down across her hips, back up to her eyes, and down to her nether regions.

"Saints preserve us," she whispered.

I shouldered Cord out of the way before he could send the young woman screaming for an exorcist and gave her a gentle smile.

"We just need directions. Then we'll be on our way."

She looked over my shoulder, peering at each of my companions in turn, then returning to my face.

"The Father will not be well pleased, but if you only mean to stop for a short while, the Inn is up yonder."

"The Father?"

"Father Frollo. He only wishes for us to be safe. Here there are no wraith or goblin, sorcerer or witch. Here life is pure, under his eye."

"What do you do for fun?" Cord asked.

"We find joy in all *natural* things provided by the gods," she said, eyes resting on Lux.

I took that for our cue to get the fuck out of the street.

"Thank you," I said, and pulled the others after me.

"Father protects," she called after us.

"Anyone else got the heebie-jeebies?" Lux asked.

"I think I pooed a little," Rek said.

We hurried down the street, putting as much distance between us as possible. Eventually, we stopped in front of a two-story building of white stucco and blue trim, neat wooden timbers decorating the exterior. A sign hung above the door, clean and orderly like everything else. Painted on it in a painstaking hand were the words 'The Maiden's Virtue'. Cord raised an eyebrow, but kept whatever comment he'd been planning to himself, and we stepped inside.

The interior was simple and clean—whitewashed walls, hardwood floors, and a bar behind which a door stood open, the sounds and smells of a busy kitchen wafting out. We took a seat at one of the sparkling tables and waited. Few other patrons ate or drank at this hour—we'd arrived just a few hours late for lunch, and yet too early for dinner, leaving only the hardcore drunks and those with little else to do.

I took a closer look. Cord told me once that the key to seeing the heart of a country was to look at its people. Here, the people were well dressed and well-fed, clean and seemingly content. At the tables where more than one sat, they carried on conversations in low tones, laughter occasionally ringing out, and though they occasionally gave us suspicious looks, they rarely lingered. I wondered how many travelers passed through this vale on their way to somewhere else, and if they ever thought of this simple village again. A barmaid came and took our order. The beer was good and cold, chilled by some unknown device or artifice, and the quiet atmosphere did a great deal to ease the tensions that still clung to us from Midian and the long flight from there.

We pushed our chairs back and kicked our feet out, sated on something that wasn't fish or hard biscuits.

"So, what's the plan?" I asked.

Cord looked around. "We could stay here a night or two, maybe take on a little honest work."

Rek squinted in suspicion.

"They call me crazy," Lux muttered.

Cord sighed. "I don't have a plan. We pulled down a corrupt monarchy. Where do you go from there?"

"Retirement?" I offered.

Cord ran a hand over his face and opened his mouth to say something. The inn's door opened, interrupting him as a trio of figures entered. They stood, straight-backed, black robes billowing around them. Each had the look of a hungry man, men made lean and angry with an ache in their gut that never went away. Each bore a symbol on a thong around their necks, though the lead figure also wore vestments of crimson that stood out like blood splashed across a stone wall. His eyes blazed with a fervor I'd only seen in the mad and the ill, and I doubted he was ill. They made their way over to our table, fixating on the four of us.

"Fuck," I muttered under my breath.

They stopped, the lead priest staring down at our empty plates and our rough clothing, a disapproving look on his face. Though, I don't know if it was disapproval, or just his natural mien. Some people are just born looking like they constantly smelled shit. He drew a breath, the sound grating in the silence. His voice was deep, though raspy.

"Brothers and sisters," he smiled, the expression like a dying rat on a hot plate. I shuddered.

"I trust you are finding our hospitality to your liking?" he asked. He didn't wait for an answer. "You should know, this is a quiet town. We prefer visitors to move on as soon as is expedient for them, as it is far removed from the intrigues and corruption at the heart of empires such as the Veldt and the Junat. It is nothing personal, we just prefer to maintain the peace without threat of... taint. Surely you understand?"

Cord nodded, but I saw in his eyes he did not. The priest smiled again, this time a thin-lipped grim thing.

"Good. Good. If you would like benediction before you pass on, please attend our service tomorrow before you go. I would be remiss in denying you at least the blessings of our sacred father. But should you choose not to attend, I hope not to encounter you again. Surely you understand?"

That simpering smile crawled across his lips again. He spun on his heel, his wordless minions following. They swept out the door, slamming it behind them. I looked at Cord, and my stomach dropped. He had that look in his eyes. You know the look, the one that tells you someone's going to do something real stupid.

"Cord?" I said.

"I have a plan," he said.

A groan went up from the group.

22

OPIATE OF THE ASSHOLES

YOU CAN UNDERSTAND why we were a bit reluctant to get on board with Cord's newest obsession. So, when he pressed several crowns into the innkeeper's hands and told her we'd be keeping the rooms above for a while, causing the poor woman to blanch like she'd just seen her grandfather's naked ghost, my shoulders cranked up tighter than a crossbow string. After we'd settled in, he gathered us in the common room, taking a table close to the fireplace.

"Okay, so what's the plan?" I asked. I figured it was better to get the question out of the way early, rather than let Cord spring one of his surprises on us.

He smirked and took a draught of his beer. His eyes lit on something, the smirk disappearing, and he lowered the mug, setting it on the table with a soft clunk. I turned to look and saw a disheveled man, scraggly beard clinging to his cheeks like a drowning man clings to a piece of driftwood. He approached, smelling of liquor, piss, and something I could only identify as similar to thing I'd eaten once in a back alley bar. It had one eye and kept trying to slither from the plate, and in the end, I gave up, stabbed it with my fork, and demanded the barkeep pay me a ransom for vanquishing the beast.

The smelly interloper staggered over and plopped into an empty chair at our table. He looked at each of us in turn through one bleary eye, Lux tittering nervously, Rek trying to move his chair away without being obvious.

"I heard ye," he said in a voice that scratched like splintered wood. Something about him tickled my gut, but I couldn't place it. "Plotting."

"What were we plotting?" Cord asked with a smirk.

"Ye're gonna piss in the church's font, if I guess right," he replied.

Cord's smile slipped a fraction. I mean, he hadn't said it, but we all knew it was coming. How this stranger kenned onto it, we had no idea.

"And I suppose you want something for your silence," Rek said.

My hand slipped toward my knives. Cord caught the motion and gave the slightest shake of his head. The man guffawed.

"Oh hells no. I want to help."

Cord leaned in, hands on the table. "What kind of help?"

"Just information."

"The price?"

"Knowing I did a good deed."

"Which is?"

He gestured toward the church and his sleeve rode up. My stomach jumped at the flash of a ridge of scars running up his arms. I took a breath. Any of the Cotard tribes would have those scars. It meant little to nothing. I forced myself to relax and sat back.

"Running those holier-than-thou fucks out of town," he said.

Cord's grin returned. "I'm listening."

TURNED out Father Frollo was a real sonuvabitch. Came to town winter three years ago. Immediately started issuing edicts. The old man, Ferd, told us the first thing Frollo did was execute anyone he suspected of sorcery. The rest, anyone he saw as impure or undesirable, he stuck on a boat and floated them on their way to Orlecht. The only reason Ferd escaped was because once upon a time, he'd been enamored with the innkeeper, and she let him stay in the basement. Now, for the most part, he lived down there.

When he was done, he wandered away, leaving us to think about the tidbit he'd shared. I wasn't entirely sure it was useful. Most of those who led the church didn't have much of a reputation for tolerance. It wasn't exactly a veiled secret. Still, most didn't have the elephantine balls it would take to put everyone you didn't like on a boat and ship them off. At least not without facing a serious civil problem. Which told us there was more to this than we knew.

If Midian taught me anything, it was that there were always two groups of people in situations like this: Those who didn't give a shit about what was happening, as long as it wasn't happening to them, and those who gave a shit, but couldn't do anything about it. That second group was good in a way. It was like kindling. All it needed was someone willing to set a fire and fan the flames.

I lit a cigar and sat back, ignoring the dirty look the innkeeper shot me.

"You guys feeling religious?" Cord asked.

"I sometimes pray when I've got the shits," Rek said.

"About what?"

Rek shrugged. "Mostly for it to stop."

"Nenn prays when she's getting laid," Lux supplied.

"What?" The word came out of me like an arrow.

"Oh gods oh gods," Lux whispered with a crooked grin.

I shot her the bird to hide my blush.

"Anyway..." I said, trying to turn the conversation back to Cord.

He wore a shit-eating grin. "Anyway. Get some sleep. We're going to church in the morning."

We groaned.

"It'll be good for your souls."

"Ain't got one," Lux said.

I looked at her. She wore a serious expression. I'd have to remember to ask about that some time.

23

A SADIST TELLS A STORY

WE PASSED AN INTERESTING NIGHT, the cats having discovered dry land. They spent most of the night yowling and hissing, screaming while they fucked in the street. We rose before dawn and made our way to the temple, amid a stream of red and white clothing and wary glances. Men wore tunics and trousers trimmed in red, the women dresses of the same. The bells in the temple tower pealed out their song, beating against the air like the wings of some terrible bird. Above, clouds lowered—the first signs of fall weather, the air sharp and clear despite the gloom.

The temple was a massive stone structure, the walls sloping toward a top that split itself into several peaks that broke off at odd angles. What looked like arrow slits decorated the top half of the building, the lower only broken by a simple set of double doors.

Cord paused to inspect the entrance. Crude likenesses of the gods stood out in bas-relief, the most prominent that of an unknown figure in the center, the robed statue grinning from its bony skull. A poster, like the one we'd found in Midian, fluttered beside them.

"That's not ominous," I said.

"The poster or the carvings?" Cord asked.

"A little of both. Put the two together, and it's like a creepy sign. 'Kill these assholes'."

"Death comes for us all, Nenn," Cord said.

"Not you."

"Well, yes, she just can't hold on to me."

"Maybe she just doesn't want you," Rek said. "Doesn't know where you've been."

"You people are ugly in the morning," Cord said.

Movement caught my eye, and I caught a glimpse of Ferd rounding the corner, but before I could point it out, Cord pushed us in. We entered the temple, rows of stone pews stretching out toward a raised dais. A pulpit stood on it, and behind that, an open apse filled with a shimmering pool. Frollo stood behind the pulpit in his black and red, his goons to each side of the dais. Hung behind him was another image of the strange figure, driven through with swords. Patrons filled the pews to the front, the entire village turned out for morning service, and we filed into one of the last in the back.

Frollo looked out at his congregation, noted our presence. He gave Cord a nod that while hard to read, was belied by the small smirk that played on his lips like a bedraggled weasel. A massive book lay on the pulpit before him, and he turned his attention to it, opening it to a place he'd marked with a red ribbon. He drew a breath and spoke.

"The Book of Oros tells us that death is natural. A gift that comes to everyone. It also tells us that those who only care for themselves, and through inaction cause undue misery to their sheep, should be punished.

"I have prepared here for you a story, one that lies close to my heart. Attend now, my children, and hear."

He took another deep breath, a windbag loading itself full, and began to read.

QOTH HATED the sound the dead men made. He scuffled his feet in the dust and stone of the yard between buildings, the creak of the Wheel drowning out his meager noise. Frustrated, he sighed and looked up, the Wheel filling his vision. It was a massive contraption of solid oak boards, pegs running its circumference. Each of the pegs held a noose, though only one was occupied at the moment, and the boards underneath the nooses were stained deep brown and yellow, remains of the men condemned there. The man currently attached to a noose made thick gagging sounds as the Wheel turned, almost matching the pitch of the bearings that smoothed its motion. His feet kicked, the black hood billowing in and out over his mouth as he struggled to breathe.

Qoth shuddered, the sight still hard to see after so many years. He wondered which sadist cum mystic first thought of the Wheel, the idea that dying men might, in their last desperate moments between life and death, gasp out visions from the other side. The Wheel turned another click, and the man in the noose sucked in a breath, then keened it out as his trachea was pinched, the sound like a fleshy teakettle. The boards beneath him took on a darker hue, the contents of his bowels spilling into his trousers and soaking through, and red-robed seers and the motley collection of peasants leaned in close.

This was it. This was the moment of prognostication. Or bullshite. The talkers that actually broke through on the Wheel tended to mutter incomprehensible trite, a fact that never bothered the seers as they carefully recorded each word and frenetically pored over every syllable afterwards - at least until the next poor cutter was hung. Qoth wasn't sure what they intended to learn. The gods were mute, blind, and deaf as far as he was concerned. He knew. He had once been a priest, a man of Oros. At least until the pox caught his family in its black grip.

The square drew quiet and Qoth glanced at the Wheel. It reached its apex and stopped, the man on it hanging at the noon position. A slight breeze stirred, rippling the hood over his head and then, a voice, creaking like branches in the wind, spoke.

"Ashen hearts
Lost and black
Do not
Grow old
Family calls
From Winter's halls
And swollen tongues"

The last came as a strangled whisper, hard to hear, and yet the words reached Qoth's ears anyway. The fabric of the hood darkened as blood gouted from the cutter's split throat. Qoth looked away even as the seers pressed in, urging their scribes to write faster. The peasants were already turning away, and Qoth joined them, heading in the general direction of the warden's office. There, they would have a wagon and the body. There, the dead would be still, and his work could start.

QOTH WATCHED a spider crawling in a corner of the room, rolling something wrapped in webbing ahead of itself. The spider rolled the ball up the wall and affixed it with a strap of web. That done, it crawled into the center of its web to wait. Qoth thought that was the envious life - eat, mate, and sleep. He wondered how things would be different if he never met Irina, if they never had Iliana. Would he have turned down a different path, been more like that spider, perhaps? Would he even now, be lounging in a *sitte* den? Would he maybe even be a predator, waiting in the alleys and warrens of the city for his next prey? He didn't know. Because he was what he was. As he had been, because of Irina. Because of Oros.

The warden that approached him was short and thick, a tree stump of a man who wore the typical leather and steel of the wardens, a dagger at each hip, and a small crossbow on his back. He cleared his throat when Qoth didn't look up right away.

"Body's ready."

"Thank you." Qoth stood to go, heading toward the door in the back that would lead to the small yard and the wagon with the body.

The warden gave him a look, one eye squinted. "What do you do with 'em anyway?"

Qoth shrugged. "All things served Oros in their time. Perhaps they will serve his soul in the afterlife as well."

"Better you than me."

Despite the fracturing of his faith, Qoth knew that the proper application of a platitude, or the appearance of a man sweeping the steps of his temple kept most from questioning him, especially if he kept that temple shuttered for some time. Some viewed him as eccentric, others necessary - handlers of the dead were rare in an age of superstition - even if everyone knew his faith had collapsed.

Qoth spread his hands in a conciliatory gesture. "I do what I must."

The warden grunted, and handed Qoth a sliver of steel. It was meager payment, but it would do. Qoth slipped it into his vest and left the room as the warden busied himself at a small desk with a pile of parchment and a quill. Outside, the sun was still and hot overhead, and the yard here as dusty as in the Wheel's square. A small row of tarps lay against one side of the building in shadow, the bodies beneath waiting purification from the surgeon inside. Behind them, a wooden cart, handles long enough for a man to step between, stood with another piece of canvas covering it. Qoth approached and situated himself between the wooden poles, grasping one in each hand. With a grunt, he kicked off, and the wagon began to roll behind him. He maneuvered it into the street and down the hill, keeping to one side of the road. As he went, men and women avoided him. Death was commonplace in the city, but no one liked the reminder. Heedless, he continued.

HIS MIND DRIFTED. It was a bit of a trot to his temple, and between the weight of the cart and the sun overhead, he wanted only to occupy his thoughts with anything other than the heat and the labor.

"What do you desire?"

They curled up in their bed, a great goose down mattress under them - a gift from the parishioners. Irina snuggled in next to him, her nose and lips against his neck, sending thrills through his chest. He shifted a bit, and looked at her, nestled in the crook of his arm.

"You."

She smiled, and her hand traced the hair on his chest.

"And you, my succubus?"

She lowered her lids and the corners of her mouth curled up, mischief shining in her eyes. "This." She rolled herself onto him and pushed off his chest until she was straddling him. He watched the muscles in her arms and belly, the inward pucker of her belly button. He grinned back at her and opened his mouth, thinking to quip at her. She leaned in, her hair falling around him like a curtain, and her lips found his. They were soft, and tasted of strawberry and wax. He closed his eyes, and-

"Watch it, you gobshite!"

Qoth blinked away the memory and stopped. A man was pacing away, gesturing, his fingers held up in a vee, muttering curses as he went.

"Forgive me, sir," he muttered, then sighed, and continued on his way.

THE BODY WAS STARTING to stink. The heat wasn't helping things, but it wasn't like winter, when you could pack the dead with ice and snow and dally for hours before the first signs of bloating appeared. Qoth stopped and walked to the back of the wagon, lifting the sheet that covered the man. He was an odd blue-yellow, the whites of his eyes shot to blood, his tongue protruding at an angle. Livid bruises surrounded his throat, and a rend in the flesh by the man's voice box was puckered like overripe fruit that had burst. Qoth poked the naked skin of the man, and it took a moment for the dent to recover. Bloating already set in. He'd have to hurry. He picked up the handles of the cart and began to move faster, trotting a little to set a quick pace. After a while, his mind drifted again, and he forgot the stink.

"I feel like a yak."

"You look much better than a yak."

Qoth curled his arm around Irina's swollen belly and pulled her close, his lips finding her neck. She swatted him away, laughing, and stood.

"That's how we got in this situation in the first place, you great horny goat."

He chuckled and watched her as she tooled around the kitchen, chopping vegetables and setting a kettle over the fire.

"Will you do the meat?"

"Will you do the meat?" he asked.

She shot a look over her shoulder, and he joined her at the table, pulling a thick shank of beef from its paper, then a knife from the block. He set to work removing the fat and slicing it into thin strips for the stew. As they worked, Irina began to hum. Qoth joined her.

"Miss Manner

So proper

Lift your skirt

But mind the copper

Mister Hammer

So randy

Drop your trousers

Mind your dandy"

They burst into laughter, and laughter became tears as they fed each other's good humor. Qoth looked at his wife, smiling, her eyes wet, and his heart ached.

The shadow of the Spire fell over Qoth, and he stopped the cart for a moment, glad to be from under the sun's thumb. He stood that way for a time, wiping sweat from his brow, letting his heart ache. Oros would have approved. *Through grief, joy. Through joy, service.*

He waited until he had his breath back, and tears no longer stung the corners of his eyes, and moved on.

———

HE WAS CLOSE. Qoth entered the warren where his little temple stood. Small homes and hovels stood side by side, often wall to wall, their graying stone and rough wood competing for every inch of space. Once, this had been the heart of the city. But as the city grew, the warren grew dim in the planner's minds forgotten. *As are all things,* Qoth thought. He thought again of how Oros abandoned him. How he ran, desperate and mad with fear, from temple to temple, begging anyone - any god - to help him, and how only silence met him. His faith and family died that day. It took him a long time - a year, maybe more - it all blended in the end. Finally, he took up care for the dead. Someone had to do it. Someone had to let the families of the lost know their loss was not in vain.

He rounded a corner, and saw the chemist's shop. Memory flooded in again.

"Please, I need wort for my family!"

"Seven shims."

"I don't - look, when your sister was ill, who brought her soup every day? Irina. You were at Iliana's baptism - this is a community, for gods' sake!"

The chemist looked at him. "Wort is expensive, preacher. I've got a family, too."

"Then loan it to me - you know I'll pay when alms come in!"

The chemist shook his head. "I cannot. Please go before I call the wardens."

Qoth let out a strangled cry and turned, fleeing from the door. He ran the distance home. He'd left them alone too long. He burst into his home, but it was too late. His daughter - Iliana, who had only been two summers, who he sang lullabies to when the moon was just growing in the sky - lay in her crib, still as a stone. Grief constricted his heart, and he managed to stagger to the bedroom he shared with Irina. He stopped in the doorway, a scream escaping his lips. Only flies moved in the room, her eyes frozen to the ceiling. He'd fallen then, on his knees, and begged for the gift of resurrection. For the ear of a god - any god - to numb him, to take him, too. No answer came. No quarter came for the grief he felt.

In the end, he decided if he could no longer do for the gods or the living, he would find solace in the dead. That was where his family was, that was where he should be, or at least he thought. Yet every time he held the knife to his breast, fear stayed his hand. So, he collected the dead. He studied each one. And he made use of them, for the day he would be brave enough to join his family.

Not this day. Maybe not the next. But one day, surely.

QOTH ROUNDED ANOTHER CORNER, and the temple was before him. It was a small thing, clapboard and brick, with a steepled roof and the symbol of Oros - an open hand - on the peak. He aimed the cart for the back of the temple. He'd kept the place because it was perfect for his work. Being a religious institution, it was somewhat secluded from the bustle of buildings shoving each other for room in the warren. It had ample room on either side, and a spacious cemetery in the back. He reached the fence surrounding the cemetery, and dragged the cart in, then shut the gate behind him. That done, he dropped the handles and made his footsore way into the rear of the temple, where his living quarters were.

It was simple inside, a small living area, a kitchen, and a bedroom. Behind the temple stood a small water closet. The church had a little money for luxuries, usually reserved for promising students, and before they installed him as preacher here, they enchanted a pipe above the sink. It brought him warm but clean water from the well, saving him some work pumping. He touched it and a stream started, trickling into the basin. Qoth ran his hands under the water, watching it come away muddy as the dust was stripped from his skin. Next, he splashed his face, washing away more of the silt and sweat that seemed to make up so much of the city.

He touched the pipe again and made his way to the living area. He sat on a small chair and looked around, listening to the buzz of flies and the drip of water. A slow throb in his feet signaled a sleepless night, but it would be that anyway. He had work to do. He stood again and took down his knife, a simple sturdy blade, made for this kind of work, and went to the yard. He uncovered the body, the smell strong, but not overpowering. Someone forgot to close the dead man's eyes, and he stared to the heavens. *Too bad there's not much to see there*, Qoth thought, and got to work.

HE DRAGGED the body into the chapel proper. Two hundred eyes stared at him. One hundred mouths hung open, their muscles slack. It was a side effect of the words he'd carved into their chests. *Calach - speak. Menoch - see.* It took him some time to gather the bodies, each a hanged man from the Wheel. This one he pulled to an open spot on the wall, beside Irina. Her eyes saw nothing, and her lips were still, yet he felt as if she'd approve. He hoisted the body and nailed it in place with a steady hammering - spikes through the wrists and ankles. When he was done, he sat back, sweating. The bodies formed an unbroken chain that covered the walls and ceiling of the chapel, a tapestry of flesh he had meticulously gathered.

It had been work, keeping the stink down. He'd had to use a small battalion of charms to keep the decay and stench to a minimum. There was nothing he could do about the flies, though. Qoth stepped back and surveyed his work. Each word carved on the dead connected to other words, but for one -

Iliana. Qoth moved to her, and with shaking hands, raised the knife. He could hear her small laughter in his mind. He carved the final word. *Yanoch - live.*

Fire raced across the words, connecting each to each, until the room glowed with it. As one, the dead groaned, and a voice spoke. It filled Qoth's ears, and its sweetness made his heart ache.

"My love. Bring them to me." In a corner, a rat gnawing at the toes of one of the dead men burst, a spray of gore painting the corpse's ankles.

Qoth fell to his knees and wept.

THE DOORS of the temple of Oros were unbarred. Qoth stood on the steps, passing out fliers, smiling and chatting with passer-bys as they went about their day. Curious, Tvent - chemist by trade - approached. Qoth pressed a flyer into his hand.

"Opening the temple again, Qoth?"

"Oh, aye, aye. Please come."

"Found your faith again?"

"Never lost it, my good man. Now scurry along, and tell the others. The temple is taking new parishioners. You'll want to hear this sermon."

Tvent looked at the flyer in his hand and back to Qoth. The man's excitement was palpable, and somewhat infectious. He walked away, and Qoth watched him go. When the last of the fliers had been turned out, he stepped into the temple, closing the door behind him. Candlelight glowed on a hundred bodies, and two hundred eyes watched as he approached Irina and stroked her cheek.

THEY CAME, one by one and two by two to the chapel. Families and friends, clutching the flyers he'd handed out, chattering of what it all meant. Inside, Qoth hung tall white sheets he'd painted with scenes of family, portraits of Iliana and Irina. The congregation settled in the pews, and Qoth waited patiently for the last of the stragglers to arrive. Children darted between the rows and people chattered while passing around small cakes the local baker made. It was a celebration, after all. A new leaf. A new life.

He saw a man turn to his wife, his tow-headed children beside him. He leaned in and whispered something to her, and she smiled, a laugh startled out of her. A beat in time.

SHE WAS IN THE MARKET. That was where he saw her first, dark hair flowing down her back, her body swathed in a dress that accentuated her hips, sandals with ties that climbed her calves. He was smitten at the first. No - that wasn't right. He was in lust at first. Then she turned. She turned, and the world stopped moving - he swore it did, men haggling at booths, their lips frozen mid-speech. Somewhere a lute played, and now it hovered on one note, hanging in the air like a bird catching a current. He could see a mouse beneath a stall, its paws paused before its whiskers, its black eyes reflecting everything.

Her eyes were green, her lips full. A small scar carved its way across the corner of one eye - later he found she'd fallen as a child, and cut it on a stone. The corner of her lips turned up, and she smirked at him, then gave a wink. His heart hammered - once. Twice. And the world scrambled to catch up. She was gone.

He spent the rest of the morning in a funk. He shuffled from stall to stall, not bothering to haggle - to the amusement and profit of the merchants. Finally, he found himself at a small jeweler's booth, fingering a jade necklace and thinking of her eyes. Who was she?

"That would look good on me."

The voice came at his elbow. Qoth jumped so hard he jostled the booth and earned an evil glare from the jeweler that he never saw. He turned, and the woman standing at his shoulder stepped back and slipped the necklace from his fingers. He stood, mouth agape, as she looked over his shoulder and smiled at the merchant.

"He'll take it." She turned to Qoth. "Pay the nice lady."

Qoth turned in a stupor and dumped out a few coins on the counter, then followed the woman who already had him by the elbow. She was already chattering at him.

"What's your name?"

"Q-Quoth."

"Interesting. I'm Irina."

"T-this is all very-"

She turned and put a hand on hip. "Do you always stutter like a buffoon?"

"Only when I'm nearly truck dumb by beauty." He blinked. He had no idea that was coming out of his mouth. Luckily for him, she smiled, and narrowed her eyes.

"What a line."

"I'm quite clever."

She looked him over, the smile slipping away. "I doubt that. But I'm willing to find out. Come, Sir Stutter."

She led him away.

THE MEMORY FADED. He'd been lucky. Somehow, he'd remained clever. He always thought himself incredibly fortunate that he'd somehow talked her into marrying him. He watched the crowd a little longer. They still chattered, but they were growing restless, he could tell. Shifting in their seats, playing with trinkets - necklaces, rings, charms. More filtered in, and he watched, waiting. The strains of an old song played through his mind, a breeze tickling the back of his neck. He wondered if it was the choir he assembled. He turned his head to hear.

Blackened moon
And bloody sun
We'll dance when all is done
Lady Black
And Jack o' Nine
Won't let you go
The sun won't shine
Scuttle out
And speak but true
For ' tis the day
Your souls are due

It was an old dance hall piece, a song the minstrels would sing to appease the gods during the harvest and the turning of the seasons. It seemed fitting to him now.

When they were all inside, Qoth closed the doors, and locked them. He carved a word into the chain of words around the jamb, closing the spell that would ensure nothing short of a giant's axe could open them. He looked around, pleased. It seemed the entire warren showed up. He took his time getting to the pulpit, stopping to greet Tvent--the man brought his entire family--and the baker who had denied him bread more than once for fear the sickness would contaminate his dough. Qoth smiled and shook their hands and asked after their businesses and extended family. Then he climbed the steps to the pulpit.

———————

SHE WAS STRONG. She didn't hate. She was smart. Smarter than he was. She could sing, she could dance, and though she had a temper and it occasionally lashed against him like a whip, he never thought he'd live up to her. He was aware of the danger of putting another person on a pedestal. Of making them an ideal instead of a person. Sometimes though, he didn't care. She was an example for him, a way to live that he strived for. He found it ironic in a way. As a clergyman, others expected a sort of paragonship on his part. He simply tried to live his life in a way that wouldn't disappoint Irina.

He remembered - they were walking through a part of the warren that even the cutters avoided - not because of any danger, but because there wasn't anything worth stealing. Irina paused as they passed a doorway, her face unreadable.

"Hand me your purse," she'd told him in a tone that asked no hesitation.

He did so, and she bent down, jingling it once, her hand extended. When she straightened, he saw the girl on the stoop, her cloak tattered, her face streaked with soot. She watched them with frightened eyes. Irina leaned in to him.

"Say something to her."

"Oros sends you his blessing."

"Something else."

He knelt. "Do you have a family?"

The girl looked at him, ready to bolt. She reminded him of a wounded and frightened bird. He rummaged in his robes and found a small lump of cheese wrapped in paper. He held it out to her. She took it and unwrapped it, pausing only for a moment to watch him, as if afraid he would rescind it. When he didn't, she devoured it. When she was finished, Qoth repeated the question.

"Your family?" He prompted gently.

She eyed him for another moment, still silent, then ran, fleeing from the doorway. He stood and started to go after her. Irina laid a hand on her arm, and he looked. She shook her head.

"Let her go. You know where we are. You know what this life is like. Be glad you could help, if only for a moment."

He watched her. "But - we could do more."

"We will. Another day."

She kept her promise. They came back week after week. They didn't see that girl again, but there were others. From that day on, he found another trait to love. Mercy.

A LOW HUMMING began in the room, and the congregation sat a little straighter, began to quiet. He took the rope tied to the sheets in his hands, and smiled beatifically. Mercy wasn't present today.

"Welcome, friends. And goodbye."

He pulled on the rope. The sheets fell. The screaming began. It did not end until the goddess he had made broke them all.

WHEN IT WAS OVER, Qoth sat on the steps of the pulpit, the bodies stinking in their pews. A low humming filled the room, sweet to his ears. It was the lullaby Irina sang to Iliana as dusk fell.

Here's the moon

I'll see you soon
In the land of dreams
Don't you cry
I'll be by
To see you in your dreams
So tell me that you love me
Love me so
And don't you cry
I'll be by
I'll see you in your dreams

Qoth closed his eyes and listened, and for a moment, he saw the sun-dappled room and his wife and daughter, side by side in the big chair, their heads pressed together as she sang.

AT LAST, Frollo finished his tale, his voice fading in echo in the stone hall. Nothing marred the silence, and I looked around. The parishioners sat with bowed heads, and sometime during the reading, more of Frollo's goons moved in, surrounding the interior. The priest let the silence hang, like a hammer dangled from a string, then he spoke.

"The lesson here, my friends, is suffer not the selfish. Suffer not the greedy. Suffer not the unclean."

He nodded, and his guards moved. Towards us. Only us. It seemed the church had a problem with newcomers. I don't know how we'd missed the signs. I cursed Cord under my breath even as Rek shoved me out of the pew. He stepped in front, blocking their path. I stumbled and found my feet.

"Run Nenn!" he shouted.

The church became chaos as Rek and Cord picked up a guard and tossed him into the pews, causing as much confusion as possible. I stood for a second, torn. Did I help? Did I dare draw blood here and risk the fate of the thieves in the river passage? Then someone's teeth flew by me like a formation of disgusting doves, and I hauled ass out of there, the church doors banging shut behind me.

Panic clutched at my heart. Where to go? I looked down the village lane, through the neat rows of shops, and deeper into the village, clean little homes in orderly arrangements. At the far end, the Codfather bobbed at anchor. For a moment, the idea of casting off, getting the hell away from this little pisswater seemed the best choice. It passed, and I prayed Camor guide me, or at least keep a knife out of my kidneys, as I sprinted for the inn.

Luck was with me, and I found a loose window leading to the basement. I opened it with a grunt, falling in amid a clatter of bottles, sending wheels of cheese rolling across the floor. The smells of piss and alcohol assailed me, and I retched.

"Oh, nice to see you too," Ferd said.

I picked myself up.

"How'd the service go?" he asked, and tore a hunk of foul-smelling cheese from its wheel.

"Piss-poor."

He raised a dirty bottle of beer. "Welcome to bed down here for the night. Mind Ton and Jer though."

"Who are they?"

"My rats."

I shuddered and tried to find a nice quiet corner, away from the stink, and think.

24

NAILED, SCREWED, I'M STILL STUCK TO A FUCKIN' TREE

LIFE TAUGHT me there are two kinds of drunks. The lover or the fighter. The fighter thinks everyone's out to get them, thinks they're ten feet tall and sword-proof. They'll take any slight as an opportunity to prove themselves, their flaws magnified by the alcohol until they needed to prove that voice at the back of their brain wrong. The other, the lover, is convinced their charisma is an all-powerful force, akin to that of a lodestone, drawing everyone near to them. Men want to be them, women want them, and if you just listen—listen—they'll tell you why.

Thankfully, the man I shared the basement with was a rare third type—the sleeper. Couldn't wake the man if I dropped a small anvil on his balls. On the occasions he was awake enough to move around, he disappeared for small amounts of time, and rarely spoke, as if he'd written me off as another rum-soaked delusion.

On the first day down, I heard the hammering. Most people hear hammering, they think 'oh, someone's building a house, maybe making a nice fence for the garden'. However, life made me not most people, and my first thought was 'oh, they're nailing my friends to a tree'.

When I asked Ferd, he disappeared without a word, leaving me to work on the bottle of wine I'd been nursing, and curse the gods that my cigars were upstairs. When he returned, it was with miserable news.

"Yep, nailed 'em to a tree."

Nenn one, universe zero, I suppose? On the upside, I only needed to wait. I hoped they didn't set fire to the boat, and said as much to Ferd. He chuckled.

"What's so funny?"

"They tried. Ran away screaming."

I tried to think of what could possibly be so frightening about our boat.

"What?"

"Yeah, shit their pants the second they got within five feet."

"Wow."

"Just uncontrollable."

"That's..."

"Looked like someone had filled their pants with pudding."

"Okay..."

"Looked like they'd had a bag of stew in their pockets and it exploded."

"Ugh."

"They were building log cabins, feeding the seagulls, giving birth to otters, hanging rats, hatching brown trout, making gravy, riding centaurs, ARSEPLOSIONS!"

At that last, he fell silent. I peeked over to see he had passed out. I breathed a sigh of relief and settled back into my little nest. I had to give it to Lux. She had a knack with curses. One less worry on my mind, I relaxed into the bottle.

———

THREE DAYS in a stinking cellar is enough. I don't know how I managed to avoid the innkeeper, or Frollo's roving patrols. On the third day, he came tumbling through the window, bursting with news.

"They took your friends down. Frollo's in the square. Got 'em piled up like cordwood."

As if on cue, the priest's voice echoed through the village.

"Woman. I do not know your name, but I know your friends have perished. I am offering amnesty. Show yourself to me in contrition, and I shall spare their bodies the flame. You may collect them and be on your way."

"It's a trap," Ferd said.

"Of course it is," I replied, and strapped on my blades.

I didn't know if my friends could come back from flame. Resurrection is a tricky thing. Trickier if you've been reduced to ash, I imagine. I readied myself and exited the inn like a lady, instead of a raccoon. Frollo stood in the town square, a torch in hand. His under priests arrayed themselves around him like an honor guard. Townsfolk crowded in front, dressed in their neat clothing. Surely the gods wouldn't begrudge them a little blood-lust? They were good, clean churchgoing folk, after all. Behind him, Cord, Lux, and Rek lay on biers of wood. I opened my arms.

Frollo smiled. "I am glad you have seen the light."

He motioned to his men, and they surrounded me, taking my weapons and binding my arms. One of the big ones led me to a pole that stood nearby, slipping a loop from the ropes over a hook there, exposing my back. The crowd's expectant silence broke into an excited murmur, and the part of my brain not anticipating pain hoped I'd have the chance to teach at least one of them a lesson about blind faith. I heard the sound of a whip loosened, and part of me clenched.

Okay, it was my ass.

The lash came down. I felt the strike as heat at first, then a

searing pain that burned its way across my nerves. It brought
tears to my eyes, and I clenched my jaw as it came down again. I
screamed, and braced myself for the next lash. Already my sight
grew dim. A retching cough stopped the lash from falling, and I
recognized Cord's voice as he rasped out a command.

"Motherfucker, put it down."

Cord's voice was like ice water. The crowd gasped and took
an involuntary step back. Their murmuring, so like starlings at
first, had shifted and now they edged toward the octave of a
panicked cat. I twisted to look, and saw Frollo and the other
priests staring open-mouthed, the whip forgotten. Cord climbed
down and straightened his clothing, ran a hand through his hair.
He gestured to me.

"Let her go."

They moved quickly, unbinding me, restoring my belongings. Cord shot me a wink, then turned, raising his hands
dramatically. Lux and Rek rose from their biers, and another
gasp went up. Several in the crowd cried out to Oros, and others
made signs and wards against evil. The back rows broke and ran
for their homes.

"Oros' chosen!" Frollo said, and dropped to his knees. "My
lord, can you forgive us?"

Cord smirked. "I can think of ways for you to make it up
to me."

The change had come sudden enough that I didn't know if
Frollo played to the crowd, or if we'd missed some piece of lore.
I thought back to the story of Qoth, and wondered how deeply
the theme of resurrection ran through their beliefs.

Rek made his way to me, inspecting my wounds. He
gestured to Lux, who grimaced, then passed a hand over them. I
winced as the flesh knit itself back together, muscle reattaching,
the bleeding slowing and then stopping. I hugged her out of
gratitude. She stiffened, then relaxed into it.

"You're welcome," she whispered.

I turned back to the others. Cord still stood above the prostrate Frollo.

"Lux?" he said.

"Yeah?"

"Make this guy regret killing us. But not to death."

"Thank you, lord! Your mercy knows no bounds!" Frollo said.

"Laying it on thick, isn't he?" I asked.

"It's fine. He's a sniveling sycophant. More pleased with his power than his duty. Aren't you, you little shitgoblin?" Cord said.

He nudged the priest with his foot. Rage tried to bubble to Frollo's lips, his face growing red. He opened his mouth to reply, then snapped it shut. The flush drained from his face, pallor replacing the beet glow as Lux approached. She stood before him and smiled. A shudder rippled through my stomach at the look. It's the sort of look you give a puppy. Right before you eat it alive.

A yellow glow surrounded Lux's hand, then detached itself like a small cloud. It floated to land on Frollo, suffusing his skin, tinging him a pale dandelion before fading. A moment passed, then the priest coughed. He coughed again, the sound like a small cloth ripping, and tears leaked from his eyes. He coughed once more, then moaned, eyes widening. His guts gurgled like a fountain trying to pump dust, and he let a tremendous fart.

"Oh gods," he moaned.

He fell face-first to the dust, and yanked his trousers down. Grunts escaped his throat as he turned red once more, straining with the effort to pass whatever wanted free. Another massive fart passed from him, and he screamed as a shit-covered frog ejected from between his ass cheeks. It landed on the grass nearby, let a quiet *ribbit*, then hopped away into the field.

The last of the crowd broke at the display of sorcery, fleeing at the downfall of their patron. He moaned once more and tipped over in the dirt, trousers still around his knees, one hand clutching his ass. Cord knelt beside him, a dangerous light in his eyes.

"Now, how about that respect?" he asked, his voice quiet as a razor through flesh.

Frollo nodded, and rose, his face a pale green. He wrung his hands, and his lips moved in silent prayer. I could only hope that in his own mind he now considered himself unclean and fought with the revelation. Cord patted him on the back, his grin back in place.

RESPECT to the Cult of Oros meant we had full hospitality. New clothing, fresh food—meat, for the first time in ages, real meat—and just about anything else we needed or wanted. We'd been guaranteed privacy and the upper floor of the inn, and Cord took advantage.

"So, what now?" I asked.

He shrugged, a puzzled look on his face. "I hadn't expected this, to be honest. But it's not sustainable. We've still got to do something about these people. Even if we did the right thing and moved on, they'd still be here. The village would still suffer."

"What if we just killed them all?" Rek asked.

"Messy. I mean, I'm on board in spirit."

"We could turn them all to stone," Lux suggested.

"That's... tempting. Can we do that?"

"I have no idea."

"That's not helpful."

"You didn't specify whether it should be actionable," I pointed out.

"That is an impressive word."

"Thank you."

"But really unhelpful."

"Stick them on a boat?"

"They can row back."

"What if it's on fire?"

"I feel like we keep coming back to this murder thing. Normally I'd be proud of you, but we're trying *not* to leave a pile of bodies."

"Why?"

"It would make me a hypocrite."

"How so?"

"I don't like being murdered."

"And?"

"Do unto others. Golden Rule. Sheesh."

"I thought the Golden Rule was they who have the gold get to bugger anyone they want."

"That's... that's better than the other way I've heard it."

"Which is?"

"Something about making rules."

"Rules are better than buggery?"

"I mean, in some cases. Consent is important."

"I'm not saying it's not. I'm saying sex is far more interesting than an ordinance telling me where I can shit."

"Point taken. But what are we going to do with these damn cultists?"

"What about a really big pit?" Lux supplied.

Cord slapped his forehead. "No. No murder. Why does this argument feel so circular?"

"Your head's circular," Rek rumbled.

"Is it murder if we just kind of... leave them down there?" Lux asked.

"First of all, fuck you, Rek. Second of all, I... don't know?" Cord said.

A knock at the door finally interrupted our argument, drawing a sigh of relief from the group. I got up to answer it, pulling it open with an irritated look. Frollo stood on the other side, wringing his hands. I noticed they were red and raw. He must have been washing them since Lux cast the spell on him. He cleared his throat and winced, as if he expected another frog to crawl from it.

"Is the Chosen of Oros available?"

"Do you have an appointment?" I asked.

"What?"

"An appointment, you shit-licking little toadstool. Do you have one?"

Anger flashed across his features, but the sight of Cord over my shoulder caused him to swallow it.

"N- no."

"Would you like to make one?"

"Yes, okay."

"And what time works for you?"

"Immediately."

"Sorry, I only have soon, later, and go fuck yourself."

"Soon, then."

"And the nature of your business?"

"An urgent message for the Chosen."

"Can you tell me the message?"

He licked his lips. "Sure. Sure."

I waited.

"Trouble from the north."

"Is that all?"

He shifted from foot to foot. "It looks like an army."

"Okay, thanks then," I said, and slammed the door.

I waited for the sound of his footsteps receding and turned back to the group.

"Bigger problems, then," Cord said.

"Yeah, I said."What now?"

"If we run, we leave things as they'd been, and it's likely everyone gets slaughtered."

"So..."

"We fight."

A groan went up from the group.

25

SO LONG, AND THANKS FOR ALL THE FLESH

FERD STOPPED us halfway out of the inn. He staggered into Cord, then reeled back. He peered out through one bleary eye beneath his mop of hair, then exhaled a cloud of alcohol in a sudden belch. Cord reeled back, but the man gripped him by the arms, holding him fast.

"Oros," he hissed. "The dead come, you must meet them."

Cord shook free, and I pressed Ferd to the side before Rek could take his head off. We moved on, Ferd hissing after us.

"Save the town!"

We swept from the inn to find Frollo and his warrior-priests arrayed for battle, dressed in mail and clutching polearms, swords, and other weapons. I was a little impressed that a small temple in the middle of nowhere managed to scrounge up this sort of armament in short order, and wondered what other secrets they hid.

We met Frollo, following his gaze north, to where a line of dust marred the near horizon.

"Any thoughts, priest?" Cord asked.

"I think it's something foul," Frollo replied.

Cord nodded. "Rek, Lux—I need you to stay here. Help the priests out."

He pulled us to the side, leaning in.

"I also need you to keep an eye on these backstabbing bastards. Rek, if you get a chance, find me a heart for that Harrower engine. We might need to make a quick escape."

"You and Nenn going to be okay?" Rek asked.

Cord grinned. "God to kill, army to stop. We'll be fine."

I moved to Lux, heart beating like a hammer. She looked wan, paler than before.

"Healing me do that?"

She nodded. I embraced her, full and hard, and she leaned into it this time. When we separated, she wore a smile. I thought of her in the deadlands, of how bright she'd been, how full of life.

"Drain them dry," I said.

She nodded, and I walked back to Cord. Rek joined us, his axe in his hand. Lux stood to the other side, Rek handing us each a pack. Then they joined the priests, who had already begun to set up crude fortifications and barriers.

Cord clapped me on the shoulder.

"Just like old times, eh?"

"Seems like there was more money then."

"Yeah, but no glory."

"You're in it for the glory now?"

"I'm always in it for the glory."

"Really."

"And the money."

"But there's no money."

"Thus, the glory."

"South, huh?" I asked. Mostly to change the subject. This could have gone on for a while.

"Yeah," Cord said.

"So away from the army of undead?"

"Yeah."

"What about the glory?"

"This again? Trust me, the glory is this way."

"Okay, why then?"

Cord shrugged. "Dunno. Something feels off about the old man. Maybe I'm being paranoid. Maybe just difficult."

"You know, if you're wrong, there's a good chance we're leaving everyone to die."

Cord glanced over his shoulder. He seemed to weigh the decision for a moment, then shrugged. "Better to die fighting, I'd think."

"Better than what?"

"Than living under the heel."

There it was again. His contempt for the oppressors and the ones letting it happen. I knew no argument I made would reach him. Midian proved that. We climbed in a small boat waiting at the shore. Cord rowed us across the river in quick strokes. We beached on the other side in short order, a long plain ahead of us, bounded by the mountains. Tall grasses waved in the winds. I looked back, across the river. From here, the line of dust from the approaching army was even smaller.

"How long?" I asked.

Cord shaded his eyes, peered across with me. "Four, five days."

We turned and headed south.

"Can we kill a god?" I asked.

"We can do anything we want. We're the Godslayers."

I made a face. "Are we?"

Cord shrugged. "Anything's possible."

"Hooray for possibility."

THERE ARE places they hang paintings of the prairie. Tall grasses, maybe a forlorn and abandoned temple, sometimes a dog. It's romanticized in the city. "Look at these places. Look at these people. Tough. Salt-of-the-earth." It's horseshit. What the plains are is boring. Nothing but grass and sky and dirt and bugs. Fart on the prairie, and the wind'll take it to the coast because there's nothing in the way. Forget privacy if you've got to piss, or worse. Thankfully, Cord still respected me enough to give me his back and silence. Nothing worse than a piss-talker. Someone didn't raise those people right. It's not chatty business.

We'd been walking for the better part of the day, the sun steadily sliding toward the horizon. It bled orange as it did, like an egg broken on a wall, until the light faded, and Cord called a halt. We'd made good time from the river, and we built a small fire, throwing bedrolls down beside it. I rummaged in my pack, coming up with a couple of sausage wrapped in paper, and a small loaf of bread. Seemed the innkeeper didn't entirely hate us.

We set to eating, chewing in silence for a while before wrapping the rest up and stretching out. Cord pulled something long and narrow from his pack, unwrapping the cloth around it. The blade shone in the firelight as he exposed the steel, and I recognized it for the one we'd found in the tomb.

"What'd you bring that thing for?"

Cord shrugged. "Figured it knew about Oros, might be useful."

"Loud is what it was."

"Ah, we've had a talk about that."

"You talked to the sword?"

"I talk to a lot of things. This one just happens to answer." he shook it a little. "Say hi to Nenn, sword."

"Hi Nenn!" the voice that came out was enthusiastic, if at a normal volume.

"Tell Nenn your name, sword."

"My name's Dyrk!"

"Dyrk?"

"With a Y!"

"Why?" I asked.

"Thought it'd be funny," Cord said. "Dirk, Dyrk. You know, stabby."

"Ah."

"Tell her about Oros, Dyrk."

"I estimate we've got an 85% chance of dying horribly!"

"Shit," I muttered.

"No, not that," Cord said, shaking the blade again. "The other thing."

"Oh! Oros is super attractive!"

"What?"

Cord was nodding. "I think we've got a chance here."

I raised one eyebrow. "I think all that dying cut off the circulation to your brain. What're you gonna do, fuck them to death?"

Cord waggled his eyebrows. "What is best in life, Nenn?"

I lay back on my bedroll, staring up at the stars. "Friends? Family?"

"Yeah, those are pretty good. But what about fucking a god?"

"Look, I know you're messing with me, so I'm giving you another chance. What's the deal with this god?"

"Hotter than shit."

"Shut up."

"Hotter than you."

"Impossible."

"It's a god."

"Have you seen me?"

"Yeah."

"What's that supposed to mean?"

"Nothing. Go to sleep, Nenn."

"You go to sleep."

I waited for a riposte, and instead long snores came back. I closed my eyes and let the prairie wind lull me to sleep.

———

WE ROSE EARLY, Dyrk slung on Cord's belt, the wind blowing its ever-annoying melody. Before long, the sword was singing along.

"I'm a swooo-rd
On this belt I ride
And I want to stab things
Dead or alive"

I shot Cord a glare, and for his part, he had the good grace to shrug. Three hours and forty-five verses later, we arrived at a stretch of cleared earth. Rain had begun to fall, making a haze of the day, and from a distance, it seemed someone set a lone rock there. As we approached, I noticed carrion birds circling above.

We stepped into the field, mud sucking at our boots, and were able to see the rock clearer. It was the desiccated head of a man, skin long dried and brown from the sun, hair and lips withered, the eyes surprisingly wet. I watched as a fat raven landed atop it and ripped an eye from its socket. The head screamed out. Blood thin as gruel ran from the wound in the rain.

"Fuck!"

Its remaining eye rolled, and the skull shifted in our direction.

"You there! Hey, you! Shoo this damn thing away, would you?"

I gave it a skeptical look.

"Whaddya think, Dyrk?"

The sword spoke up. "There's a 25% possibility this is a trap!"

I sighed in exasperation and charged the bird, shouting. It spread its wings, and with an indignant squawk, took flight, splashing me with water.

"Dirty fuckin' birds," I muttered.

"Gods, thank you. Those only regrow once every few years. Little bastard was just waiting. Hey, I don't suppose you're going to see Oros?"

"Well..." I started.

"Yeah, we are," Cord interrupted. "Why?"

"I can be useful."

"How?"

"I know things. Like how to get into the tomb. How to get out of the tomb."

"Interesting."

"Wait," I said. "You're not going to trust this thing, are you? I mean, it was probably planted here for a reason."

Cord turned to me. "Are you saying you're prejudiced against the dead?"

"What? No. But people don't just get themselves buried for being friendly."

"Not true," the head said. "My friend, Gen, was once buried for giving a squirrel a nut."

"Why?" I asked.

"It was a fifty-foot squirrel."

"Hmph," I said, resisting the urge to roll my eyes right out of their sockets.

"Well?" Cord asked.

"I'm leery," I said.

"You're an anti-deadite," Cord said.

"What?"

"You're a rabid anti-deadite!"

I threw up my hands and turned, yelling to the prairie. "Fine, fuck it, bring him with. I mean, I haven't got a shovel, and there's no reason for an undead monster to betray us at all, but sure—"

When I turned back, Cord was already sawing at the corpse's neck.

"This is super yucky!" Dyrk chimed out.

He was through in a matter of seconds, and held the dead guy's head up by the hair. Gristle hung from the ragged edge of the severed neck, and rain made rivulets in the muddy skin.

"This is mortifying," the head said.

"No, that's your body. Now which way?" Cord asked.

The head spun in his grip to point a bit to the west, and we set out.

"Are there others like you?" I asked.

"No. Dead. Long dead." A note of sadness tinged his voice, and I let it drop.

We left the field not long after, and the grasses gave way to a broken road, the stones discolored and sharp at the edges.

"This was the Tevint Way. At one time, it spanned the entire empire."

"What was that like?" I asked.

"Beautiful. Did you know this was all forest and pastoral fields? Oros so utterly wrecked the land, they left little else than this flat waste."

We fell silent again as we walked, and I tried to imagine it. A village here, rolling hills there, beautiful copses of pine and maple and oak. Farmers leading their livestock out to pasture, lumberjacks working in the forest. The sound of children at play, of mothers calling them home. The sounds of laughter and love in the night, accompanied by fiddle and drum. Now only the wind played, and the grass rustled in time.

"What the hell is it with men and hubris?" I asked. "Why do they think they always know best, and when they don't, claim it so anyway? What is it about the urge to break and remake and break again, to reforge the world until it looks like the thing in your head instead of the thing handed to you?"

"The pity of that is any artist will tell you no matter how steady their hand, no matter how long they refine the thing they've created, it always falls short. Inability to appreciate beauty as it is might be one of the universe's greatest tragedies," Cord said. "And they're dicks."

The stones in the path began to appear more whole, the grasses shorter. Ahead, an edifice rose from the flat plain like a lord in his seat. Cut from red rock, the sides sloped together until they met a flat roof. Carved in the face of the building was a single glyph, but as Lux wasn't here, it was impossible for any of us to read. Around it were arrayed several smaller buildings, and I suspected they housed the families of those who'd been interred here as guards.

We approached the flat face of the rock, and Cord held the head up.

"Okay, where's the door?"

The head frowned. "It's right here."

It swung forward until its nose bumped the rock, banging into a hidden switch. The rock slid to the side with a rumble, revealing a round portcullis of black iron, etched with runes.

"And this?" Cord asked.

The head frowned. "I have a name, you know."

"Ah, sorry. And after I accused my friend of anti-deadism. What's your name, friend?"

"Omen."

"Oh, that's good," I muttered.

"Shh," Cord replied.

"Okay, Omen, how do we get this open?"

"See those depressions on the sides?"

"Yeah."

"Fill them with blood."

Cord looked at me.

"Fuck you," I replied.

He shrugged and sat the head down, cutting a shallow groove into his forearm, then letting the wound drip into the depressions. The gate slid to the side with a screech, and he picked the head back up, the cuts already healing. He bowed to me. I glared at him for a moment, then decided not in the rain was better than in the rain.

"After you."

I pulled my blades from their sheathes and stepped through the door.

THE INTERIOR of the tomb was lit. Well-lit, for that matter, a fact that surprised and annoyed me. We wouldn't be able to get away with hiding in the shadows. It also meant that even if someone wasn't waiting for us, they sure as hell had been busy. This tomb had none of the trappings of a typical mausoleum. The floors were swept, new torches stood in the sconces, fresh incense placed in small holders in the walls, and the cobwebs cleared away. Sarcophagi lined alcoves in the walls, their denizens sealed safely away. Where the walls hadn't been cut for the dead, lines of runes and glyphs marked the stone.

A door at the far end of the antechamber waited, but Cord was busy holding Omen up to the writing on the stone.

"What's it say?" he asked.

Omen muttered to himself for a couple of seconds before replying. "I'll need some time."

Cord nodded and placed the head on one of the incense shelves, then walked over to me.

"You ever wonder why a god would be in a tomb?" I asked.

"It's their prison," he said.

"Yeah, but you know... god. They don't have to be anywhere they don't want."

"That's a good point," he said. "That's a really good point. Shit, why didn't you bring this up earlier?"

"Well, you seemed sure of yourself, and there was the whole thing with the sword..."

Cord snorted. "Dyrk? I'm 90% sure he's full of shit."

"Hey! That's really hurtful!" the sword chimed in.

"What about the dead guy?" Cord asked.

Omen interrupted him by screaming. "INTRUDERS! INTRUDERS!"

"Ah. Fuck," Cord said. He strode over to the head and picked it up.

Omen's mouth clamped shut, and Cord set him on the floor, to which the head responded by screaming an alarm again. Cord drew Dyrk, holding the blade point-down over the head.

"I don't like this plan!" the sword shouted.

Cord ignored it and impaled Omen through the top of the skull, the blade passing through the parchment skin and brittle bone with a crunch, embedding the steel in the floor. Omen's mouth shut with a clack of teeth, and even the sword seemed subdued. I walked over and knelt beside the skull, tipping a blade against its eye socket. The eye rolled frantically, as if trying to escape, and I rammed the knife home, letting the orb pop, thick vitreous fluid running down the skull's cheek. I stood and found Cord staring at me.

"Sicko," he said.

"I told you not to bring it."

"But you're notoriously racist against the undead."

"By whose standards?"

He pointed to the impaled, blind skull. "His, to start."

I rolled my eyes and shoved the door at the end of the room open.

———

"THIS IS MORE LIKE IT," I muttered.

Cord blinked, and looked at me. "What's more like what?"

I gestured at the tangle of veins and flesh blocking the hall. It spread from wall to wall, a spiderweb of gore, sheets of skin making drum-like patterns, veins feeding the flesh. In each square of meat sat a mouth, and they all seemed to be about their own thing—licking, yawning, coughing, and speaking words in a language I couldn't understand.

"This is more like it. You enter the lair of some sort of evil, and there should be a horror waiting for you. Not that ladies garden society travesty out front."

Cord approached the monstrosity, and poked at various sections of it with his pinky.

"You trying to lose that one, too?" I asked.

He poked it again, and the structure shuddered.

"Uh... Cord?"

"Yeah, yeah. Okay." he backed away, until he stood behind me.

A popping sound echoed down the hall, and the thing blocking our way quivered. It drew in on itself, the popping growing louder as it balled up, then reshaped its form. Slowly, it took the shape of a man, but for the mouths marking its body like freckles mark a redhead. It turned, and I saw it had two wobbling dicks for eyes.

"Well, that's..." I started.

"Really unsettling," Cord finished. He shuffled from side to side, then stopped beside me. "It's eerie. No matter where I stand, it's like they're following me."

The golem shook its head, sending the dicks to bobbing like apples in water. It turned, and the voice that came from it was surprisingly melodious, if not melancholy.

"Walk this way, please."

It shuffled off down the hall, obviously expecting us to follow. I looked at Cord, who shrugged, and proceeded to imitate the golem's shuffle, waggling his head back and forth.

"What are you doing?" I hissed.

"What he said."

"You know, every time I'm next to you, I get a fierce desire to be alone."

"You just hate fun."

"We might die. What about that is fun to you?"

"The only thing dead here is your sense of humor. You are a fun assassin. An assassin of fun. A killer of mirth. An antijoyster."

"That's not even a word."

"It's a perfectly cromulent word."

I made a strangled sound, shook my head, and followed.

***

THE GOLEM LED us through a series of chambers filled with all sorts of things I'd rather forget. Most were unrecognizable clumps of flesh. Others were entire bodies—man, woman, and all manner of other creatures—splayed out and vivisected like insects. In one room, a man stood connected to another by a fleshy tube at the navel, and another stood in the corner playing a song on a broken fiddle while they danced. In the last room before we came to another open hallway, there was a goose. Bones littered the floor of the goose room. Even the golem gave it a wide berth as it softly honked in warning at us.

"What's with the goose?" Cord asked.

The golem shrugged. "He was already here. No one wants to fuck with him."

We passed from the goose room into another long neat hall,

finally arriving at an open arch. The golem ducked through, and we followed. The room beyond was wide and spacious, carved in a round dome. Space for a table had been made by pushing the sarcophagi into one corner of the room. Arcane tools and books covered the surface of the slab of wood. A figure stood behind the workbench, hooded and grim. The golem stepped to the side, and the man acknowledged him with a curt nod.

"Thank you, Elvis."

Cord jerked his head almost imperceptibly to one side, then stepped forward, drawing the figure's gaze. I sidestepped slowly, trying to circle around.

"So, hey... come here often?" Cord asked.

The figure stared at him, silent and grim.

"What are you doing?" I hissed.

"Rying oo educe eh reepy izard," he said out of the side of his mouth.

He sidled up to the table, leaning against it, then picked up a pencil. He dropped it, and with a wink at the wizard, bent over, wiggling his hips as he did.

"I am so embarrassed for you," I whispered.

"Cord!?" the figure said, and swept the hood back from his head.

Cord shot up and spun around, and I took a breath.

"Holy shit, the sword was right."

This guy was hot. Not normal person hot, but like if a beautiful person had sex with the idea of a beautiful person. I forgot to move. Cord was gobsmacked.

"Tug?" he said.

"You two *know* each other?" I said.

Cord laughed as they embraced. "Yeah, Tug and I went to the same school."

"You went to school?"

Cord looked hurt. "Of course I went to school. I'm not a complete lunk, Nenn."

"Huh. I thought you were just the walking embodiment of a libido."

"The walking embodiment of a libido who's read all of Heronocus' works," Tug corrected.

"So, what're you up to these days?" Cord asked.

Tug shrugged. "Mancin'. Necromancin'. Makin' with the dead guys."

"Why?"

"Got bored with the whole making flaming swords for minor lords thing. Turns out terrorizing the countryside pays better."

"So you're the one responsible for that army of the dead up north?"

"Yeah. Have you been? Those priests are total dicks. Figured I'd just raze the village and maybe open a nice little B&B."

"You? An innkeeper?"

"Guy's got to diversify. Stealing dead peoples' shit doesn't pay as well as you'd think."

"Oh no, I'm familiar."

"Tell him about the sword," I said.

"What sword?" Tug asked.

"It was a magic sword," Cord said.

"Oh?"

"Useless," I interjected.

"That's unfortunate."

I cleared my throat.

"Ah, yeah, okay," Cord said. "Soo... here's the thing. I kind of need you to not destroy the entire village."

"I'm gonna need a reason."

"Friendship?" Cord asked.

"I love you, Cord. And I really love your ass, but we haven't talked in fifteen years. If you're going to cut into my profit margins, I need a compelling reason."

"What about morality?"

"What about free will versus determinism?"

"Are you telling me it's your destiny to murder these people?"

Tug shrugged. "Maybe it's their destiny to be murdered, and I'm just fulfilling my own predetermined path as a tool of the gods. Think of me as a hammer, and these people the squishy melon that needs to be mulched so that beautiful flowers can grow."

"The only thing that's gonna grow from that bullshit are weeds. What about their own right to live, to pursue happiness?"

"They kind of gave that up when they threw in with the cult."

"You don't think people have a right to survive?" Cord asked.

"It's not enough to survive, it has to be fulfilling. Just surviving makes us less than animals, Cord. Even animals play and fuck and have a sense of family."

"I seem to remember you making a similar argument not that long ago, Cord," I interjected. He shot me a look that could have melted good steel. "I'm just saying, what you did in Midian—you left those people to just survive."

"I left them to live. How they do it is up to them. But I didn't just murder them," he growled.

"Do I get a say in this?" Elvis asked.

Cord and Tug both responded. "NO."

"Irony is dead," Elvis muttered.

Cord whirled on Tug. "If everything is predetermined, why do we even bother then? If we have no control over our own lives, why not just let the world come to us, and let things happen as they may? If everything is already written, then nothing matters, and if nothing matters, life isn't worth living, or even surviving, anyway."

Tug blinked, and fell silent for a few minutes. Finally, he heaved a sigh and spoke. "Well... shit. If I don't kill everyone, what do I do with this army I raised?"

Cord walked around the table and put an arm around Tug. "Don't think of it as an undead army. Think of it as a *fun-dead-* army."

Cord picked up a pencil and began to write on an empty sheet of paper.

WE LEFT the temple a few hours later, Elvis escorting us out. He bobbled his eyes at us as we left, passing the now-silent sword and Omen on the way out. Cord was quiet for a long stretch while we walked. On the upside, the rain had stopped. Not one to shy away from a confrontation, I finally broke the silence.

"Pissed?" I asked.

He sighed and pinched the bridge of his nose. "Yeah, but not at you. Midian's weighed on me for a while now. There's righteous rage, then there's self-righteous rage, and I may have been too caught up in the latter to realize that what I needed was the former. If we ever run into that sort of situation again, we'll be more cautious."

"Again?" I asked in mock horror, though it was only a little mock.

"Well, we've got a reputation to build. We are the Misfits, after all."

He looked at me with one eyebrow raised, a half-smirk curling the corner of his lip. I returned the eyebrow raise.

"Not entirely shitty," I said.

"I aim to please."

We walked until the stars showed in the pale dusk.

"Wanna hear a story?" he asked.

"Is it about that thing in Pied?"

"The donkey thing? No. It's about how Camor lost their eye."

I lit a cigar. "Sure."

Cord's grin widened, and he began.

IN THE BEGINNING, there were the fox, and the raven, and the spider, and they all lived together, though not always in harmony. In those days, the spider had eight eyes already, but wanted more, because spider had always been wroth and greedy. So it went to the raven first, for they were closer in nature.

"Sister Gren," it said. "Though I have seven eyes, I only see so well, as some see here and some see there, but none see far. You however, see near and far, much further than is necessary. Would you lend me one of your eyes? Surely you do not need both with their strength."

And while Gren understood his plight, she was not willing to part with it. She let him down gently, explaining that seeing far didn't mean just distance, but the future as well, and she needed to see the death of all things so she might shepherd souls when that time came.

"Unless you would like to shepherd those souls?" she asked.

Spider declined, as he would rather feast than shepherd, and they parted ways amicably, notwithstanding spider's disappointment.

Time passed, and he watched. He watched Camor, the bright eyes of the fox, the way they picked out the slightest tremor of the grass, the way they caught the furtive movement of prey.

Finally, he went to Camor, and as kindly as he was able, asked the same question.

"Brother fox, surely you could spare an eye. Yours are so strong, and mine so weak I need many."

Camor, always wary for the next deal, the next advantage, squinted at him.

"And brother spider, what will you give me in return?"

The spider thought for a while. What could he give Camor? Web strong enough to bind any prey? Venom to paralyze his foes? An extra leg, to make the fox faster? None of these things seemed sufficient. Finally, he fell upon it. He would share the dark with Camor.

For the spider, the dark was always there. It whispered secrets, it showed him the things others did when they thought no one was watching. There were hands in the dark, voices. For spider, it was an easy trade.

"I will give you secrets," he said.

"And what do you get?"

"I can see prey ever so easy then, I can see riches to build my homes from spun silver and gold."

Camor thought for some time on it, but finally agreed. Spider plucked an eye from his head, placing it into his own, then from his own mind spun a strand of pure black, and filled the hole with it. Thus, it's said that Camor knows every dark thing you've done. They are the Watcher in the Dark and the Saint of the Unlighted Path.

And that is how Camor came to have only one eye.

———

"SO, how did spider lose the eye?" I asked.

Cord shrugged. "I suspect one of the other gods plucked it out. Or it just got tired of him. Gods and parts of gods are fickle things."

We walked until the light went out, then made camp one more time. The sense of urgency was behind us, though with Cord you never really knew if it existed in the first place. We lit a fire and ate in silence, enjoying the simple company of one another. It'd been a while since we'd been on our own, and while I loved our extended family, Cord had been my first, and best friend.

When we finished, he dug a pipe from his pack, and we passed it back and forth. The smoke was good—clean tobacco and slipweed, and it took the edge off the past few weeks. We'd been sparing with the drug, as outside the cities it was fairly hard to find, so to have it now was a simple pleasure.

One moment, only Cord and I occupied the fire, the next a third figure sat with us. I blinked. I knew Cord's slipweed was strong, but this was a new level of *oh shit*. Robes the color of sand wrapped them, and what little I could see of their skin was pale. They radiated cold, and when they turned their face my way, each eye was black, from edge to edge. They regarded me for a moment, and I felt my soul weighed. Finally, they turned to regard Cord.

"A proposal," they said without preamble. Mist escaped their lips as they spoke. "Stand aside. Allow my work to finish. Surely you cannot hold love for the remains of a long-dead empire?"

"And what's in it for me?" Cord asked.

Oros gestured, and the sand at our feet stirred, whirling into life. It formed thin spirals that joined one another in a grainy tapestry. We saw Cord, perched on a raised throne. At his feet, a thousand adoring fans. Scattered around the base, gold and treasures unheard of. The scene blurred, showing fields verdant with life. Another shift, and the inside of a home, a happy family feasting. The visions faded, the sand drifting to simple motes.

"What makes you think I want this?" Cord asked.

"I think you want more than you are willing to admit, but if this does not please you," Oros shrugged, "you may sift through the ashes for whatever riches will sate your bottomless heart. Unimpeded."

"And if I disagree?"

Oros looked to the stars. "I cannot be held responsible for the things that fate decrees is your punishment for defying a god."

"Let me sleep on it."

"I see your heart, thief," Oros warned.

"I see your crotch," Cord replied. "Really, wrap that robe tighter."

Oros let a long-suffering sigh, and as quickly as they'd come, left the firelight. We had little time to consider the conversation.

"Was that real?" I asked.

Cord shrugged. "Good pipe, right?"

"If you like not feeling your feet, great pipe."

"I hate my feet."

We took another few draughts, and the moon rose. With it, a figure on the plains ahead, slender, with a graceful walk. I sat up and watched them approach, their walk steady and unhurried. As they neared the firelight, features clarified and coalesced. Skin the color of mahogany. A high forehead and an intelligent eye the color of gold, the other a black pit where one once sat. Fine cheekbones and full lips. A word escaped Cord's lips.

"Camor."

They took a seat beside the fire, making a triangle with the three of us. They smiled, and looked at Cord.

"Cord, my most precious fuck-up." Their voice carried hints of music, the lute and the fiddle, the drum.

They turned to me and smiled as well. "Nenn. I owe you a debt. I think that if not for you, Cord would be far more broken than he is."

"What can we do for you, your..." Cord trailed off.

"Camor is fine. You can listen for a while. Then I would ask a favor."

They lifted a hand and placed it in the fire, tracing symbols as they did so. Pictures formed in the flames, and we leaned in to see better.

Cord, on the throne. He glanced at Camor, a question on his lips, but they shook their head and motioned for him to watch. We turned back, and the scene shifted, revealing the back of the high seat. Shadows lurked at the edges, dark things with silver eyes. Behind the façade of rich wood and gold, bodies twisted beyond recognition supported the throne. They cried out for succor, but those cries were lost as the vision shifted again, revealing the adoration Cord received was that of a thousand slaves chained to a vast machine of blood and bone.

Again the scene flickered. It dipped beneath verdant fields that seemed so enticing, revealing a plot of corpses that fertilized their greenery. Then in, into the home of the happy family, to show the roast they devoured. In this vision their eyes were too wide, their skin too sallow. In a room behind them, stained like an abbatoir, a man sat weeping and clutching the crudely bound stump of one leg.

"What is this?" I asked.

"Truth in the lies," Camor said. "Watch."

The flames grew more intense, and another world, that stone and water came into focus. A thin man wrapped in tight furs slipped between shadows, a blade out. He paused at the edge of an alley, waiting for a guard to pass. Before they did, something the color of spilled ink separated from the shadows behind him, engulfing him. When it passed, only the desiccated husk of a man remained.

Another world, this one lush and green. Homes sat nestled in treetops, while great lizards trundled below. A small woman, her skin the color of oak, slipped from roof to roof, in a window here, out another. A small pouch at her side grew with each excursion. Darkness waited within the walls of the last home, and I cried out as she slipped inside. The scene paused, but no one emerged, and finally, it moved on.

The last, a city of such beauty I wondered who or what could have built it. Graceful spires, delicate steel. Water running through it all in a way that made me think of music. A child, no older than I had been when I joined the orphanage slipped in and out of crowds, purses seeming to drop into their hands. A smile marked their lips, the light of unhindered joy in their eyes. They passed an alley, and they were gone. Silver eyes stared from the dim space between buildings, and then that too was gone.

The images faded from the flames, and we sat back. Camor looked us over, each in turn.

"Go home, Cord. Go to Orlecht. Oros' imprisonment has driven them mad, and they mean to burn this world to ash. We are jealous gods, and each of you little shits are precious to us. To me."

"Not to be blasphemous here, but I just had an entire argument about free will versus determinism, Camor," Cord said.

"You, blasphemous? Perish the thought. But there's this—I have never forced one of my own down a path, and I won't now. If you refuse this burden, so be it. There are a million other thieves and assassins in the world. One of them's bound to get lucky."

"Luck? Luck?" Cord sounded indignant. "Fuck that, you need skill. I'll do it."

Camor smiled.

"For a price."

Camor's smile exploded into a laugh. "I would expect nothing less. Get it done, and we'll talk."

"Deal." Cord spat on his palm. Camor did the same, and they shook.

Then, the god just... disappeared.

"Huh," I said.

"What?"

"Well, they could have just done that instead of walking all slow toward the fire."

"You're high. Besides, theatrics are important."

"I'm a big fan of getting to the point."

"I have so much to teach you yet."

"Can you teach me what it's like to have five minutes of quiet?"

He laid back on his bedroll. "Fuck you."

"Fuck you too, buddy."

We fell into silence, and sleep claimed us.

WE STROLLED into the village just past noon the next day, the undead army that came to destroy the town no longer armed with blades and pikes, but hammers and saws. The sounds of hammering and sawing and digging filled the air. The temple had already been all but dismantled, the pieces used to build some sort of wheeled contraption on a tall scaffold, others used to create small booths. Some townspeople kept a respectful distance, others acted as though the dead were simply newcomers. None of either group spared us more than a passing glance, and they made a wide circle around where Cord and Lux sat beside a pile of corpses.

"What the fuck is this?" I asked.

Cord grinned. "I call it an amusement park."

"What's amusing about it?"

"There's rides, for one. And a dunk tank."

"I don't know what any of those things are."

"It's because you wouldn't know culture if it bit you in the ass."

"Maybe. But I also know you have a knack for annoying people in the most efficient way possible."

"That too," he conceded.

Rek and the Lux looked up at our approach, Rek raising a hand in greeting. I looked at Lux for a moment, heart in my throat. I was suddenly ecstatic there hadn't been any killing—well, not any killing of people I cared about—and I swept her up, planting a massive kiss on her lips. She swooned a little, then straightened, a smile creeping across her face.

"Made a decision, then?" Lux asked.

"Yep," I said, and reached for her hand. She clasped my fingers tightly, and we went to join the others.

The corpse pile became clearer as I inspected it. Every priest in town was piled together in a lifeless heap, Frollo's body on top, suspiciously large holes where their hearts used to be. Not a single undead occupied the pile.

"What happened here?" I asked.

Rek shrugged. "The dead stopped a few yards from the town. Figured you guys must have been successful. These idiots still wanted to fight, and when we didn't, they tried to attack us."

"Extra-crispy dumb," Lux said, and pointed to a blackened limb poking from the pile.

"Yep," Cord nodded in agreement.

"Got your heart," Rek added.

"Thought you might have. The townspeople?"

"They're wary, but Lux here whipped up a couple of charms to make them feel better, and once they saw the dead were building and not killing, they relaxed. They might still run, but I don't think there will be any violence here."

"What about the old man?" I asked.

"Who?"

"Ferd?"

Rek shrugged.

A scream from the far end of town interrupted him, and we turned to see. A figure rode between the shops, townspeople scattering before the newcomer. It drew closer, and I sucked in a breath.

"Is that?" I asked.

Cord nodded. "Yep. Horrific man-thing."

"At least it's not a horse," Rek muttered.

It approached at a trot, long legs stuttering against the cobbles of the street. Its torso sat high, and as it drew close, I saw the Harrower had twisted a man to do his bidding. Its ribcage rode the top of the body, long limbs moving from knobby joints. Legs ended in four-toed hands, and the movement reminded me of a crab. Nearer still, and I made out the flesh was stretched over bone and muscle, as if too small for its body, and nailed in place. Strips of gore glistened in the light, and it left a trail of wet redness behind as it moved. Its face was a torn rictus of agony, eyes rolled to the whites. I tore my gaze away and spotted Ferd atop a blanket strapped to its back. Dried blood streaked his lips and beard, and he swayed dangerously atop the beast. He tugged the reins, and it skidded to a stop a few yards from us.

"Okay then," Cord said. "Everybody on the boat."

We turned and started the walk toward the docks. Ferd's

mount let out a screech and a shadow passed over our heads as it leapt, landing once again in our path.

"What is it with this guy?" Rek asked.

I squinted. "Harrower, if I had to guess. But it looks like he fucked up his throat calling this thing."

Fred tipped his head to one side. "You. You have stepped into my path. Is it not enough to harry you to the ends of the world? Is it not enough that you have pulled my would-be empire down around my ears?"

"Who the fuck *is* this?" I asked.

"YOU DON'T KNOW?" Ferd screamed. Blood spilled from his lips, and he coughed. He moved them again, and no sound came aside from a wheezing gurgle.

"No fuckin' idea," Cord said. "Lux?"

"Right, roast weirdo coming up," she said.

She stepped in front of us, hands aflame. Blue balls of fire launched from her palms, leaving behind a *woosh* and a searing heat that dissipated as they streaked toward the beast. Ferd juked the flayed man to one side, and it lashed out, smacking Lux in the face with thick fingers. It knocked her back, and she sprawled out, spitting in disgust.

I stepped in, Rek to my left, and as the monster lunged for the big man, I ripped my blades through its rear leg. Blood gouted from the wounds and the horror gave a keening cry, spinning toward me. Its jaws snapped, lightning-quick, catching a bit of my armor. I lashed out, opening one of its eyes. Vitreous fluid spilled down its cheek as it screamed.

The monster wobbled suddenly, then collapsed, Rek's big axe chopping two legs from it. Lux swooped in, placing a palm on its head with a look of disgust. She spoke a word in her arcane language, and black fire exploded behind its eyes. Smoke curled from it as it withered.

A weight hammered into my back, and I stumbled forward as Ferd beat at my head and neck with furious fists. I fell, teeth chattering as I collapsed onto the street. Another keening wail came as Ferd opened his mouth. The sound was corrupted however, the damage to Ferd's throat causing it to sound like a rusty hinge.

"Somebody get this weird fucker off me!" I shouted.

"On it!" Cord shouted, and the weight disappeared, the wail cutting off.

I worked my way up on unsteady feet. My head rung from the noise and the beating. I looked around, to see the others standing nearby, then down at Ferd's motionless form. Cord had beaten the man unconscious with one of the beast's legs, and now the Harrower lay in an unceremonious heap, face obscured by the wounded flesh.

I shook my head and we made our way back to the boat.

"Gret's balls, Cord," I said.

"You needed help," he shrugged.

"I didn't mean bludgeon him with a leg."

"Hey, I get results."

"He's got a point," Rek said.

"Maniacs," I said, as we arrived at the boat. "You could have just stabbed him."

"Where's the fun in that?" Cord asked.

"So, are we just leaving him here?" I asked.

"What do you think he's going to get up to?" Cord asked.

"I mean, he's a Harrower."

"That Cord just humiliated," Rek said. "Would you stick around after that?"

"Good point," I agreed.

We gathered our things and boarded, pushing away from the docks with Rek's usual skill. No crowd gathered to see us off, no cheers of joy. Lux slipped below deck to install the heart in the Harrower engine, while Cord staggered downstairs to sleep.

When she'd finished, Lux and I found a cabin, and spent some time doing the opposite.

Later, when night fell, we stood on the deck together, and listened to the river rush by. The wind whispered through the sails, and clouds hid the moon and stars. Rek piloted with a steady hand, and Cord rode the crow's nest. Ahead, the city. Ahead, uncertainty.

But here, family.

26

THIS ASSHOLE AGAIN

WHEN FERD CAME to on the other side of Tremaire's lake, he'd spent an hour probing the raw red scar on his throat. Finally, he found his feet, screamed an unintelligible word at the trees, and began to walk. Somewhere in the western reaches of the forest (and he'd been fortunate here--the beasts didn't love the Harrowers) Oros opened a gate, and showed him the way.

Now he lay on the far side of the river again. He'd nearly drowned, again. And this time, he was sure he'd lost his ability to Harrow at this point. His voice had been destroyed beyond all recognition. First the bitch with the knife, then his own attempt at vengeance. Once again, Oros opened a gate. Ferd hesitated at its threshold.

Why do you stop? Oros asked.

"I need a moment," Ferd replied. His voice sounded like nails in a tumbler.

Have you been broken? Do I need to find another champion?

"No. No. My will remains the same. I will simply need a new approach."

And what is your will?

"Vengeance."

That will do.

The gate shimmered before him. Ferd stepped through, the gate snapping shut behind him. He hesitated in the face of the swirling chaos, like fractal breaks behind his eyelids. He hated this part. He took the first step.

THE RITE WAS UNIRONICALLY CALLED *The Harrowing.* Ferd expected little else from a humorless bunch in the humorless depths of the black spire of Tremaire. His instructor, a large man with folds of skin that hung beneath his chin like a turkey's waddle, paced back and forth in front of him. Voluminous robes hid the bulk of the man, though the disciples of Oros doubted that it was all fat beneath the thick velvet. There were times, they whispered, that those robes moved on their own. There were times, they said, in the dark of the Hive, when the Commune was to be observed, that *things* reached from beneath the hem. Thick and tenebrous, slick with the plasm of other worlds.

Now though, the man seemed simply *large* in the flickering light of the torch at the entrance to the catacomb. He stopped pacing and looked at his ward, the young Harrower trying to focus his gaze on the big man. The new eyes he'd been gifted with had taken some practice in control. Granted, the world still seemed to decay and shift about him, but if he concentrated, Ferd could see the normalcy that hung on everything like a gauzy facade.

"Are you listening?" Hret asked.

Ferd nodded. Hret's gaze lingered on him a moment longer, then shifted away. "Then you are ready."

He stepped away from the yawning mouth of the tunnel leading down, and swept an arm out.

"Begin. Do not return until you have your fetish."

Ferd stepped forward, unwilling to show fear. That had been his first lesson. Fear earned you a curse, and in the beginning, Hret had cursed him many times. He'd spent time as a turnip, with boils on his penis, with tiny faces that cried out in fear each time he tried to sit, and as a scrub brush for a wizard whose bathroom proclivities ran from the obscene to the horrifying. He stepped into the dark without a glance back.

The tunnel swept quickly downward, and his feet moved almost of their own accord at the steep angle. Faces carved into the walls leered and winked as he went, and some reached out with questing hands, probing for weakness. He ducked and dodged, and they called out insults and hoots of glee at his pace, until finally the slope deposited him in a wide chamber. Bones lined the walls, made up the floor and ceiling. A thick red moss held everything together, and as he stepped in, the room wobbled a little, as if he walked a rope bridge.

Ferd's eyes saw the truth of the place--the great throat he'd passed through, the stone teeth carved with faces. He saw that this ossuary was the guts of some great beast, half in and half out of this world. Faces of its victims crawled across their own skulls, the skin shivering and wrinkling, jaws open and jittering as they burbled mad laughter.

He paused, listening. He only needed one thing here. A hand from that corner? But as he watched it crawl the wall like an eager spider, it paused long enough to flip an obscene gesture. No, then. Maybe that femur? Ferd walked over and gave it a tug, but the bone was stuck fast, the wall puckering outward with his pull. He released it and the room let a sound like a rippling fart, the noise sending the skulls in the corner giggling.

"Idiots. Cretins."

There, in the corner. A lone skull, its face still motionless, the skin clinging like a cobweb. Ferd approached and knelt.

"Ah there, you boy."

"Me?"

"No, the other boy," the skull said.

Ferd whipped his head around and caught his own shadow passing from wall to wall, as though pacing. The skull chuckled.

"Yes, you. Pick me up."

He did as asked. The skull felt warm against his palms, the skin smooth as leather.

"Ah, yes," the skull chuckled. "This is well-made. Come now, to the surface. We don't need these others."

Ferd nodded and departed, taking the tunnel upward, the direction and slope different again. As they passed from the room, the skull finally spoke above a whisper.

"Later, shitbrains!"

THE MEMORY FADED, and the gate tunnel shimmered. Ferd stepped from the gate into a rainswept street. In the distance, a black spire. Closer, a lake filled with boats. Not Tremaire, somewhere further. Somewhere new. Another chance.

PART III

If you see that stranger
Coming on the track
I can hear your mama just calling you back
Hit you like a fever, fever deep
And I touch you like a thief
And leave your pockets clean

Rival Sons - Do Your Worst

27

CANNIBALS, PEDERASTS, AND
FUCKMOUTH SAUSAGE

I LEANED over the rail of the Codfather, staring into the foamy wake of the ship as we sped west, toward Orlecht. Lux repaired the Harrower engine, and while Cord lobbied for us to use it immediately, flinging us toward the city, I had little to no interest in being plunged into the deadlands again. To be honest, my capacity for horror was damn near full, and if I saw one more unspeakable nightmare, I was gonna crawl into a wine cask and not come up for air for several years.

Cord joined me at the rail, leaning on the weathered wood with both elbows.

"Whatcha thinkin' about?" he asked.

"How wizards seem to be obsessed with dicks. I mean, they're everywhere. Not once have I seen a vagina monster, Cord. Why?"

"Have you met a wizard? You think those guys have ever seen one?"

"That's unkind."

"Buncha stinky longbeards. Gods help you if you ever get something wrong around them. The sheer weight of the 'well, actuallys' would suffocate you. When I was in university, some of them even had a club. The Unfucks, they called themselves."

"Unfucks?"

"Involuntarily unfuckable. Try explaining that if you just shave, bathe, and stop wearing those weird-ass robes and pointy hats, you'd at least have half a shake at it. Oh, and stop blaming everyone but yourself for your inability to socialize. Own up to it, Gern. You have a shelf full of intestinal parasites, and you've named them all. You have a straw mat you've painted the queen's face on. You refer to everyone you meet as either Lord or Lady."

"Yeah, but why dicks?" I asked.

Cord shrugged. "Some people take up philosophy, some people navel-gaze."

"But in this case, the navels are..."

"Yeah."

I grimaced. The landscape changed since our passage through the Godsteeth. Where before the continent had been almost overwhelmingly long grasses and hills, this side of the mountains the spaces north and south were thick and woody. Bird cries and other calls hung in the air, and occasionally, a deer or a boar appeared from the tree line, staring at the boat as we passed.

"You notice how few ships sail this side of the river?" I asked Cord.

"I hadn't until now," he said. "But if I had to guess, there are a couple of reasons. One, we burned down Midian. That'll put a cramp in trade. Two, most of Orlecht's traffic is coastal. Three, there are other cities, but they're smaller, and at the end of tributaries too small for this boat."

"What about piracy?"

"Aside from the assholes in the valley? Hell of a lot of work on a river. You're better off on the seas, where you can maneuver. One wrong move here and you beach both boats, run them against rocks, or worse, find yourself locked with an enemy you hadn't expected to lose to." He shook his head. "Not worth it."

I watched the forest roll by for a few minutes before another question came to mind. "I'd always heard this side of the mountains was filled with monsters. I don't see any."

"That's probably for the best."

"Why?"

"If they see you, they want to eat you."

"Ah. But one or two can't be bad, right?"

"Most of the things in there are clannish. Tend to bond together for safety. There are supposedly even carnivorous trees in there."

"Why the fuck would those exist?"

"If I had to guess, because the world exists to fuck with us."

We watched the water pass for another few minutes. Cord sighed.

"Bored?"

"Yeah. Can we turn on the engine?"

"No. Fuck no."

"Aw."

"Go whittle something."

"I'll whittle you a nice dildo."

"The last thing the world needs is more dicks. Whittle me a whistle."

"Fair enough." he wandered away.

I made my way over to Lux. She raised her head from the bird she'd been toying with. I tried not to notice what she'd turned it into. She waggled the wings, and I looked despite myself. It wore a grin instead of a beak, and a scorpion's tail curved over its back. I shuddered and remembered I loved her.

"Coming to the cabin tonight?"

She looked out over the water. "Maybe."

"It's been a month. I'd like you to move in. It's a big cabin."

"I need time. I need space. I need you to understand those things."

"I need you to understand I won't wait forever," I said.

I turned on a heel and made my way to the other side of the boat. I stared out at the woods a little longer, then sighed. I felt the tension in my shoulders, my back aching despite having nothing to ache for. Whatever was coming in Orlecht had me on alert, my nerves keyed up like the strings on a lute. I almost missed the days working in the mill, the nights at the Dripping Bucket. Then I thought of our little family, and realized I would have missed them more. Even had I never met them, there would always have been a piece gone from my life.

I turned away from the rail and slipped below deck to get some sleep.

LUX WOKE me just after dawn, her face pale and lovely in the dim light of our quarters. She'd conceded a little. I had her in the private moments and the small hours, and though I knew Lux was not a thing to be owned, a selfish part of me was still glad she gave of herself.

"We're here," she said, and pulled me up.

We walked to the top deck to see the sun peeking above the horizon, setting the sea beyond the city on fire, the clouds and sky pink and blue the color of robins' eggs. Ahead, the city. I'd never seen anything quite like it, and cursed myself for a fool for thinking Midian was what passed for civilization. It shared similarities—it straddled the river, a great curtain wall, wide roads leading into massive gates.

Here though, the forest had been cut back, and extending from the tree line to the banks of the river, a massive bazaar held sway, all manner of people shopping, hawking wares and food, and even performing filled it to the brim. Wooden stalls stood on earth worn bare by the passage of thousands of feet, and a series of posts carved with wards marked the edge of the forest.

More people approached or left the city from the north and south, wide roads populated by peoples on foot and horseback. On this side of the wall, the river spread out, the deltas long ago dredged and cleared out, leaving a massive lagoon where ships bobbed at anchor or maneuvered into slips on the dock. Smaller boats—fishing trawlers—worked the areas closer to where the river spilled into the sea, and others, sleek rowboats with official-looking seals, delivered messages to and from the city proper.

Tall buildings of stone and wood filled the city, and above them all, a spire of black marble quarried from somewhere distant. As we approached, the smells of the bazaar and the city mingled and filled the air—perfumes and spices, the press of bodies and animals, the odors of craftsmen—blacksmith and tanner and charcoal-maker—and created a scent that I would have associated with an offal pit in summer.

"Woof," Cord said, coming to stand beside us.

"Smells like hot ass."

"Smells like someone set a pile of vomit on fire, then vomited on that fire," Rek said.

Lux took a deep breath. "Smells like heaven," she said.

We turned and stared. She grinned and shrugged. Rek moved the boat to an open spot on the water and Cord spun the windlass, dropping anchor in the depths. We piled into the rowboat and made our way to the city.

THE GUARD at the river gate was about thirty, pudgy, and had the sleepy eyes of a habitual slipweed user. He glanced at our group, waving us through one by one until he got to Lux. He straightened and smiled, holding up a hand.

"Just a minute there, honey. Where you going so fast?"

Lux shrank back, and he leaned in, putting one hand across the postern gate, the leer on his lips growing wider.

"There's a tax to get in, you know. Beauty tax. It's just, ah..."

He reached down to grab his package, and found my knife at his balls. He froze, and I whispered in his ear.

"Unless you want the next meal you eat to be fuckmouth sausage, I'd suggest letting her pass." I pressed the blade into his thigh, not stopping until he winced as the tip pierced the skin. "As a matter of fact, I'd forget this tax altogether. I'd even consider reparations."

He nodded, and I pulled the blade away, the guard sucking in breath like I'd just tried to drown him in a mound of shit, and he'd managed to come up for air. Lux gave him a sweet smile and passed through, taking my hand on the other side. He stared at us for a minute, hate on his features, so I shot him a wink and a kiss, and we continued on.

"I'm so proud of you," Cord said.

"Me too," Rek chimed in.

"Our little girl's growing up," Cord said and wiped away an imaginary tear.

"I haven't been little in years."

"I'm not even entirely sure you're female," Cord said.

"Let's not get wrapped up in labels. What I am is a badass. And a great lay."

"Gods, you *have* been spending too much time around him," Rek said.

"One of us. One of us," Lux chanted in a mock-whisper.

The river entry widened out to a large street, every manner of shop and craftsman. The near end featured a fish market, the stalls packed with ice and layered with fish of in every shape and size. Shoppers browsed the aisles, picking out bits of what they liked, and having them packaged into simple sacks.

"Smells like a fish orgy," Cord said.

"Probably tastes better than fuckmouth sausage though," Rek replied, drawing a laugh from the rest of us.

"Okay, where to?" I asked.

"Well, Camor sent us to stop a cult. Who belongs to cults?"

"Cannibals," Lux said.

"Probably pederasts," Rek supplied.

"Rich people," I said.

Cord touched his nose and smiled. "Winner. But first, I have to make a detour. Rek, Lux, find us lodgings. Nenn and I have to visit someone."

CORD LED me through a warren of streets I couldn't track on a good day, navigating through thick crowds and wide avenues until I thought my head would spin. Finally, we emerged onto a clean street, modest homes with small patches of green kept around them.

"Where are we?" I asked.

"Home," Cord said.

"It's weird to think of you as having parents," I said.

"You didn't think I just sprung from a rock, perfectly formed, did you?"

"More like under a cow flop, mostly deformed," I said.

"Wow. All this fame is making you mean."

"Wait until I actually get rich."

"Perish the thought. Let's be poor heroes forever."

I made a face and he laughed, leading us up the street.

We stopped in front of a small cottage, clean shingles and paint that had just begun to flake with time. Weeds dominated the yard of the still sturdy home. Cord pulled a key from a thong around his neck and led us in.

Sheets covered the furniture, and a thick layer of dust coated everything else. He closed the door and stepped to the fireplace, running a hand across two urns on the mantle.

"Hey mom. Dad. I brought Nenn. She's a great person, and if you don't like her, well, tough fuckin' nipples. But I know you would. Camor sent me home, and even though I know they meant Orlecht, I doubt they'd be upset about this little trip.

"Anyway, there's something fucked up going on here, and we're going to stop it *before* it gets bad, for once. I just wanted to tell you, in case I can't come back again. But if Nenn does, you can't haunt her. I promised to do that. Okay, I love you guys."

He turned to me.

"Nenn, you want to say anything?"

I thought for a moment. "Your son's a shithead, but he's the best kind."

Cord nodded, looking back at the urns. "I told you she was great."

We stepped out of the house. He locked the door and tucked the key away, and we were on our way once more.

"Tell anybody about this, and I'll cut your nipples off and use them for thimbles," he said.

"Your secret's safe with me, you momma's boy," I said.

He slung an arm around my shoulders and we went in search of the others.

WE'D PASSED into a section of the city Cord called the Narrows. Every city has its shantytowns; it just seemed this one was on the inside. Buildings leaned against one another in haphazard fashion, putting me in mind of Midian. Narrow alleys appeared and disappeared seemingly at random, and though Cord led us through with confidence, I suspected if I came here alone, I'd be hopelessly lost for days. Cord stalked through the quarter with a sour look.

"What's up, buttercup?" I asked.

He gestured around us. "This. I've been gone for half as long as I am old, and nothing's changed. It's just... doesn't anyone care, Nenn?"

I shrugged. "Sure, they care. They care about themselves. Everyone else can get fucked."

He nodded. "I used to think I could make a difference, you know."

"You? Caring?"

"I had a kinder, gentler blade-wielding hand back then. Thought picking up a sword would make a difference. If I could protect the kingdom, it'd have a chance at fixing itself. When that didn't work, I thought if I educated myself, I could apply that. And when that didn't work, I decided I'd get myself paid, and let the whole thing rot."

"And now?"

"And now I'm inclined to let it rot, but only after I burn it down."

We turned a corner, then another one quickly. Cord pulled me deeper into an alley with only room for us to fit sideways. I opened my mouth to ask what he thought he was doing, and if he wanted me to ram his balls all the way up into his stomach or only part way. He shook his head, cutting me off, and nodded at the entrance. I waited, and a group of men passed us on silent feet. They wore short blades or daggers, leather armor, and short hair. They looked like professionals.

We waited another minute, then Cord pulled us out. He led us away from the party that passed.

"What was that?" I asked.

"When I left, it wasn't on the best of terms," he said.

"I'm so surprised."

"I'm wounded. I'm very likeable."

"What'd you do? Rob them? Kick their puppy? Fuck their horse?"

"I would never kick a puppy. But yes, I sort of robbed them. Then burned down their hideout," his face screwed up in thought. "But I also paid reparations. They shouldn't be after me."

"Then, what? They just decided to hunt you for sport?"

"If I had to guess, not them. But somebody. Someone here wants to send me a message."

"Which is?" I asked.

Two of the men appeared from the end of the alley we'd been walking down. I shuffled back and stopped, another two appearing from the other side. A fifth stepped forward, blades in his hands, a pinched look on his thin face.

"Welcome to Orlecht," he said.

The leader turned to Cord and nodded. "Cord."

"Mict. I uh, I see you've been busy. Don't suppose you'd tell me who hired you?"

"Nah, fuck you. Easy or hard?"

Cord raised his hands and backed against a wall. "Hey now, we're square. Bell said as much when I paid her."

Mict shrugged. "Bell ain't around no more. New management."

"I hate these godsdamned corporate structures," Cord said.

The men from each end moved in, Mict standing his ground at the mouth of the alley.

"Got any ideas?" I asked Cord.

He set his back against mine. "Yeah, STAB THAT GUY IN THE BALLS," he shouted.

As a battle plan, it was shit. But as an intimidation tactic, it was incredibly effective. The man facing me stiffened, his eyes going wide as my blades came out. I went low, ripping one into his thigh and leaving it there as he collapsed to one knee. I felt an impact and heard Cord grunt as he took on another attacker, then it was chaos.

The second man tried to trip me up, bringing his blade in an upwards sweep, but I slipped to the side as I rose and slashed a cut along his forearm. Blood slicked his weapon, causing him to fumble, and I rammed another dagger into his eye. He fell away, leaving me facing Mict.

Behind me, I heard one man wailing, and no sound from the other. I glanced back, seeing Cord had taken a nasty cut along his ribs, a move the assailant paid for. His own dagger jutted from his crotch, and he wept on the cobbles.

Cord joined me, and he grinned.

"Now, Mict. Care to renegotiate?"

The would-be assassin paled and sprinted away.

"Nenn?" Cord said.

"On it."

I flipped a blade as he fled. It sailed end for end and nailed the back of his head with a *thunk*, the hilt hitting his skull with a sound like a melon dropped from a roof. Mict collapsed, and Cord walked over, grabbing an ankle.

"What're you up to?" I asked.

He winked. "Grab his arms. I got questions."

WE DRAGGED Mict to a blacksmith shop closed for the night. I tied the would-be assassin to a chair in one corner while Cord rummaged around in the tools. I tried my best to ignore his cursing, and the subsequent shout of joy as he found what he was looking for.

"Wake him up, Nenn," he called.

I grabbed the smith's quenching bucket and splashed Mict in the face. He blinked and sputtered, then groaned in pain. Cord walked over to stand beside me as the assassin tried his bonds.

"Nice knots," Cord said.

"Thanks. What's that?"

Cord held up the tool with a grin. "Hammer."

"Whatcha' gonna do with it?"

Cord frowned, and turned the hammer head to face him. "What are we gonna do, Mr. Hammer?"

He tilted the tool toward his ear as if listening, then nodded and pulled it away again.

"Interesting. But won't he walk funny after that?"

"What's he doin'?" Mict asked. Panic tinged his voice.

I turned to the man. His eyes showed the whites, and they flicked from me to Cord. I shrugged.

"Talking to Mr. Hammer. Shush."

Cord was addressing the tool again. "But I don't know if you'll fit in there, Mr. Hammer."

"WHAT DO YOU WANT?" Mict bellowed.

Cord grinned and leaned in, setting the hammer on Mict's thigh. The assassin flinched. "Who paid you?"

"Rook," the assassin whined.

"Not good enough. Why aren't the guards on my ass? The Leashmen?"

"I dunno! He's got some sort of beef with you. Wants to make it personal."

Cord slid the hammer closer to Mict's crotch. Sweat stood out in bright droplets on his forehead.

"So why send you?" he asked.

"He wanted you riled up, maybe hurt."

Cord pressed the hammer into Mict's balls, and the man let out a whimper.

"That's all I know, oh gods oh gods oh gods."

"Nenn?"

"Right."

I threw a fist into Mict's jaw and he went boneless in the chair. Cord dropped the hammer on the straw floor.

"Let's meet the others."

WE MADE our way back to the hotel as quickly as possible, avoiding three more groups of men out for blood. Once we made the high street, we relaxed, blending into the crowd as well as one can when covered in blood.

"That went well," Cord said. He sounded almost cheerful.

"I'd hate to see your version of the opposite."

"There's a lot more screaming and oozing, to be honest."

LODGINGS WERE a suite of rooms in a massive two-story stone building with tall columns decorating the front, and frescoes carved across the face. They depicted all manner of recreation, from food and drink to dance, to other, more graphic depictions, of certain pastimes. Rek and Lux waited outside.

"It's like they built you a monument, Cord," Rek said.

The interior was marble and stone, the floors lined with plush red carpeting. Tapestries and art hung on the walls in tasteful-adjacent arrangements. Our rooms were on the second floor, including a small kitchen, a parlor area, and bedrooms. Lux and I claimed ours while the others settled in. I broke into a small chest in the kitchen area, discovering that an enchantment kept the bottles of light sweet beer inside cold. I sat back with Lux on the divan and sipped, then lit a cigar for the first time in days, the smoke swirling out a nearby window in lazy spirals. The others joined us shortly.

"What's the plan?" I asked.

"We've got two options. One, we insert ourselves into high society—parties, balls, dinners, the whole shebang—and hope for an invitation."

"That sounds suspiciously like an excuse for you to be drunk for a month," Rek said.

Cord grinned. "Option two is we join one of the cults around here, and work our way up to the inner circle, where an invitation is almost guaranteed."

"That seems like the more direct route," I said.

"It does. Except the cults are more likely to kill and eat you than just uninvite you from their parties if they sniff anything suspicious."

"That's convenient for you," Rek pointed out.

"And more fun," Lux added. "I can't stand the dreary priests with their dreary ritual and their guilt and their hypocrisy."

"Then we go after Rook," Cord said.

"The man who tried to have you kidnapped? Isn't that a bit, I don't know, suicide-y?" I asked.

He shrugged. "The Gentians have a saying. 'Show a man a wolf, and he will run screaming. Make a man a wolf, and he'll piss on your carpet.'"

"What the fuck does that even mean?" Rek asked.

"It means we'll be wolves. And I just ate a bag of asparagus," Cord said.

"How do you know Rook's high society?" I interrupted.

"Because you can't just hire a bunch of assassins with a giant penis and promises. I've tried."

"Wait," I said. "Are you implying you have a giant member?"

"They used to call me Cord the Thick," he said.

"That was in Agrest. And it's because you're a moron," Rek pointed out.

"Thanks, man," Cord said.

"You know an awful lot about politics here for just stepping foot in after a couple decades," I pointed out.

Lux nodded in agreement. Rek found a bag of chilled carrots and crunched one thoughtfully.

"That is kind of weird," Rek said.

"Well, yes," Cord hedged. "About once a month I get messages from a wizard I keep on retainer."

"Aha. Cat's out of the bag, then. What were you, son of nobility? Merchant's kid?" Rek asked.

"Student. Then a soldier, and a prisoner."

I cleared my throat to break up the tension in the room. "What's the Harrower situation like here?"

"Sparse, but they're here, too. They tend to be a little more expensive, so harder to come by. Besides, the cults aren't fond of them, so they like to stay out of sight."

"Tell me about Rook."

Cord shook his head. "I don't know a lot. He's a mover, but most everything he does is obfuscated. There are rumors he was once a thief that used some of his knowledge to move up, but the people spreading those rumors tend to wake up less than alive."

A knock at the door interrupted our conversation, and Lux answered it. A woman in slicked-back hair and well-fitting leather armor stood at the door, a naked blade on her hip. She bowed and extended an envelope, then turned smartly on a heel and left.

Lux brought the envelope over, cracking the seal and reading the contents.

"Well?" I asked.

"An invitation," she said. She handed the letter over to Cord.

"Looks like the decision's been made. Rook is inviting us to dinner tomorrow."

"Trap?" I asked.

"Trapitty trap trap," he said.

"What do we do about it?" Rek asked.

Cord shrugged. "Bring a lot of knives."

"You'll have to be more specific," I said. "Like, is ten too many?"

"Gret's balls Nenn, I said *a lot*. Not 'enough to commit a murder for each day of the week and double on the weekend'."

"Hey. Not all my knives are for murder."

"No?"

"Some are for slicing. Or flaying."

"Have I ever mentioned there isn't at least one day a month you don't scare the shit out of me?"

"Have I ever mentioned that you've got a pretty mouth?"

"What's that even mean?"

"It'd look good with an apple in it."

"Yikes."

"Yes, yikes," Rek conceded.

"You're all just jealous of my knives."

CORD SENT the others ahead to 'procure' a coach for our arrival at Rook's estate. In the meantime, we helped each other into our formal wear—a clean tunic, waistcoat, and trousers for Cord, and a dress with simple skirts, flat shoes, and a whalebone corset for me. I slipped my knives into the garters on my thighs, and two more into the back of the corset, letting the short pearl handles stick out like decor.

I straightened Cord's jacket, brushing off the shoulders while he looked at me, a strange expression on his face.

"What?" I asked.

"I love ya, Nenn."

I smiled. "I know."

"This might be the last one."

"I don't believe that for a second."

He shook his head. "No, really. I think when a god asks for your help, you kind of have to hang it up after that."

"What then?"

"If we live?"

"Whaddya mean, *if?* You can't die."

"I don't know if that's true anymore. That thing with the cult in the valley—when they sacrificed us to Oros—coming back *hurt*. It was like something being pulled out of me. Like losing a piece of myself."

"But I saw you heal at the temple."

"It's slower now."

I fell silent. "Well, fuck."

"Anyway, this is all conjecture. For all I know, the only thing that can kill me is a full-on bonfire. So yeah, if we live? I think I'll go back to the Veldt. Settle down in the country, maybe try my hand at wine-making."

"That seems so... anticlimactic."

He smiled, a little sad. "After you've lived the life I have, anticlimactic is kind of a welcome change."

He took a breath and stepped back, holding out his arms, then spinning. "How do I look?"

"Pretty damn good, for you."

"Fair enough."

Rek opened the door and poked his head in. "We're ready," he said.

We shared a look, and left.

THE CARRIAGE SAT PARKED beside the inn's exit, black-lacquered, with four horses hitched to it. We descended the stairs, crowds already beginning to gather in anticipation of attending the nightly parties. One of their member broke free, a pale man in black robes and a wide-brimmed hat, symbols on chains around his neck. He pointed at Cord and started shouting.

"My god has seen! My god has seen you and weighed your worth!"

"Yeah, well my god can beat up your god!" Cord shouted back.

Cord grinned at Rek, the priest forgotten. "You brought horses!"

"Nearly shit his trousers," Lux muttered.

"They. Are. Terrifying," Rek said.

Cord pet the nose of one. "They're sweet."

"Not my problem if he eats your arm," Rek shrugged.

We climbed into the carriage and in moments, were on our way.

28

EXCUSE ME WAITER, I DIDN'T ORDER THE MURDER

CORD PRESENTED the invitation to the door guard with a flourish.

"Cord and party," he said.

The guard leaned in to inspect it, then glanced up at Cord, then at each of us, suspicion written on his features.

"Problem?" I asked. I hated waiting.

The man sneered down his nose, and pulled out a list attached to a board. "Simply assuring you're *supposed* to be here."

"What the hell does that mean?"

"It means I am the arbiter of taste, and you are a lowly petitioner. You want to play, you gotta play my way first."

"Lemme make a door," Rek said.

"Lemme make a door through this guy," I said, hands itching for my blades.

Lux produced a dove from somewhere within her dress and ripped its head off, popping the skull into her mouth like a fried morsel. The guard turned green as she chewed noisily, but otherwise remained steadfast.

Cord waved us off. "Patience. Some day, probably soon, he'll have horribly violent diarrhea. Right, Lux?"

She grinned through a mouthful of red teeth and feathers.

After what felt like a ridiculously long time, all while other guests tapped their feet and cleared their throats behind us, he waved us through. Lux touched his hand as she passed, and his eyes widened in panic.

"Well, that was insulting," I said.

"All part of the act," Cord said.

"What act?"

"The great play, the grand design. We're new here, so we have to wait. I can guarantee anyone who actually matters would have been waved through with a glance. Instead, we have to deal with the pantomime."

Behind us, the guard cried out in dismay, followed by a loud wet splatter. I smiled to myself and kissed Lux on the cheek on impulse. The interior of Rook's manse was well done. Understated decor with hardwood accents, tasteful hangings, and unobtrusive servants who lurked in the shadows, waiting to cater to your every whim. One such led us to a long, wide hall with parquet flooring, fireplaces flanking each side of the room, and a massive dining table, probably as long as the Codfather. The servant led us to a row of chairs, each with a placard bearing our names, then left.

Lux leaned in. "This is really fancy."

"What is?"

Lux picked up the card, turning it back and forth. "The lettering. I can't tell the font. It must be handmade. And this paper—it's amazing. Thick, but not too thick, good stock, ink doesn't bleed..."

Other groups filtered in, speaking in low tones among themselves. All wore fine clothing, none smelled like shit. Cord once said that's how you could tell the nobles from the common, no matter the clothing. The rich could afford hygiene. Another servant entered from a door at the far end of the room, and rang a small bell, indicating we should take our seats.

We sat, waiting in silence. Cord winked at a tall matron in a silver dress, causing her to roll her eyes so hard I thought they might just pop out. He chuckled softly, and turned his attention toward a small dark man at the end of the table, but before he could cause a scene, the first notes of a song filled the air. We turned to see a young redheaded man in a silk shirt and blossomed-out trousers enter, a lute in his hands. He played a few more notes, then let the lute drop to his side.

"Ladies. Gentlemen. Others. I am your entertainment tonight. My name is Koot, and I aim to inspire and amaze and bewitch."

He lifted the lute again, playing a beautiful series of notes.

"Let me regale you with my tale. When I was but a wee lad, I 'twas the smartest around."

Another set of notes.

"I killed a king and made the world weep."

More music.

"I am a master pugilist and a cunning linguist, my tongue as deadly as my fists. Ladies."

Another set of notes.

"My will is like iron, my rod is like wood, and my skill with a lute literally unbelievable."

This went on for a while. When he finished, the group applauded quietly, and he bowed, stepping from the room, but not before throwing me a wink.

"I think someone's trying to bugger you, Nenn." Cord leaned in and whispered conspiratorially.

"From that display, I'd be willing to bet he buggers himself quite enough."

Rek snorted at that, blowing a noseful of wine across the

table and onto a fat man in a brocaded jacket. We spent the next five minutes laughing while Rek apologized and servants appeared as if by magic to clean up the mess.

Finally, another bell rang, and the door at the end of the hall opened. A pause, and a man, tall—maybe taller than Rek—his skin alabaster, entered. He wore black clothing, and a black mask fashioned like that of a raven, feathers around the edge. When he spoke, his voice was clear and carried throughout the room, making me think the mask was probably enchanted.

"Friends, welcome. Repast will be served soon. But first, business."

He raised a hand, and servants appeared behind almost half the chairs, glittering knives in their hands. I tensed, and tried to feel any presence behind me at all.

"Ohshitohshitohshit," I whispered.

Rook's hand came down, and the servants quickly and effortlessly slit the throats of their charges, blood spraying out in a hot gurgling wave, coating every inch of the table. The smells of shit and piss filled the air as the newly dead voided their bowels. Just as quickly as they'd come, the servants disappeared, leaving the bodies to slump forward in their places.

Rook surveyed the room, then turned his mask our way. "You four. With me."

We stood and followed as he led us through the door. The room beyond was a simple stone room, devoid of anything but another door at the far end. Two Leashmen entered from the other side. Servants moved to close and block both, appearing from the shadows again, and I wondered at that ability. I thought it would be especially handy in situations like this, when I felt something hard and sharp pressed against my spine.

Rook turned and regarded us.

"I need three of you. No more. You choose. The other stays as my guest."

"For what?" Why? What the actual fuck is happening?" Cord asked.

"I'd like to know as well," I said. "For future reference."

"I think she means so she can stab you later," Cord clarified.

"Thanks, man," I said.

Rook's eyes glittered behind his mask, and he spoke again.

"You left something behind in the Hollow Hills," he said.

Cord's look sharpened, a man on the edge of glaring daggers. "How do you know that?"

"I know a great many things. I have friends. Some who share information willingly. Some... share it anyway. All I need is for you to return there and retrieve it. In the meantime, your friend will stay, to ensure you return."

"And if I don't?"

"I would think fire would do for your friend. But this one," he tipped his head to indicate me, "I think a knife in the back should work as well."

Cord looked around. I could see him calculating odds, making decisions, jaw hard and tight. Finally, he slumped.

"Nenn, Rek—you're with me." He looked over at Lux. "Behave. Don't, I don't know, burn the entire fucking city down when I'm gone."

He gave a wink and spun on his heel, and Rek and I followed. I hated Lux behind— and not just for the obvious reasons. I'd come to love our little family, and splitting it up put a splinter of ice in my gut that was damned hard to ignore.

"Six days, Cord," Rook called after us.

———

CORD LED US OUT, a disgusted look in his eyes. He ushered us past the guards and into the street, the carriage long since sent on its way—before the local constables could trace its theft to us.

"I know that look," I said.

"Power," he spat. "It's always about power with these assholes. They amass more money than they can spend in several lifetimes. They find themselves isolated from anyone who might do them good, because they don't trust anyone, because greed has told them that everyone wants what they have. So they get bored. And because they don't know humanity anymore, it no longer holds value for them."

We stopped in the street, and I looked at the Rek. "Go on. Get the boat ready. I think we need to walk around for a while."

Cord nodded, and Rek left, making his way down the street. When he'd turned a corner, I took Cord to the side.

"Does this city have any parks?"

He blinked. "Odd time to sightsee."

"Sure. I like flowers."

"Huh."

"What?"

"I had always pegged you as more of a burnt-out brewery type of person."

We'd started walking again, and I slugged him in the shoulder. "I like pretty things."

"Mmm," he said.

We walked the streets for a while, passing tall lamps on poles, yellow stones inside glowing gently. A soft mist sprung up, bringing the scents of pine and the ocean in a mixture that cleansed the smells of blood and shit from my nose.

A figure approached through the mist, staggering slightly, the lute in his hand clutched by its neck. His red hair shone in the light of the streetlamps, and as he drew close, a grin plastered itself across his face. I groaned.

"Ah, milady!" he called, hurrying over to us. "I had hoped to meet you here."

"Don't you have a sorority to raid somewhere?" Cord asked.

"Another snipe like that, and I'll show you my fearsome skill," the youth bragged.

"Is that your skill with your left or right hand? Surely you don't use both. I don't believe your weapon is large enough," Cord replied.

"Silence, cad! I have bested knaves twice your size and thrice your wit," the young man said.

He lifted one hand, the palm flattened, and chopped the edge into Cord's neck. Cord blinked and looked at me. I shrugged, and he turned back to the redhead, slamming his fist into the kid's nose. The youth staggered back, a fountain of red spraying from his hands, his lute forgotten on the ground as he attempted to staunch the flow of blood.

"My face! Alas, my visage shattered!"

Lute abandoned, the boy began to weep, fleeing for the quay. We watched as he climbed the stones, standing over the sea as it crashed around him.

"My heart is struck in twain! Dehna!" he shouted before jumping from the wall and disappearing.

"Holy shit," I said. "That was dramatic."

"It's fine. There's a beach on the other side. When he sobers up, he'll be back to annoying everyone in a fifty-mile radius," Cord said.

We turned another corner, and found ourselves in a small wooded area in the center of the city, neat grasses and carefully cultivated flowers planted at the borders. The mist and the late hour cleared the visitors out, and we found a bench under the spreading branches of a sturdy oak.

"Okay," I said. "Talk."

He shrugged. "I hate the way the world chews people up. I

hate the way the rich, the powerful rape and take and nothing ever happens to them."

I shook my head. "It's more than that. You've been... different since Midian."

He laughed. "Yeah. Wow. That got out of control. Wraiths, who woulda thought?"

"You said that."

He fell quiet, looked off into the trees. When he finally spoke, it was subdued.

"I feel like I'm tumbling from thing to thing, and just barely fucking holding on to a thread that keeps slipping through my hands. When I do manage to grasp it, it moves so fast it cuts and bleeds."

He looked up to the black spire towering over the city. "You know what that is?"

"Mage tower?" I guessed.

He shook his head. "Prison. I spent four years there. It's a rough place. Gangs, lunatics, rogue wizards, fuck knows what else. They put the worst up top. That way, if they think of escaping, they have to work their way down or jump. No one's tried either, yet."

"Anyway, I saw the worst of humanity in there. Inmates and guards. I saw men bleed out over simple things—an apple at lunch, the wrong word spoken. I saw guards beat a man so badly he'd never walk again. I saw a lot of injustice, too. People in for simple offences beside murderers. Men who couldn't afford to pay whatever tax the local lord came up with that week."

"In there, you have two choices, Nenn. You either live like an animal—you just survive, moving by basic instinct—or you find that spark of humanity they've tried to take away, and you nurture it. You make yourself better. Because the people that put you in there don't care if you ever are. They just care that you're no longer their problem."

I let him talk for a while, then we fell into another silence.

"So, this Rook. What does he want?"

"An artifact. Once upon a time, we'd explored the Hills, and we found a ruin. And in the ruin, something we felt was better kept there."

"Which was?"

"Camor's eye."

"Wait, you found the eye of a god, and you just left it there?"

"It was really icky."

"You declined godlike power for 'icky'?"

"Hey, it's also a lot of responsibility."

I looked at him for a long moment. "Good point. Okay, well, we have to be responsible now."

"Then can we burn this fucking city down?"

"Sure. I'll even buy you a cake after."

WE CLIMBED ABOARD THE CODFATHER. Rek watched us board, and inclined his head.

"Good talk?"

"Good enough," I said.

Cord went below deck to get some rest, and I took the bench behind Rek as we pulled from the lagoon and swung east.

"Six days, huh?" Rek asked.

"Yeah."

"Gonna have to use the engine, aren't we?"

"Yeah."

"That'll suck."

I lit a cigar, blew a plume of smoke, and watched his cats play. "Fuck yeah."

29

AS FUN AS A GENITAL PAPERCUT

A FEW HOURS LATER, I crawled up from my cabin into the bright moonlight. Rek had retired, and Cord stood at the wheel. For a while, I stood on the deck and listened to the wind snap the sails, the water rush against the hull. Finally, Cord called to me.

"Nenn."

I climbed the stairs to the quarterdeck, and took the bench behind him. Rek's cats disappeared, presumably making their way below deck to toy with mice, curl up in cabins, and generally be a nuisance, albeit out of the way.

"When are we starting the engine?" I asked. I knew it had to be soon.

Cord looked up at the moon. "First light. As soon as Rek's ready to navigate. Even I'm not comfortable slipping into the deadlands in the dark."

We sat in silence until light flooded the east. I played with my knives, spinning and sharpening, until Rek stomped from below deck, followed by a small herd of cats. He yawned and stretched, then unpacked a small meal for us on the bench—

hard biscuits, dried fish, a pungent cheese, and skins of mild wine that helped kick the senses a little alive. We ate for a while in silence, and when we finished, Cord and I smoked while Rek took the wheel.

"If we're gonna do this, let's get it over with," Rek said.

Cord shrugged and motioned for me to follow. We descended to the cargo hold, stepping lightly around barrels of supplies and random loot we'd amassed. The engine sat at the far end, as horrific as ever.

Scratch that. I as I drew closer, I saw Lux had been busy. The engine still held a beating heart at its center, but arrayed around it in glass jars connected by what looked like thick veins were more hearts, at least twenty in all. I pointed at them.

"Do I want to know where you got all of these?"

"Probably not."

"I don't suppose they were donated."

"Let's just say the owners weren't using them anymore."

I noticed another change—a lever set just a foot or two in front of the machine.

"Now this, this is good," I said. "Don't need a wizard to unfuck this thing."

"You'd hope," Cord said, and before I could respond, threw the switch.

The rings on the engine spun, and the hearts beat in time, suddenly loud as hooves on stone. The world went gray, the sides of the boat becoming transparent. Colors began to bleed and stream around us, and the world elongated.

"Coooooooord," I said, my words strung out. "Whaaaaaat the fuuuuuuuuck?"

"Luuuuuuuux caaaaaalled iiiiiiiiit tuuuuuuuuuuurbo."

Strains of haunting music played from somewhere unseen, and outside, scenes from worlds I couldn't begin to recognize. I moved my hand, and the image blurred, stretched in front of my eyes, and then snapped back to itself. I giggled involuntarily. At least until Cord started singing.

"Neath the eaves
Black as night
Slips the shadow
Of the wight
On its shoulder
Raven black
On its skull
Eye of black
Red of tooth
Long of claw
The fox god
Watches all"

By the end, he was screaming the verse, and I clapped my hands over my ears. Above, Rek howled at the wheel as the world came undone. Cord screamed and wrenched on the lever, and the world suddenly *stopped*, slamming into quiet focus with the force of a hammer blow to the skull. We collapsed, and for a time, lay on the boards of the hull, stunned. Finally, I stood, and helped Cord up.

"That woman is a genius," Cord said. "Bent, but a genius!"

"When we get back, if Rook hasn't killed Lux, remind me to," I said.

We climbed above deck. Rek greeted us with a wide-eyed stare and a nod. Had he any hair, it would have been standing on end. He just blinked, walked calmly to the rail, and vomited his entire breakfast. When he was done, he took the wheel and steered us as close to shore as he could. A series of hills rose to the south.

"Nice job," Cord said, and clapped Rek on the back.

The big man swiveled his head and fired a stream of puke onto Cord. He coughed once, and grinned.

"Thanks."

30

IN WHICH I MAKE FUN OF IDIOTS

WE'D BEEN FORTUNATE. Just a mile down the shore, masts and hulls clotted the river, the exodus from Midian brought to a halt by the sudden onset of cold and a narrowing of the banks. The air took on a chill since our own flight, and as we disembarked, we kept watch for signs of wraiths.

It was a four-hour hike to the ruins where Cord had found the eye. We fell into a companionable silence for most of it, content to walk in one another's company without the need to fill it with nonsense. I suppose that was the way with friends. You grew comfortable enough with one another to not feel the need to fill the dull moments with useless speech.

A wind kicked up, and an eerie howl echoed through the landscape, like a pack of lost wolves. The hair on the back of my neck rose, and I tensed.

"What the fuck was that?" I asked.

"The hills," Rek said.

We crested a rise, and I saw the reason for the sound. Holes riddled each hole, and as the wind blew, it kicked up the moaning, like an oboe gone wrong.

"Holy shit. I thought it was ghosts." I said.

Cord laughed. "There's no such thing."

I paused and grabbed him by the arm. "Hold the fuck up."

"What?"

"You don't believe. In ghosts."

Cord shrugged. "Ever seen one?"

I frowned. "No, but that doesn't mean they don't exist. What about goblins? I've never seen a goblin, but that doesn't mean they don't exist."

"She's got a point," Rek said.

"Oh yeah?" Cord said.

"Yeah," I said.

He pointed toward an object nearby. "Then what's that?"

I turned and looked. It was a squat humanoid with green warty skin, a crooked hooked nose and large yellow eyes. It watched us while clutching a short spear in one hand. It wore brown rags and oversized shoes.

"A goblin?"

"Right. They exist."

I opened my mouth to argue further with him, when the goblin called out in a crackling voice. "Bro!"

"Ah shit," Rek said.

"What?"

"You'll see," Cord said.

The goblin approached, spear held out cautiously, until it was only a few feet away.

"Bro?"

"Why's it keep saying that?" I asked.

"Well actually," it said.

"Kill it now," Rek said.

The goblin frowned and took an aggressive stance, steadily advancing with its spear. I backed up a step.

"Well actually, bro," it said, speech becoming agitated. "Bro, actually. Well, bro."

"Eek!" I said, and flung a knife at it.

The blade flipped once and embedded in the goblin's skull, sinking to the hilt. The goblin dropped, and I pulled the knife free, wiping bits of blood and a shockingly small amount of gray matter on its robes.

"Their heads are surprisingly soft," I noted.

Rek nodded, trying to speak over Cord's laughter. "Wel'ctually goblins. The most annoying tribe the gods ever dropped onto the Veldt."

I put the blade away, and we advanced up another hill. In the valley below, a large group of the goblins gathered, and we heard their annoying speech as a jumbled mess from our vantage point. Cord pointed just past them.

"Ruin's there."

I saw a small temple, four decaying walls, and a collapsed roof. It didn't look like much. He pointed again, and I followed the new line he'd traced out.

"But it looks like they did our work for us."

A totem stood in the middle of the goblin swarm, a tall brown thing in the approximation of a man. Its face was nondescript, though where one eye should have been carved, a wet glistening orb stood out. Even from this distance, we could smell what they'd made it from.

"What's the plan?" I asked.

"No plan," Cord said.

"Yep, no plan. Goblins suck," Rek replied, unlimbering the axe from his back.

"Fuck," I breathed, and pulled two of my longer blades out.

Without waiting, Rek leapt from the crown of the hill. For a moment, he hung in the air, like a thrown brick, then like a thrown brick, fell among the goblins. His axe rose and fell in workmanlike strokes and goblin screams filled the air.

"ACTUALLY!" they yelled as one, and charged him.

I slipped down the hill while they were distracted by the big man dicing them up like particularly aggressive vegetables. I reached the back of the line and began to cut my way forward, blades ripping open kidney and spine, skull and groin. They fell like wheat before a scythe, and in a matter of minutes, any remaining were groaning on the ground, or fleeing for the relative safety of anywhere but here. Rek wiped the gore from his face and shook his axe clean.

"Okay, Nenn," he said. "Grab the eye."

I gave him a look with one eye squinted, and reached into the dung heap, pulling the orb free with a squelch. It was warm, and I had the distinct feeling it was trying to see me. I hurried back to Cord, Rek in tow, and tossed it to him. He caught it easily, and washed it off with his waterskin. He inspected it for a long minute, then held it up to his own.

"I have an idea," he said.

"This sounds like a terrible idea," I replied.

"You haven't even heard it yet."

"No, she's right. This is a terrible idea," Rek agreed.

"Fine," Cord sighed.

He lowered the eye, then with a quick motion, ripped his own out. His scream echoed across the hills, putting even the low moaning to shame. Before he could collapse, he shoved Camor's eye into the now-empty socket. The optic nerve squirmed and twitched, then sucked the dangling orb into his skull.

"HOLY SHIT," I said. "You fucking lunatic."

Rek coughed once, a hard, wet sound. "Bleurgh," he agreed.

"Okay. Okay, that wasn't my best idea," Cord said.

"How does it feel?"

"Got a hell of a headache."

"Yeah, but any godly stuff going on?"

Cord shrugged. He pointed at a goblin's body. "RISE," he commanded.

A low ripping sound came from the corpse, followed seconds later by a horrid stink. Cord coughed and waved it away.

"Nope."

I shook my head. "Let's get back to the boat, before you conjure something more disgusting."

WE'D JUST CLEARED the hollow hills when the first of the wights crested behind us. They were preceded by their own wave of sound, setting the hair on the back of our necks on end and gooseflesh rippling. Rek looked behind us, and broke into a trot.

"Where's he going?" Cord asked.

I glanced back and joined Rek. "Wights," I shot over my shoulder.

"Whites?" Cord glanced back. "Oh."

He broke into a run as well, though trailing a little.

"Slow down," he panted.

"So they can kill us all at once?" Rek asked.

"Just enough to distract them."

I flipped him the bird and put on speed, pulling ahead of the two of them. I glanced back and saw the first row of wights gained ground, long alabaster limbs thrashing in their effort to catch us. Black eyes gleamed in the sun.

"If that eye can do something, maybe make it do it now," I shouted.

Cord puffed a curse and spun. He planted himself in the path of the wraiths, and stuck out his chest.

"Fuck off, the lot of ya!" he shouted.

They gained ground, and he blanched. Rek and I paused, Rek unlimbering his axe.

"Ohfuckohfuckohfuck," Cord spat. "Thinkthinkthinkthink."

"Cord!" I shouted.

The wights gained ground yet again, the closest within arm's reach. It drew back a claw to swipe at the stocky thief when he pointed.

"LOOK OUT BEHIND YOU," he bellowed.

A roar sounded from the hills, and the wights turned as one. Something--something enormous and prehistoric in its size rose from the crest of the hill, jaws open and slavering. Ivory teeth the length of a man's arm jutted in savage rows in its mouth. Above that, a snub nose and yellow eyes and a crest of spines running down its massive body. It screeched, shattering the relative quiet of the hills, and unfolded massive membranous wings.

The wights scattered as it launched itself into the air, a deep intake of breath sounding like a massive bellows. Cord stared at it a moment in shock. I grabbed his collar, yanking him along with us as Rek and I sprinted away.

"What the actual fuck, Cord?"

"I don't actually fucking know," he replied.

"Typical," Rek rumbled.

We ran for some distance before I risked a glance back to see both the sky and the plain were empty. I paused, snaking an arm around Cord. Rek skidded to a halt alongside us. We peered around at the now-silent hills.

"Huh," Cord said.

"Understatement of the year," Rek said.

"Holy shit. You didn't fuck that up," I said.

"I stand corrected," Rek said.

Cord just grinned and turned, making his way back to the boat. After a moment of stunned silence, Rek and I followed.

WE REACHED the boat by late afternoon. Three days already passed, and we were just getting started back. We knew we'd have to use the engine once more, and no one was happy about it. Rek pulled the ship into the current, and we drifted west, Cord and I entering the cargo hold to inspect the engine.

It sat as it usually did, squat and menacing. The hearts chained to it looked scorched, but still beat in their containers. The central heart however, was blackened and useless.

"Fuck!" Cord swore.

"What now?"

Cord shifted from foot to foot. I could tell he was keeping something from me.

"Spit it out," I said, finally.

"We'll need Rek's heart."

"Why Rek?"

"Because he'll come back."

"We can't just go cutting hearts out every time the engine dies."

"I beg to differ. Why not your heart?" I asked.

"I have the eye. Besides, it's me Rook's expecting."

"He's expecting the eye." I fingered my blades and Cord backed up a step.

He raised his hands. "Now is not the time to go around dismembering people. Look, I didn't want it to come to this, but here—" he drug a bloodied sack from behind a crate. It smelled like three-week old carcass.

"What. Is. That."

"Goblin hearts."

"Oh, all fucking right."

We got to work. Rek had collected about ten of the things, and with a little thread and a lot of gore, we were able to stitch them into the engine. We stepped back, looking at our handiwork.

"Looks like someone made a meat atrocity."

That's the idea," Cord winked. He called up the stairs. "Ready?"

Rek's voice echoed back. "Fuck no."

Cord shrugged and pulled the lever.

The world flicked and went to black. In its place, a new world flickered in being, lives never lived and only half-seen in dreams.

———————

CAMOR FLICKERED INTO MY VISION. A flame, then a body without substance. Their voice echoed as if from a distance.

"What I'm going to show you is the last secret of Oros, Nenn."

"Why not Cord?"

Camor sighed. "I love him, but he needs guidance. He needs a reason. You are that reason. Should he falter, tell him this story."

They faded without further discussion, and worlds opened before me.

The barbarian tribes that fled from the icy northern corridors named him when the first of the green things took their flesh and fed on it, verdant life thriving on carmine vitality. *Oros*. It was a fitting name, brutish and short in their language, the glottal stop hard on throats burned with spore and bitter liquid from the trees they tapped for water. They sat around their camps and heard it in the buzz of flies in the soft decay of the greenery and other, wetter things. The vines that strangled their children in cribs fashioned from leaf and branch spelled it out in twisting sign. It was there in the sound of rain pounding the broad leaves of the canopy, *OrosOrosOrosOros*. He was the whisper and the shout, the choke and the crush. He was pervasive and insidious, and now, he was perplexed.

Behind the veil of flies, beneath a crown of wizened thorns, his brow wrinkled. He stared at the child in confusion. She was small, curly hair spiraling out from her scalp in a whirlwind, her gaze fierce. For all her size, she held herself as someone not to trifle with. She leaned back on the mat of vines she co-opted, shooing the scuttering and slithering things away.

"Who *are* you?" he asked, his voice like the sound of kudzu in silence, a creeping, creaking thing.

He had no recollection of her entering, none of her sitting. She simply seemed to *be*, and it was disconcerting, even for a thing like himself. She tilted her head to one side and tipped the end of the staff she held toward him. For a moment, she looked older than her few years, though he dismissed it as a trick of the light, chiaroscuro deepening lines and shading flesh until she looked a woman.

"Your end." It was a statement, said plain and clear in the dark of that place, and not for a moment did Oros believe it. This was flesh, pink and soft and warm. His was the cold of the night, the dark of the cave, the heat of venom. He relaxed into his throne, the black wood creaking under his weight, and smiled behind his veil. He would entertain her. It had been so long since anyone visited. So long since the last of the beasts bent the knee at his foot, since the green consumed his thought and action. He thought maybe he would entertain this small pink thing, and in return, perhaps she would entertain him. He let her words hang in the air, and when he didn't reply, she went on.

"Would you like to hear a story, Eater?"

He flinched at the name. Though he held no love for the

fleshlings that found their way to his jungle, their hatred still stung. *Eater* was their way of deriding him, of reducing him to a maw that only consumed. Mindless, small. He swallowed the rage that boiled up and raised a magnanimous hand in assent. The girl settled herself into the vines, thrusting her staff into the ground beside her. She leaned forward, elbows on her knees, and spoke.

"My family was the last to come over the shelf- the place where the ice meets the warmer places of the world. We were five - mother, father, sister, brother, and myself. At my birth, the ice was close, but not too close. It hovered on the edge of our village, but there was still room for us to move, to get to the caribou and rabbit and fill our larders. That year, the ice moved a few feet closer, but it seemed a warm summer. My parents named me Elysh, 'hope' in the language of our people. There's a unique cruelty in that - naming a child something that means nothing in a broken world. The ice claimed my brother that winter. He was out tracking rabbits. He didn't come back."

A spark of envy lit in Oros's chest. Death was his demesne. The right to pluck life, pink and squalling from the green and crush it. A question formed on his lips.

"Who is your god?"

She paused. "Was. Rhyn, the White. The Cold Knife."

"Was?"

"Even the ice took him, in time."

Satisfaction rose in Oros's chest, replacing the envy. Hubris was unfortunate, but necessary to survival for those who knew its signs. It was an abject lesson in the ways of men and gods— become comfortable, become complacent, and you soon found that power turning inward, eating, chewing at bone and sinew until it reached your heart and stopped it cold. He would do neither. These pink things, these scaled and green things, obeyed. They feared. They trembled on the cold fringes of night. As they should. He raised his hand again, indicating she should go on.

"When we saw the fringes of the jungle, we rejoiced. Here was shelter from the dead brown lands between the shelf and the sea. Here was life, abundant. Here was survival and warmth," she spat, and Oros tasted it through the vines. Salty, thick. He wondered if she would be enough to feed his vines when she finished.

"And what did you find, little one?"

"More death. Our father was next. He climbed a tree to pull at the gourds there—great yellow things with thick shells - we suspected they contained perhaps meat or water. Instead, a thousand stinging bodies emerged, piercing his flesh. He screamed as he fell, his body swelling with their venom, his eyes mercifully shut to the horror of impact."

"My mother wept for four days, and in that time, my sister wandered to the edge of our camp. Something cold and slithering, something black of scale and sharp of tooth took her. She never screamed. After, my mother took her own life, cutting her own throat with a sharpened piece of flint."

Oros snorted. "This is less a story, and more a recounting of your unfortunate genealogy."

It was Elysh's turn to hold up a hand. "You wish to hear a story, or prattle on like an old man?"

The girl's bravado impressed him. He thought it interesting to see someone so small embrace what would surely be a tragic legacy. "And how did you survive?"

"There is another story you must hear to understand mine."

Layers on layers, like a wasp's nest—despite himself, Oros leaned forward in his chair, and even the black flies that swarmed and buzzed for his veil stilled while he listened.

"In my homeland, they tell the tale of Huska. When he was perhaps no older than myself, he joined a ship's crew hoping to learn the sea, of feeding his family, and making some coin. He was young, but strong, and in his own way, clever. So, he found a home on a small vessel and set out among the fjords.

"It was three days they were at sea when the first of storms hit. Though the captain was good, he was also greedy, and hoped to fill his pockets before the frost came that season. The snow and wind blew in great gales, and ice seized the hull in a matter of hours, like the fist of Rhyn punishing a heretic. For a time, spirits were even—they had provisions and whale oil for a week. Everyone agreed to cut rations, to light the lanterns only when needed. For a time, they were fine, if cold."

"They were there for four weeks. The depredations that happened in that third week—Huska would not speak of them, but when the boat returned, he was at the helm, and a mass of burned bones lay in the ship's furnace. He was hale and hearty."

Oros was enraptured. "What happened?"

"I heard my father ask him, when he was well into his cups. Huska looked up from his drink and shrugged. 'Meat is meat,' he said."

Oros looked at the girl, at her pink skin and full limbs. At her sharp eyes and white teeth. His hand trembled a little. This he understood, eating, devouring—but not family.

"Why are you here?" the question nearly rose to a shriek.

She tipped her staff again, and this time, he heard the slosh of liquid. He turned his gaze on it and noticed a gourd attached to the top, liquid spilling clear. It tasted oily to his vines, wicked and sharp. He willed them into action, but they lay still, perhaps in fear, perhaps poisoned.

"To end you," she replied, again as matter-of-fact as stating that the sun was hot, or the wind chill.

She tipped her staff again, and he saw it was bone lashed to bone, long femurs held together with vine. Liquid poured from the gourd—a wasp home, he thought—and brought the sharp smell again.

"There are no whales here."

Her statement took him off guard.

"You might ask why they didn't use the lanterns to melt the ice. Whale blubber doesn't burn that hot. It would have been a waste."

She tipped the staff again.

"But this—what a gift. Something the wasps leave behind when they abandon the nest."

She lay the staff down and the last of the liquid dripped and pooled at her feet. From her tunic she withdrew two stones and knelt. She struck them together, bringing a spark and the acrid smell of smoke. She looked up at him, and horror filled his heart. He struggled to escape his throne, but vines grown long and strong and old in his complacency held him in place. He fought, commanding them to free him, but they only slept. She struck the stones again, and a flame blossomed, and he gibbered. It was so *bright*. *So hot*.

As the flame touched them, the vines withered and smoked, and fire crept along their length, reaching blazing fingers toward his crown. He screamed and screamed again. Through the flames, he saw the girl, flesh melting like tallow from her bones, grinning.

———

I BLINKED as the world slipped into focus again, the hull of the Codfather regaining solidity. Cord looked at me, and pushed his hair back.

"Okay, goblin hearts make things weird."

We went above deck, Rek greeting us with a raised eyebrow.

"That was less fucked up than normal."

The Codfather sat in the same spot we'd departed from, just outside Orlecht. We gathered on the quarterdeck, wind in our hair, the world eerily quiet, aside from the call of gulls and the occasional splash of a wave.

"Rek, I need you to stay here," Cord said.

"What? Why?"

"Because he doesn't plan on coming back," I said.

Cord nodded. "And if everything goes to shit, you and Nenn need to get out alive. I owe you that much for dragging you into this."

Rek looked like he might argue, then with a heavy sigh, nodded, and sat on the bench, drawing Mr. Meowington into his lap. Cord turned to me.

"Ready?"

"I thought you wanted me to live."

"I do."

We jumped in the rowboat and Rek lowered us, Cord taking us to shore.

"Got any pithy Gentian sayings for this one?" I asked.

"A man on fire doesn't ask why. He simply screams until he can't," Cord said.

"That's... morbid."

"Yeah, they're a dour people. Just really miserable. Want to hear a Gentian joke?"

"Do I have to?"

"Trust me, it's the worst."

"Try me."

"The king of Gentia is riding through the woods with his hunting crew and on that day, they were out hunting elk. All of a sudden, a naked beggar comes running through the forest and sees the king and his hunters, throws his hands up in the air, waves them around and starts screaming, "Don't shoot! I'm not an elk! I'm not an elk!" And the king raises his bow and shoots the beggar dead. The prince taps the king on the shoulder and says, "Your Majesty, why did you shoot that beggar? He was screaming 'I'm not an elk!'" And the king replies, "Ohhhhh, I thought he was saying, 'I'm an elk! I'm an elk!'"

"Thanks, I hate it."

Cord chuckled. "Ready to have some fun?"

"Fun, huh?" I asked.

"The most," he said, and his eye glittered.

31

THAT'S A FILTHY JOKE, YOU DICKHEAD

THERE'S AN OLD SAYING. It goes something like 'man makes plans, and the gods laugh, then burn them down, piss on the ashes, then mix them with shit and paint the walls with the leftovers'. Or something like that. Cord told me once, but he was drunker than six sailors, so he may have gotten carried away.

When we arrived at the docks, one of Rook's pale servants was waiting for us. He handed over a card, then disappeared into the crowd the way they'd been able to slip through shadow. It read one word, in that same calligraphy Lux admired so much at Rook's estate.

BLACKGATE

Cord swore and threw the letter into the sea.

"You know that whole trap thing?" Cord said.

"Yeah?"

"Massive fuckin' trap, Nenn. Trappy McTrapface."

"Gonna walk right into it, aren't we?"

"Yep. But first I have to visit an old friend."

WE FOUND ourselves in a part of town made of squat stone buildings and thatched roofs, the people preferring to stay inside, and the guards out of the street. Cord made his way through the neighborhood with confidence, navigating like a man who knew the stars better than his own hand. The few people on the streets either kept their heads down and hurried by, or slunk through the alleys, eyes averted. Here it was prey or be prey, and our appearance apparently heralded the second instinct.

"Who's this friend?" I asked.

"An old campaigner," Cord said. "He was an officer when I served. He's holding a few things for me. Oh, and he's jumpy, so keep your hands away from those knives."

We stopped in front of a building much like the others in the row, though it bore signs it received better care than the others. The stone walls bore the signs of a recent wash, the thatch on the roof was fresh, and the front door looked like the planks were of a thicker build than others on the street. Cord knocked and waited.

No answer came, and he knocked a second time, this time calling out. "Clane! Open the fuck up, you old pigsticker!"

A small door opened in the door, and a pair of eyes framed by bushy eyebrows peered out.

"Cord? Gret's sack, I thought you were dead sixteen years ago."

"I get that a lot. I need to pick up my belongings."

Clane's eyes widened, and the door opened. He peered both ways down the street and ushered us in. The interior was neat and well maintained, the floors swept, and the ceilings web-free. He slammed and bolted the door after us, then walked to a nearby chair, a pronounced limp in his step.

"You must really be in the shit if you've come home," he said.

"Doing a favor for a friend."

"No shit? Some friend. Who's this?" he jerked his chin at me.

"Nenn," I said.

"Of?"

"Myself," I said.

He grinned. "I like her. Few words. Nice tits."

I glared at him. "Can't I cut him a little?" I asked.

Clane laughed. "I really like her. Got any sisters? About twenty years older than you?"

"Nope. Just me."

"Thank the gods," Cord muttered.

"Your shit's in the closet there," Clane said, pointing to a small room hidden behind a hanging sheet.

Cord swept the sheet aside and after a moment, pulled a large chest out with a grunt. He undid the clasp and started pulling items out. A black leather cuirass. A pair of matched short blades. A pair of bracers, and a matching pair of greaves, and finally, five small orbs, each with a silvery finish.

"Gods above, those were in that chest this whole time?" Clane said.

"Yep. Safest place for them."

"What are they?" I asked.

"Really unpleasant," Cord said.

I helped him into his armor, making sure his swords hung right, attaching the orbs to a harness he pulled from the bottom of the chest. When he was finally geared out, he looked every inch a fearsome warrior. With Cord's face, so it was a bit of a wash. Finally, he reached into the pack he'd been carrying, and removed a sack, handing it to Clane.

"What's this shit?" Clane asked.

He opened the sack, the jingle of coins giving it away.

"Payment for storage. Buy yourself a nice house in the country."

He pulled one more item from his pack, then let it drop. It was a small silver vial.

"Is that the bottle from Midian?" I asked.

Clane cackled. "Always said the fucker's a pack rat."

He stood, and Cord shook his hand. We left the way we'd come in, taking the long way through town. The plan was to hit Blackgate at night, when the guard count would be lowest.

"Hey Nenn," Cord said.

"Yeah?"

"What's brown and sticky?"

"Is this a poop joke?"

"No, really. What's brown and sticky?"

"Rek's dick?"

"A stick, Nenn. A stick. Holy shit. That is fucked up."

"I'm not the one who told the joke."

"You are severely damaged."

"Says the lunatic storming a five-story prison."

"Context matters, Nenn."

32

I SEEM TO BE BLEEDING FROM THE EVERYWHERE

WE HALTED JUST outside the tower. A small army of corpses, armed and armored to the gills were arrayed in neat rows before the gate.

"They really don't want us in there," I said. "Why? I thought he wanted this eye."

"If they kill us, they can just take the eye, and they don't have to fight."

"I hate logic."

"And it hates you."

"What?"

"Never mind. How are we gonna get through this?"

"Cord?" the voice came from the back ranks of the soldiers.

"You're fucking kidding me," I said.

The soldiers shifted, the rows moving like corn in the wind, finally disgorging the owner of the voice. Tug came into view, grinning widely.

"Tug?" Cord said. "What're you doing here?"

"Freelancin' and necromancin'," he said.

"What about your amusement park?" Cord asked.

Tug shrugged. "They unionized."

"The dead. Unionized. For what? An increase in brains?" I asked.

Tug shook his head. "Some bigwig showed up. Jesh? Yosah? Jesah? Said he was their king. Got them all together, had them picket the city."

"So you just left?" I asked.

"Well, not at first. Then someone threw a rock, and well..."

"Well, what?" Cord asked.

"City's dead. Rampaging horde of undead. Had to make a getaway."

"What about Elvis?" I asked.

"Oh, he's uh..."

"Right here," the golem said, hoving into view. He tossed his head toward the undead army, sending his dick eyes wobbling. Cord giggled, and I elbowed him. "They're getting restless, boss," Elvis said.

"Yeah, yeah." He turned back to Cord. "Anyway, what's up?"

"I have to get in there."

"In there? They hired me to keep someone out. That's weird."

"That's me, Tug."

"Well, shit. I can't kill you."

"So you'll let us in?"

Tug rubbed his chin. "They're paying pretty good."

"I'll pay better," Cord said. "I just need you to be a bit flexible."

"Aw man, you know I'm flexible."

"Not that. I need you to slow down anyone who tries to follow."

Tug rubbed his chin again, looked at Elvis. The golem shrugged.

"Whatever," Elvis said.

"Okay," Tug said.

Cord shook his hand, then pulled him into an embrace. He whispered in the necromancer's ear, and when they parted, Tug wore a grin. I assumed Cord just gave him the address of a stash.

"Go on then," Tug said.

Cord nodded, and we passed him, brushing past the undead ranks.

"What'd you tell him?" I asked once out of earshot.

"I told him that if I lived through this, we'd get away to a nice island for a while."

"You know we're probably not going to."

Cord shrugged. "I also told him that if he finds the old man, there's some cash in the closet. Assuming he isn't cut to ribbons first. Clane hates necromancers."

"You're a shit."

"I'm bad at goodbyes."

CORD HAD BEEN RIGHT. The guard station was practically unmanned, and once the acid from Midian ate through the locks "Like shit through a small angry badger", Cord commented, it was little work to cut down the three guards eating their midnight porridge. Cord milled about for a moment, digging through sheaves of papers. Finally, he gave a nod and joined me.

"I'd always thought that shit was going to be the death of someone. Does anyone even know what's in it? The consistency's like ground-up babies."

"See a lot of ground-up babies?"

"Not a *lot*, no."

We made our way up the stairs to the second level and arrived at the landing, opening the door slowly. A long hallway greeted us, lined on each side by cells. At the end was another two doors.

"The one on the right is for the guards. The left are the stairs. Keep an eye out."

I squatted beside the door while he moved to each cell, peering inside, pouring a little dribble of the acid on some, leaving others locked. The ones he freed, he ushered to my end of the hall, where I let them know the way ahead was clear. He came back and stood beside me.

"How is this thwarting Oros' plans?"

"Most of these guys are slated for execution. I let the best of the worst out, to hopefully keep living. Besides, if we create enough chaos, we keep the city guard busy enough to get our friends back."

"And the others?"

He grimaced. "Gren can have them. Some people are just beyond saving."

"I still don't see how this relates outside of that."

"The guard room. Paperwork marked with the seal of the Warden. Every death here is a sacrifice."

I nodded. "All right then. Let's go."

Cord picked up a stone from one of the cells, whipping it at the guard's door. It swung open, disgorging three Harrowers, thin bastards with cruel faces and brown robes. Each held their particular fetish—a severed jaw, a loop of dried intestine, several vertebrae connected by a cord. They raised their hands, a high-pitched whine issuing from their mouths. Cord grinned and pulled one of the orbs from his harness, tossing it lightly.

It crashed to the stones, the globe shattering and causing the Harrowers to leave off their screeching. They leaned in as yellow smoke swirled from the remains, coalescing into a cloud that wrapped itself around their ankles.

"What the fu—"

Something leaped from the miasma, yellow and shaggy. It had teeth the size of small daggers, and claws black as onyx. It ripped the eyes from the first, sending him screaming and spraying blood across his companions as two more of the beasts emerged, ripping bellies and groins open, spilling liters of crimson across the flagstones. Then they were gone, and the room was silent, the Harrowers nothing more than inert meat.

"That was..." I said.

Cord nodded. "Fuckin' awesome, I know."

"I don't know if that's the word I was looking for."

"Spectacular? Astounding?"

"Sure. Not horrifying."

We opened the door on the left and climbed to the next floor.

I COULD TELL you about how we cleared each floor in much the same way. I could tell you about the gore and the horror—things came from that mist I'd rather not remember. Children with flat expanses of skin instead of faces, and where they touched you, your flesh decomposed on the bone. A snake covered in barbs that entered in one end and exited the other in a shower of viscera. A whirring crown of sentient thorns that dismembered its victims limb by limb.

I could tell you about the human guards we put down, blades in their guts or their spines, knives in their eyes, or under their ribs, and into their hearts. About the way a man chokes when blood fills his lungs or clots his airway. About the way piss mixes with blood at a man's last, and everything stinks. About the way some of them wept, pleaded for their mothers or their children or their wives, the sound like a saw on a fiddle, because they knew the last time they'd see them was the last time forever.

I could tell you about how death isn't a glorious or a clean business, but when it comes down to it, some people need to die in order for you to live. About how no one in a story is an extra, how everyone has a life, and no matter whose is snuffed, you were never the star of their story, just the villain. About the small hours years later, when you wake in the night and they stand by your bed, and you can't sleep again for a long while because you're shaking so hard you worry your heart might burst.

I could tell you all these things, but I won't. Because this isn't that kind of story.

WE STOOD on the last floor, and in the center, Rook. Someone finally raised the alarm, and we could hear the pounding of footsteps as cultist and guard came, eager to kill. Lux laid out on a table against the wall, her insides open to the world. Somehow she'd kept her promise to not burn the city down, despite the cost. I thought of a cottage in the country that would stay empty, of fields of gold that would never know our boots. I thought of a dog that would never be pet, and a laugh that would never leave a throat. Rook held a long silver knife in his hand, the edge stained red, his mask impassive. I looked to Lux, and my heart sent up an ache, a perfect silver note of sorrow. That note turned sour, and rage blossomed in my chest like the spark of a wildfire. I flicked a glance at Cord.

"Hold the door."

He nodded and stood before it, blades still slick with the deaths before. I held my own knives akimbo, and Rook watched as I approached.

"You've chosen poorly, Cord," Oros' voice echoed from behind the mask.

"He usually does," I said.

"I usually do," Cord agreed over his shoulder.

Rook tilted his head like a bird.

"Hey Cord. This asshole thinks he's a bird."

"Really? What kind?"

"Some sort of fuckwarbler, I think."

Rook feinted, and I stepped back. He tilted his head to the other side as the door burst open. The sounds of battle began, Cord cutting would-be complications down as they tried to enter.

"You know what we do with birds, Nenn."

"Yep. Gut 'em, roast 'em, and eat 'em."

I moved forward, bringing the blades around with a series of quick jabs, forcing Rook back. The sounds of battle ebbed for a behind me as my focus narrowed.

"You know what I miss, Nenn?" Cord asked.

"Not having to deal with insane dickbags every weekend?"

I moved to Rook's right and swept a blade out, watching for him to duck. When he did, I brought the second up and under his mask, cutting it away from him face. It peeled off, along with a line of flesh, and I stepped back in sharp recognition.

"Holy fucking shitballs," I said. "Ferd?"

Rook stood before me, unmasked. A ragged scar ran from one side of his neck to the other, a souvenir from our encounter in Tremaire. It made sense why he hadn't used his magic against us since our last encounter. I'd damaged his ability to create the Harrower sound, and he'd broken it completely calling his spider mount.

"Ooh, nice twist," Cord called out as a second group of cultists approached.

The former Harrower's face twisted in rage, and he lunged at me, blade out.

There are moments you have to make a decision. You know the big ones, because time seems to slow, like the universe is giving you a chance. Left or right. Up or down. Life or death. I saw the blade coming for my ribs, and knew that if this went on much longer, I'd likely die of old age before I killed this dickhead. As Cord had taught me over the years, sometimes you have to make the wrong decision for the right outcome. I moved into the blade. I immediately regretted it because holy shit, a knife in the ribs hurts, but it got me close and trapped his weapon, and that was what counted.

I winced and heard myself cry out, then slammed both my blades into his skull with a crack of bone and a scalding rush of blood. I let the hilts go, and his knife clattered to the floor as it fell from nerveless fingers. Ferd followed, boneless. He hit the stone with the finality of a single drumbeat.

"Did you get him?" Cord asked.

I kicked the body. "Yeah."

"Is he dead for sure this time?"

I pulled another blade from my tunic and rammed it into his spine. "Extra dead, yeah."

Cord came to stand beside me. He looked tired, and blood covered him from head to toe.

"Holy shit," I said.

"Don't worry. Most of it's mine."

"That eye didn't do much, did it?"

"You think *I* did all that? I'm good, Nenn, but I'm a terrible soldier. That's why I gave it up. I mean, look."

I saw the gaping hole in his ribs where a blade opened him like a pig for slaughter. He staggered to the window, pushing me along until he'd forced me to the sill. I heard another round of boots coming up the stairs. Cord left a good-sized pile of bodies behind, but it wouldn't slow them for long. He pulled another globe from an inside pocket and grinned.

"Get the fuck out of here," he said.

Far below, in a small courtyard, a pool of water shimmered. I turned back.

"What about you?"

"We'll be fine. You know how it is. Hard to kill." he paused. "Almost forgot."

He rummaged around in his tunic, pulling out a small wooden object. I took it, and saw it was a dick-shaped whistle.

"If you ever need me, just whistle. You know how to whistle, right?"

"You're the worst."

"Yeah, but you love me."

"I do."

I looked down, at the water far below, and wondered how many bones I'd break. I wondered if my heart would recover. I wondered what would happen if I missed the water, and none of that mattered anyway. Just a splat on the stones some poor pimple-faced kid had to shovel up while puking in the bushes. My hands trembled, and I almost slipped. Cord brought me back to the present.

"Hey Nenn?"

"Yeah, Cord?"

"I still like the Kingkillers."

"Yeah, me too."

The din of voices broke into the room, angry cries and threats. Cord chuckled once and gave me a wink, eye glittering, and I felt something in the air, like a powerful gaze turned our way. He shoved me. Not long after, a great explosion came from above, the stones of the tower blasting outward, and I was fall-ing, falling, and then—black.

33

I AM NOT PUTTING MY LIPS ON THAT

I'D LIKE to say I know how this story ends. I know how *that* story ends. Rek pulled me from the water. He was terrible about taking orders, and I was thankful for it. Fire gutted the tower, but worse, the loss of half my family gutted me. We spent some time sailing down aimless tributaries while I recovered, but after six weeks of moping about, Rek finally picked a direction and sailed us toward gods knew what, guiding the boat from the river to the sea.

I'm not sure there's a lesson here. Maybe it's don't steal. Maybe it's don't make friends with strangers in bars. Maybe it's never trust a god. But to be honest, following those rules never made life any more interesting. What did was the little family I'd made what felt like a thousand miles and years ago. We were the worst kind of people. For the best reasons. We understood that, even if no one else did.

I recalled a conversation Cord and I had that first night away from Midian. I'd asked him how dooming an entire country to a long hard winter because its ruler was a tyrant made sense in light of Camor's first rule. He said it was because even if he didn't wish harm on the Veldt's people, they failed it as much as Mane had. You didn't suffer tyrants to place their boot on your neck, to hold you down in the mud. You fought back. Even if the last bit of mud was made from spilled blood, you fought. To do anything less was a disservice to the gift of life given to you.

He'd said something then, and it stuck with me, lodging in my brain like a knife in the heart. "Love is simple, Nenn. The truth isn't. Sometimes you have to draw a little blood to wake the dreamer."

That was Camor's second rule. The third? Cord never told me that one. Gods were ineffable, after all.

When I described that to Cord, he just winked.

"You'd think that," he said, and laid on the deck with his hands folded behind his head.

I felt a bemused expression cross my face and wondered if he knew what that word meant. I decided it didn't matter, and joined him.

Whenever I asked Rek about it, he just shrugged and told me that Cord worked in mysterious ways. Which sounds like a great heap of bullshit, but I knew it to be the truth. Wherever the fucker ended up—either as a carpet of meat across Orlecht, a star beside his god, or in some dirty backwater, winding up the locals, I think it didn't matter. Any of those things would have been good enough for him. Any of those things would have bored him, and he would have found a way to make them interesting.

There's a hole cored in my heart from the loss of Lux, and sometimes I wish I'd had the chance to know her better. We'd had something good, or maybe the start of something good. Maybe when I see her again, in that place beyond the deadlands, we can pick back up, and it won't be so lonely.

Still, the water rushes against the hull, and the orcas swim beside us. Sometimes they're fucking, sometimes just guiding us.

The ocean is big, and the world larger than that. I know there's a plan in mind here, but for once, I wasn't let in on it. Are we ever, though? The best you can do is hope to notice as the universe sets you up, then act like you'd meant for everything to happen the way it did when it does.

I still wondered what might happen between Oros and Camor. There was history there, but sometimes you don't get all the answers. Maybe it's the universe's way of keeping you on your toes. Maybe that's just how life works out. Shit like that will keep you up at night if you let it.

As a rule, I don't. Cord taught me that. There's enough to deal with in the now that dwelling on the what-if will drive your brain right into the nearest cask. It was a lesson I only took half to heart. I still think of Cord. I think of the thing I'd seen at the last moment as I tumbled through the air, that of a flash of light and something fleet, like a fox, slipping across the outside of the tower. I think of Cord's last words, and sometimes wonder, when it's very quiet, if I whistle, will he come running?

Then I remember I threw that horrible whittled dick in the ocean.

ACKNOWLEDGMENTS

There are a lot of people to thank for making this book happen. Alternatively, you can curse them. My beta readers: Justine, Angela, and Krystle. My editor-in-a-pinch and all-around good idea person, Krystle again. Twitter, for ideas that had me laughing so hard I had to add them to the text, and to Sadir for the tomato bandit. To the fantasy community, for having the kind of sense of humor that lets me poke a little fun. Finally, to Shelly. I wrote something that made you laugh. I told you I'm funny, damn it.

36984513R00197

Made in the USA
Lexington, KY
19 April 2019